CORY ANDERSON

WHAT BEAUTY THERE IS

PENGUIN BOOKS

PENGUIN BOOKS

UK | USA | Canada | Ireland | Australia
India | New Zealand | South Africa

Penguin Books is part of the Penguin Random House group of companies
whose addresses can be found at global.penguinrandomhouse.com.

www.penguin.co.uk
www.puffin.co.uk
www.ladybird.co.uk

First published in the USA by Roaring Brook Press
and in Great Britain by Penguin Books 2021
This paperback edition published 2023

001

Book design by Michelle Gengaro-Kokmen
Printed and bound in Great Britain by Clays Ltd, Elcograf S.p.A.

The authorized representative in the EEA is Penguin Random House Ireland,
Morrison Chambers, 32 Nassau Street, Dublin D02 YH68

A CIP catalogue record for this book is available from the British Library

ISBN: 978–0–241–44173–2

All correspondence to:
Penguin Books
Penguin Random House Children's
One Embassy Gardens, 8 Viaduct Gardens, London SW11 7BW

www.greenpenguin.co.uk

For Brady and Kate,
who showed me what to put in my heart

I

My life has faded to floating bits of black and white, but I remember the minutes with Jack in color, in a vivid haze of red and yellow and blue. Sensory things. The sound of his voice. The smell of him, like a forest in winter. I can see him lying beside me with the moonlight on his face. His hand holds mine, and I'm warm all over, despite the cold. I can feel his breath on my skin.

I don't forget these things.

I told Jack to stay away. He'll make you hurt, I said. He'll take what matters most. He'll do it with a smile and then he'll smoke a cigarette.

Jack didn't listen.

But I get ahead of myself. I go to the end when, to understand the truth, you have to start at the beginning.

When Jack opened the door, Mom wasn't sitting in the rocking chair by the stove. Her rainbow blanket formed a barren heap on the rocker, except for a tattered corner that slunk down to the worn carpet. She wasn't in the kitchen either, staring glass-eyed out the window above the sink, all bone and skin in her frayed pink nightgown. Cold clung to the house's scant walls and crouched in dim corners where sun never hit. She'd let the fire go out. She never did that. Not even in one of her dazes.

In his mind, a steel clamp tightened.

He kicked snow from his boots and slung his backpack off his shoulders and hitched it over the peg of the kitchen chair. He took out his earbuds to see if he could hear her upstairs, but he couldn't. She hardly ever left that rocker these days except to use the bathroom. Once she'd have greeted him at the door when he got home from school, but that was in another time.

"Mom?"

He stood there listening for an answer, and one didn't come. Wind blew at the windows and rattled down the stove flue. He needed to get a fire going. If they had no fire, they'd be bad off. Matty would be home from school soon. Mrs. Browning let the second graders stay after and shoot hoops in the gym, but only for a while. He needed to get supper going for Matty. Night coming.

Still he just stood there and listened for her.

Snow melted under his boots and made puddles on the linoleum. He took off the boots and socks and lined them up by the cold stove out of habit. When he looked back toward the rocker, he saw the pill bottle on the table. The cap was off and most of the little round pills inside were gone. In the beginning, some doctor in town said the pills would help her rest from the pain after she got hurt, but that all happened a long time ago, and from then on she got the pills any way she could. Now she slept in the rocker day and night and didn't greet him at the door or eat or take baths or say things that made sense.

Wind, or something else, rustled upstairs. He went to the stairwell and stood looking up. The light dimmed halfway and shrank to darkness at the top.

"Mom?"

She had to be up there, in the bathroom. Maybe sick again from taking too many. He climbed the creaking carpeted stairs and flicked on the hall light and waited. No sound. A gust of air along the roof.

He crossed to the bathroom.

He imagined he'd find her hunched by the toilet throwing up, eyes sunken in cups of livid shadow, or standing in front of the mirror, starving-thin, like a crumpled paper doll. But she wasn't there.

Bathroom empty. Rose-pink porcelain.

Octagon tile, dingy white.

He thought of her lying somewhere outside in her nightgown with the life seeping out of her into the frigid snow. *Stop it*, he said to himself. *She's okay. Somebody came and got her and maybe took her to the store. That's all.*

But this was a lie. Of course it was.

He left the bathroom and stared at the closed door at the end of the hall, and that door got bigger as he looked at it. Only one room left in the house, and she wouldn't be in there. No, she never went in that bedroom. Not since they came in the night and hauled Dad away.

No. That room was a grave. And she wouldn't go in.

He put his hand on the doorknob and turned it.

She was hanging from the ceiling fan. A belt was coiled around the fan's downrod and cinched around her throat. One of her frail hands twitched.

He tore to her and raised her up by her legs, but she was limp all over. Beneath her lay a wooden chair on its side. He let her go and shoved the chair up and stood on it and lifted her but her head lolled forward. Her eyes didn't blink. *Oh God.* He yanked on the belt and the fan shuddered. Plaster dusted his face. *Please*, he thought.

Oh, dear God, please.

He lurched down and rattled through the dresser and found Dad's hunting knife and unfolded the blade and got on the chair and hacked at the leather. Slash the strap, find a notch, and saw. *Dammit. Oh, dammit damndamn.* When the leather broke he caught her by the waist, but she fell sideways out of his arms and thumped to the floor. The chair tipped and sent him sprawling. He dropped the knife.

He crawled to her and turned her over. She lay there in the dull gooseflesh light with her face blank and little specks of blood in her open eyes. Her hair fallen over. A lump of bone knobs on the green shag carpet. One slipper on her foot and dried drool on her chin.

Such quiet.

He stood and hit the wall with his fist. There wasn't any force in the first hit, but the second time he scraped his knuckles on the drywall so they bled. Noise shook him, broken sounds of hurt and shuddering breath.

He sat by her on the floor.

He touched her hand and held it.

He just sat by her.

When the window darkened and the cold crept through the walls, he straightened and gathered her up. She couldn't have weighed more than a hundred pounds, but she was heavy. He got her to the bed and laid her there and then just stood looking at her. Shadows pooling violet on her skin. Her yellow hair. He closed her eyes and straightened her nightgown down around her legs. He folded her arms. He found her other slipper on the carpet and put it on her foot and sat by her on the bed.

He sat there a long time.

He locked the bedroom door and washed his face and then he went downstairs and got a fire going in the stove. The cold kept coming, and now the night too. He threw the pill bottle in the garbage and opened the cupboard by the sink and got out the yellow Tupperware bowl. He pulled off the lid and counted the money inside. Fifteen dollars and thirty-six cents. He counted it again.

Yup. Right the first time.

He rubbed his eyes with the heel of his hand and opened the pantry door. Half-full sack of potatoes. A couple jars, beans and peaches. Canister of sugar: almost empty. The potatoes were good Idaho russets from Mrs. Browning. He took three and washed them and cut them up. In a fry pan he melted a pat of shortening and then dropped the potato pieces in. His heart stitched pain in his chest and he ignored it.

The front door squeaked open and Matty clattered inside, stomping snow, bright cheeks, damp wool hat pulled down to his eyes and coat zipped up to cover his chin. The coat had once been

Jack's and, before that, somebody else's. A rip in the front exposed stuffing, but inside was flannel and warm. Matty slammed the door shut and pulled off his coat and hat and smiled.

"Jack, you'll never guess. I got every times table right. All the way to the twelves. I didn't miss even one."

The potatoes sizzled, and Jack turned them over to brown both sides. Salt and pepper. For a second things felt normal. Except his eyes. The hot sting at the edges. In his head a pulse began to beat. "Nice work, short stuff. Now hang your coat and wash up."

"You think we can have peaches tonight?"

Jack nodded. "To celebrate your times tables."

Matty hung his coat and bag on the wall hook by the stove and placed his boots carefully by Jack's, lining up the heels. He looked at the rocker and stood there a moment. Thoughtful. An expression of concentration on his face. He turned and went upstairs, and Jack heard the bathroom faucet turn on. There was a tang in his mouth. It tasted like gunpowder.

The door is locked.

The door is locked.

After a minute Matty came back down. He watched Jack cooking. Then he dragged a kitchen chair to the cupboard by the sink and got out plates.

Together they laid out everything and sat at the Formica table. Fried potatoes and peaches and cups of hot instant coffee. Jack knew what was coming and readied himself.

"Where's Mom?" Matty asked.

"She went on a trip."

"I checked the bathroom and she ain't in there."

"I told you. She went on a trip."

"Well, who'd she go with?"

"A friend. Somebody you don't know."

"Like who?"

"Eat your potatoes," Jack said.

Matty didn't eat. He looked at her rocker. He looked at Jack. "She didn't take her rainbow blanket."

Jack glanced at the blanket. Rows of crocheted yarn. The edges pulled loose and faded to orange where the red used to be. A gift from Grandma Jensen when Mom was just eight. Stupid, to forget that blanket. "No. I guess not."

"I don't think she'd go nowhere without her blanket."

"Maybe she forgot it."

"You think she's okay in the snow?"

"Yeah. I think so."

"When will she be back?"

Jack drank a little coffee and burned his mouth. He ate his potatoes.

Matty watched him. "Are we okay?"

"Yeah. We're okay."

Jack ate. Chew and swallow. Sip of coffee. *You will do this for him. You will not let him know. You will not.*

Matty sat watching him. Then he picked up his fork and started eating.

Good.

Jack heated water on the stove and plugged the sink and

poured the hot water in and washed everything and let it dry on the counter. After Matty finished his peaches, Jack asked him to get out his homework. Spelling.

"*School*," Jack said.

The concentration returned to Matty's face.

"*S-C-H-O-O-L*."

"Good. Now *pencil*."

"*P-E-N-C-I-L*."

Outside the kitchen window, wind smashed snow flurries against the glass and gusted them in circles and shoved them to the earth. An iron cold out there. Jack put his hands over his eyes. Dark pressed down on the roof and in on the walls of the fragile house, and she was lying up there on the bed.

II

What do I remember?

My father is a thief and a killer. He robbed a pawnshop with Leland Dahl when I was ten, but nobody ever caught him. No evidence. No trial. That started everything. A long scar jags across his forehead and down his cheek from the time my mother came at him with a knife. She paid for that. He's a killer, but he's something worse.

His eyes are hooks. They dig deep. They snare the soul.

Some people have ice in them. I know I do. It's what my father made me. Frost-covered, black inside. Even now, when I think of him, I go cold all over. Like I just stepped into a freezer.

But Jack—sweet, angry, quiet Jack—he burns me up. He breaks me to pieces.

We knew each other nine days.

They pulled out the sleeper sofa and spread nubby blankets and a quilt over the sagging mattress. Jack stoked the fire and locked the doors and made sure they had enough firewood to get through the night while Matty stripped off his clothes and put on pajamas in front of the stove. Batman PJs and a tattered cape. The sight of him shrank Jack's chest. His ribs poking out, and his knees. Like some poor orphan. And so it was. Jack picked up the clothes and folded them and put them on the bed.

Just breathe, Jack.

Breathe in and out and then do it again.

Matty burrowed under the blankets. He kept glancing at the rocker. Jack switched off the lamp and tucked the blanket edges around him to keep in the heat. Moonlight gleamed in through the window. He sat on the mattress.

"Can we watch TV?"

"No. It's past your bedtime."

"Sure is cold."

"Yeah."

The fire crackled. He sat there, breathing. In, out.

"Jack?"

"What?"

"Do you think Dad will come home soon? Like Mom said he might?"

"I don't know."

Matty was silent. Then: "You remember that Services lady?"

Jack remembered her. The lady from Child Services. He got under the covers and looked at Matty. His face streaked with dim bluish light from the moon and the snow. His pale cheeks. His hair still matted down and fluffed up in spots from the stocking hat. He needed a haircut. Jack pulled him close. "I remember."

"Do you think she'll come back?"

"I don't know. Probably."

"You think she'll bring that sheriff like she said she would?"

"If she or that sheriff comes around and I'm not here, you just don't answer the door. You keep the door locked, and you don't answer."

"Okay."

"I'll take care of it."

He could feel Matty's heart beating.

"If they hear Mom's on a trip, do you think they'll take me somewhere?"

"I won't let that happen."

"Okay."

"I won't let that happen," he said again.

"Okay."

Matty didn't sleep for a long time. He fidgeted. He curled into Jack and then rolled over and huddled in the blanket with his back to the rocker. After a while his eyes closed. Jack thought he was asleep, but then he opened his eyes and looked at Jack in the gloom. He didn't say anything. Just looked at him. Jack pretended to sleep. *You will not screw this up. You will not. You will do what needs doing. Like you always have.*

After a while Matty's breathing turned steady.

Jack lay there and didn't sleep.

Hours passed.

When he rose he laid a pillow over Matty's ear and hoped it would be enough. The house was mostly dark. Outlines of shapes.

Kitchen table. The rocker and the stove. He pulled on his coat and then his boots. Matty didn't move.

He scooped up the rainbow blanket and walked upstairs to the bedroom and unlocked the door. She lay there on the bed with her arms folded and moon shadows playing over her. Almost iridescent in the leaden light. Like some emaciated Sleeping Beauty waiting for her prince. *Well, he ain't coming. And he never was any prince.*

He spread the blanket over her and pulled the bottom corners together and knotted them under her feet. Her skin was cold. Her hair in yellow wisps on the pillow. He looked at her face one last time. Then he knotted the blanket's top corners behind her head and rolled her over and pulled the edges tight. The sculptured blankness of her face hidden by yarn, a drift of colors across the bed. He tried to swallow but couldn't.

How can you do this?

You are a monster.

He hefted her into his arms. She was stiff, and he knew he couldn't carry her down all those stairs. Halfway through the hall he stopped with her in his arms and leaned against the wall to catch his breath. When he got to the stairs, he crouched and rested her flat on the floor and moved to her head. He gripped her shoulders through the yarn and lifted her partway up so she bent a little at the waist. With the weight of her on his knees, he dragged her down, one riser at a time. Sluggish thumps on carpet. *Drop her slow. Soft so Matty doesn't hear. There. All the way to the bottom.*

He looked at the sleeper sofa. It floated like a barge in the dark. Matty's shape lay swathed in the quilts. The pillow still over his ear.

Silence.

He crouched and lifted her. He could not hold her long.

Quiet. Be quiet and quick.

He faltered to the front door and opened it and stumbled through. Every noise loud as an axe cracking. He thought he'd wake Matty, but he didn't. When he got the door closed, his legs gave out and he dropped her. She banged down and slid from the porch into the snow.

He sat by her.

You will never see her face again. You will never see her. You will never.

He got up and looked around. Starless night. Frozen and hushed. A single flake floated down. Frigid blue, this wasteland. The stubble of desolate fields on all sides. No one around for miles.

He went to the shed and got the wheelbarrow and pushed it on its tire through the snow to her and heaved her in. Snowflakes light as lace dusted the rainbow blanket. He stood there, his breath a faint plume. The cold and the quiet. Ten heartbeats, twenty.

The moon stared down at him.

He wheeled her around the Chevrolet Caprice to a nice spot behind the barn, where the roof hung over and tall old pine trees wore coats of fresh whiteness and a patch of ground wasn't frozen too bad. A peaceful spot. He got a shovel from the shed and started digging. He'd forgotten gloves, and he didn't go back for them. He kicked the blade through layers of snow to the packed dirt, and he tried to dig. He dug and kept digging. Deep, so the dogs in the fields wouldn't get at her. So she wouldn't come up in the spring. He dug, and he didn't think. He flicked off his mind like a light switch.

Cold burned into his skin.

On the shovel, his hands went slippery.

Lift, slash. Dig.

When he got done covering her with dirt, he sat next to her. Swollen earth. Churned and blackened snow. Cold as it was, he just sat there. Nothing watching his back but the moon. A gray dawn curdling over the land. He wiped his eyes and got up and walked to the house.

In the living room, Matty still slept, the pillow over his ear. Jack took off his coat and boots and opened the stove and put a log on the coals to feed the fire. The faint light fell on the walls, brief and quivering. The palms of his hands were throbbing. He closed the stove and got down to his underwear, shivering. Then he climbed beneath the covers and pulled Matty close. His small body. In the darkness, Jack listened to each shallow breath.

What will I do now? he thought. *What will I do?*

III

Life can be brutal.

Jack knew it.

So did I.

I wonder sometimes why things happen the way they do. If there's any rhyme or reason. People say a butterfly in Brazil can flap its wings and set off a tornado in Texas. One little butterfly makes a storm halfway around the world. I think about that. Did I feel the flutter of wings when Jack and I met? Did I sense the coming tornado?

Looking back, I think I did.

Jack walked in front of my eyes, and everything changed.

I hear locker doors open and close. Metal clangs. Voices shout and laugh in the hall. Bright colors flash by. T-shirts and jeans. My first day at a new school. I'm about to open my locker. I've just finished calculus, and I'm thinking about limits at infinity.

I'm distracted.

I don't see it coming when Luke Stoddard walks up and starts

talking to me. I find out his name later. Luke wears a football jersey.
He has straight teeth. He's big, and he says something about showing
me around, and he gets close to me, too close, so I back up against my
locker. The metal presses into my shoulder blades. My elbow. The back
of my head. He takes a step closer. He's going to touch me. I know
he is.

    I drop my books. Loose papers drift and scatter. They decorate the hall,
squares of white confetti at a ticker tape parade.

Then I see Jack.

Leave her alone.
    Jack says this to Luke.
    Stay away from me.
    I say this to Jack, a few minutes later.
    I don't mean it.

I replay that memory in my head sometimes. The minute I first saw Jack.
    Sweet, angry Jack. Quiet Jack.
    Looking back, I think the butterfly flapped its wings then.
    Winds started swirling.
    Everything changed.

Jack woke.
    Matty lay wrapped in the blankets, watching him. Silence. In a
dream, Jack had been running through a field dressed in snow with
the moon looking down. Smell of cold dirt in his nose. Something

lost he had to find. Waking, it all crumbled in the gray daylight, the colors decaying fast.

He ruffled Matty's hair. "Hi."

"Hi."

"Everything's okay."

Matty nodded. His eyes shining in the ashen light. Something nameless and binding.

Jack could feel the shovel in his hands. He got up and lit a fire while Matty put on clothes. The air felt brittle as bone. Grim daylight slanted through the window and crawled over the mattress. Matty looked at the empty rocker and didn't say a word about the missing rainbow blanket.

Snow fell in hard chunks and piled up on the windowsill. Jack sprinkled cinnamon over oatmeal and ladled it into bowls and brought the bowls to the kitchen table. Matty sat holding a blue paper in his hands.

"What's that?" Jack asked.

"Nothing."

"It looks like something to me."

Matty wouldn't look at him. "We got a field trip today."

"Sounds like fun. Where to?"

"I don't want to go."

Jack studied him. He wore one of Jack's old woolen shirts. Two of the buttons were missing. A threadbare plaid. He'd combed his hair with water, but it wouldn't lie flat. "Why?"

"This paper says you can stay at school if you don't want to go."

"Why don't you want to go?"

"I just don't."

"Why?"

Matty sat there holding the paper. He looked almost in tears. Jack took the paper and read it. The field trip was to the Museum of Idaho to see dinosaurs, and it cost two dollars. Gas for the bus. A vise closed around Jack's chest.

"Is the two dollars why you don't want to go?"

"I don't care if I don't. That's all."

Jack walked to the cupboard and got the Tupperware bowl. He pulled off the lid and counted two dollars and handed them to Matty. "Look at me. We aren't going to die if I give you two dollars."

Matty looked at him. Those eyes gripped him. "Okay."

"Do you believe me?"

"Yes."

"We're all right."

Matty looked at Jack's hands and looked away. *There is no description of stupid*, Jack thought, *that you don't fit*. He said again, "We're all right."

"Okay."

They ate the oatmeal side by side. Jack signed the permission slip and put it in Matty's backpack. He warmed Matty's coat by the fire and held it out for Matty to reach in his arms, and then he zipped it up. He watched Matty wait for the bus and watched him get on and watched the bus rattle down the road. When it disappeared over the hill, he still watched. All he could think was that he'd lied to Matty. They weren't all right. They had thirteen dollars and thirty-six cents. They had a foreclosure notice in the kitchen drawer and a broken water heater and an empty pantry and a dad in prison and a mom under the snow in the backyard.

He sat at the kitchen table and listened to the clock above the oven tick. "You need a plan," he said. "You damn well need a plan."

Everything depended on money. If he had money, he could buy food. Milk. Bread. He could pay bills. A job meant money, so he would get a job. Where? Somewhere in town. He'd have to make it happen. Find a way. But there was school to think about. He'd be missed if he didn't go to school. And he couldn't be missed. Being missed meant Child Services. Nope. Not an option. *They will take Matty. They will take Matty.*

So.

School.

Then job.

And what will you do with Matty while you're at work?

No answer.

The clock ticked. Counting down the seconds to some invisible zero moment. Each tick louder than the one before. Time moving in the narrow space between. Pulsing slowly. Blood from a wound.

His hands hurt, so he went up to the bathroom and bandaged the blisters. He combed his hair and brushed his teeth. He slung his backpack over his shoulder. Then he got in the Caprice and drove to school.

A substitute teacher talked about history. All the presidents over the years and who was best or worst. Jack stared out the window.

Images in his head—they kept coming. He would not look at them straight on but instead saw sharp, fractured bits reflected off the backs of his eyelids. Incomplete pictures. Like pieces of a fallen mirror.

Her slipper on the carpet.

The knife in his hand. Cutting leather.

His eyes burned, and he closed them. He crossed his arms on the desk and shoved the images down to some unspoken place and leaned his forehead on his arms.

Go to the grocery store and then the diner. Gas stations next. Both of them. What will you say? I'm a hard worker, sir. I have no experience, but I work hard. I will do what you need. I'll do it well, I swear, whatever you want—stock shelves or mop floors or clean toilets, I'll work hard—

The bell rang.

He raised his head and swallowed. Pain in his throat. Hell. *You cannot get sick. What will happen if you get sick? You know what.*

In the hall, he opened his locker and crammed in his history book. Students passing him. Talking and laughing. Some in groups and others alone. Lunchtime. If he went out to the parking lot, he might sleep for maybe twenty minutes in the Caprice. He turned and headed for the doors. *You just need some rest. A little nap. That's all.*

". . . prettiest thing I ever saw."

Luke Stoddard stood by the lockers with his back to Jack. A senior. Quarterback. Talking sweet nothings to some girl. He wore tight jeans and a ball cap with the bill cupped so it lay over his eyes. He had a reputation for his touchdowns on and off the field.

"I could take you places," Luke was saying. "Show you around."

Jack kept walking, but when he saw the girl he stopped. She stood there, holding her books to her chest with no expression at all on her face. Mostly it was her eyes that stopped him. They were like looking into deep water. At once glistening and dark. Far down in those depths, something flashed and disappeared as if swallowed. Jack knew that flash.

Luke moved closer to her. "You're kind of a shy one, aren't you?"

Jack stood a little off to the side, watching. The girl dropped her books. Papers drifted and scattered, and Luke laughed. The girl didn't move. Her hands were clenched at her sides.

Luke reached out to touch her cheek. He was slightly bent over when she raised her arm and jabbed down with knee-jerk quickness and, in the same motion, dropped her hand. It was something Jack felt more than saw. The pencil stuck out at an angle from Luke's forearm.

Luke recoiled sharply. He looked at his arm, gulping air, and yanked the pencil out and dropped it. A splotch of red expanded on his sleeve. He was choking on his own gasps.

She stared at him. Still as a stone. The pencil lay at her feet.

He shoved her against the locker. "Bitch!"

"Leave her alone," Jack said.

When Luke turned, he saw Jack standing there, quiet. "What?"

"Leave her alone."

Luke's breaths slowed. He spread his feet and smiled. "Josh Dahl. Or Jack. Right? What do you want?"

"I said what I want."

"You did."

Jack didn't answer.

Luke looked at the girl and looked at Jack. "Do you know who I am? Because I'm not somebody you really want to mess with."

"I know you," Jack said.

Luke flushed. A few kids had stopped and stood watching. The girl said nothing. She hadn't moved at all. She might have been mute for all Jack knew.

"How's your daddy, Jack?" Luke said. "How's he doin'? You see him much?"

Jack waited and didn't answer.

Confusion passed over Luke's face. Doubt. "What do you want?"

Jack felt very separate from himself. Far away. As if he were observing himself talking to Luke from a distance. He looked at Luke's hands. "You need good hands in football, don't you? Quarterback's gotta have good hands. To throw the ball."

"What?"

Jack just stood there, watching him.

Blood dripped down Luke's arm and spattered on the floor in droplets. He licked his upper lip. "Is that some kind of threat?"

Jack just waited.

Luke looked down the hall in both directions, as though there might be some friend there. No one moved. Quite a crowd now. No more talking. No laughter.

Quiet. Somewhere a locker creaked open.

Luke gave a little shrug. His mouth labored to find words. "Whatever. Asshole. You're not worth the time." He glanced at the girl. "Neither is she."

He studied Jack a moment longer. Then he stepped backward and turned and pushed between kids and blundered out the door.

A murmur rose from the crowd. Faces from the past. Kids who had once been his friends. Years ago. Jack could hear bits of conversation.

"Damn. Did you see Luke?"

"She stabbed a pencil—"

"That's Jack Dahl. His dad's the one who—"

Jack gazed steadily at the students he saw talking. Their voices died at the sight of him, until there was no sound anywhere. He stared at them. Each one. Their faces. What would it be like? To be like that? So normal? He watched them until, one by one, they glanced away. He knew who they were thinking of. *You are just like him*, he thought. *Backed into a corner, you are just like him.*

A bell rang, and the crowd stirred to life.

Noise now. Spectators, moving on.

He looked at the girl. Her head was down, and her dark hair hid her face. He crouched and gathered the loose pages and picked up one of her books. The cover showed a hot-air balloon, with faded letters across the top. *Calculus, Fifth Edition.* He straightened and held out the pages to her.

"Are you okay?"

She lifted her head and met his gaze. He saw her clearly for the first time. Apple cheeks and naked skin. Eyes an aching hazel. Her voice rasped from her.

"Stay away from me."

He stepped back.

She snatched the pages from him. He saw a tattoo on the inside of her wrist. It was a heart. Black as onyx. A small, black heart.

She turned on her heels. Her back very straight, her hair a riot of kinks and twists. She headed down the hall to the girls' bathroom in long strides and disappeared inside.

Jack stood there stupidly, holding her book in his hand. The hall empty now. Then he opened the cover. Her name was printed in black letters at the top, with her phone number written beneath it.

AVA.

He stood for a minute, examining the book. And he wondered why Ava was so afraid. Then he opened his backpack and put the book inside.

IV

Stay away from me.

What a lovely thing to say.

I should have thanked Jack. He tried to help me. He picked up my book. I should have thanked him. But you have to understand. I knew who Jack was. I knew as soon as Luke said his name.

Jack Dahl.

How's your daddy, Jack? How's he doin'?

Jack was Leland Dahl's son.

Leland Dahl, who robbed a pawnshop with my father and went to prison. Leland Dahl, who knew where the money was.

In the bathroom, I washed my hands. I washed them once, scrubbed. Washed again. Then I went into a stall and locked the door. Breath flinching and jittering through me. Thoughts striking in quick, sharp jabs.

Jack Dahl is dangerous.

Stay away from him.

Stay far away.

As far as you can.

I have said a little about my father. His name is Victor Bardem. I do not call him Father. I was ten when he robbed Lucky Pawn. It was a Tuesday in August. He came home real late in the night with a man I'd never seen. I should have been asleep, but we didn't have air-conditioning and I was hot. My nightgown stuck to my skin even without the blankets on. At the time we lived in a trailer outside of Rigby. Mom was gone by then.

Here is what happened.

Bardem shuts off the Land Rover's engine and gets out. He stands in front of the trailer, looking at it. A pale outline of aluminum siding. The moon a slit in the sky. The other man gets out on the passenger side. He wears a mustache that hangs down over the sides of his mouth, and there's a tattoo on his arm of a pair of hands clasped in prayer. He carries a shotgun with the end sawed off. He looks at Bardem and waits.

Bardem stands there, studying the trailer. Dim windows. Nothing moves inside. The light fixture above the door casts a glare over the front porch.

"You figure he got out with the money?" the other man says.

"Yes. I do."

"You figure he stashed the briefcase somewhere?"

Bardem smiles in a distracted sort of way. He walks across the dirt to the porch and sits in a green plastic lawn chair. Casual. Relaxed. He watches the man.

Silence.

The man spits on the raw dirt. Sweat beads his forehead. No air moving. He limps to the porch and leans against the rail. He holds the shotgun in one hand, the barrel pointing to the ground. A dark blot stains the left thigh of his jeans. He nods toward the trailer. "You got a bandage in there?"

Bardem doesn't seem to hear. He cocks his head toward the trailer as if listening for something.

All quiet. The hoot of an owl.

"You want to go look for him?" the man says. "We could try and find him."

Bardem doesn't move at all. "Do you know where he'd hide something?"

The man shakes his head. "No. But you know him better. Where he lives." He wipes the sweat from his brow and gimps onto his good leg. "I'm bleedin' bad. You got a bandage?"

"Are you certain?"

"What?"

"I said, are you certain? You don't know where he'd hide something."

"I don't know."

Bardem puts his eyes on the man. The smile lingers on his lips.

"I need to see 'bout this leg." The man steps up to the porch and looks at the trailer again. "You got antibiotics?"

"What good are you?"

The man glances at Bardem fast. "What?"

Bardem leans back in his chair and studies the man. The smile is gone now, but the voice remains untroubled. "I said, what good are you? You don't know where the briefcase is."

The man's fingers tighten on the shotgun, but there's already a pistol in Bardem's hand, pulled from his belt and leveled at the man's head.

"Drop it," Bardem says.

The man doesn't move. Bardem watches the panic flare in his eyes. He has seen this panic before.

"I think you understand," Bardem says, "your chances in this situation."

The man drops the shotgun. It clatters off the porch and whiffs up a puff of dry dirt. "There's no need for this."

"But there is."

"I could leave—"

"Do you ever tire of hearing your own voice?"

The man's mouth quivers.

Bardem leans back in the chair, holding the pistol. "Do you know how many people have knowledge of this night? I'll tell you. Three people. Me. You. And Dahl. That's too many. I don't like it."

"I said I'll go."

Bardem looks at the trailer. He lowers the pistol.

"I'll tell you what," he says. "We'll settle this like men. Let's go for a ride."

They get into the Land Rover and roll out across the dirt in the dark.

A half hour later, Bardem returns alone.

He sits in the lawn chair. He pulls a cigarette and a lighter from his shirt pocket and lights a Marlboro and smokes. The lit end glows a faint red circle in the dark. There is blood on his ostrich-skin boots.

He drops the cigarette butt and smashes it. He whistles softly.

With a water hose, he washes out the trunk. The rubber mat atop the carpet. He comes back and shifts dirt over the blood on the ground with the side of his boot. Crickets chirp in the distance. He climbs the porch steps to the trailer.

He doesn't turn on a light. In the kitchen, he washes his hands and dries them on a clean towel. He wipes the blood from his boots. The refrigerator hums. The trailer smells of herbs. There is basil by the sink. He looks at himself in the reflection of the window. His appearance is neat. Unruffled. He listens again.

He walks to Ava's bedroom door. He stands with his ear to the door, and then he touches the knob and turns it.

Ava lies in bed. Curled up under the sheets. Her eyes closed.

She has been peeking out the window.

She lies very still. Breath flitting in and out of her. Almost soundless. Her face smooth. In the bed beside her is a stuffed animal: a little monkey with brown fur. She wants to reach for it, but she doesn't. She doesn't move.

His footsteps are silent, but she knows he's there.

She smells his aftershave.

He sits in the chair by the bed. Quiet. She feels his darkness there. She waits. She breathes. Heart flapping against the walls of her chest. She lies in the shadows and thinks about blue skies and palomino horses and happy things. She waits, she waits.

He stands and crosses to the bed. He waits there. He leans down and brushes his lips against her hair. She doesn't move.

The room is still.

He sits in the chair again.

When she wakes, he is gone.

V

They found that man out somewhere off Route 20. Everybody said it was Jack's dad who killed him. But it wasn't.

It seems like most people don't believe in good and evil anymore. They smile at you funny if you talk about those things. Like you've seen too many movies or something. But I can tell you, evil's real. I've seen his face. Pure and simple. I've heard his voice. I've looked in his eyes. And once you look evil in the face, you know. You don't even wonder.

I told myself to stay away.

Jack's dangerous, I said. Stay away from him. As far as you can.

And I planned to stay away.

I did.

But Jack pulls me to him like the Earth pulls the moon.

And I don't stay away.

I saw him four more times.

★   ★   ★

After school, Jack walked Main Street from store to store, looking for somewhere open. Most of the buildings were abandoned. Broken glass. Boarded doors and crumbling brick.

Snow whispered down from a crouching gray sky. Frail bits getting thicker. Drifting like ash in some apocalyptic world. Already starkly cold. Jack zipped his coat and blew on his sore hands and shoved them in his pockets, every part of him sore and tired.

The girl from school kept stealing his thoughts. Her hair the color of a black walnut shell. Her downturned eyes, her lips. Something about her was beyond his understanding. He said her name in his head and then said it out loud. Ava. She must've been new. He'd never seen her before. He tried to figure out why she'd run away from him in the hallway, but he couldn't. She was scared. Why? *Doesn't matter*, he thought. *You've got more to worry about than a girl. A whole long list of things.*

Matty.

Money.

Job.

If he didn't find a job, they'd be out of food in two days. Maybe three.

Could be the Caprice ought to be sold.

He plodded along the sidewalk, peering in windows. A barbershop with a faded sign above the sloping metal roof: $5 Cuts. The candy-striped barber pole was dead and rusted. A furniture store advertised in weathered red paint on the windowpane: Everything Must Go. The whole street slowly decomposing.

He checked the gas stations, but there was no work to be had.

Nothing at Big J's Burgers either. He went on. White chunks sifting down over everything. Dusk darkening to night.

At the corner of the second block, a hazy yellow light beckoned from inside a storefront. Hunter's Drug & Hardware. He walked over and stopped and looked in the big front window by the door. A display of beef jerky and cigars and whiskeys. On a red checkered tablecloth lay a radiator hose next to a baking sheet. A KitchenAid mixer. Put up against the glass in the corner was a cardboard sign with two words written in black marker.

HELP WANTED

He pushed open the door, his legs weak. A bell jangled on the handle. Inside he saw rows of aisles cloistered under the glow of fluorescent lights. Cough drops, fever reducers, pain relievers, antacids, thermometers. Canned goods on another set of shelves. Beans, corn, chili, soup, tomato sauce. Jam and Wonder Bread. A wire stand of greeting cards for $0.99 each. Sleepy music from a radio somewhere. Patsy Cline's "I Fall to Pieces." He stood on a black doormat and kicked snow from his boots and unzipped his coat and smoothed his snow-dampened hair. Nerves: sliding in like garter snakes. He jammed them down. *You can do this. You can.*

"I'm closin'," the owner said from behind the counter. "Storm's comin' in. Newsman says we'll have least a foot by mornin'."

He stood wiping the countertop with a shabby barmop towel. Old and bent and paper-thin, eyes shrouded under creases of wrinkled and spider-veined skin. He wore a checkered button-front shirt with brown suspenders and a vinyl apron tied over the top.

"I saw your sign," Jack said. "I'm looking for work."

The owner quit scrubbing and stood up straighter. He frowned and inspected Jack. Squinting under white eyebrows. "Well. Come on over and let me look at you."

Jack held the old man's gaze and went to the counter and knew he could not mess this up. No matter what. "I can do whatever you need. Sweep, dust, stock shelves. Anything. I'm real reliable too."

"How old are you?"

"Eighteen." A lie, but it was only off a year.

"Ever had a job?"

"No, sir. But I'd work hard. I swear I would."

"I expect hard work."

"Yessir. I'd work hard for you."

"You'd be liftin' heavy boxes."

"I don't mind. I can lift whatever you need."

"I don't take any back talk. None."

"No, sir."

The old owner grimaced and looked out the window at the snow. His yellow fingernails tapped the worn marble counter. His beak nose twitched. "Pay's seven an hour. Off the books. It's all I'll do."

Jack didn't breathe. "That's fine."

Behind the counter a cuckoo clock on the wall chimed six times. The owner scratched his chin. His buried eyes scrutinized Jack, sharp as a crow's. "Well. You might fit the bill." He nodded and held out a hand to shake, though his scowling face didn't change. "Deal."

Jack blinked. Everything blurred a little. The owner's whiskered face. The marble counter and the cuckoo clock. Far down in him, where the constant worry paced, he hadn't thought this would really happen. Finding work. Money was always on his mind. That and food. Work meant money for meals, bills, a new pair of shoes for Matty. *Remember this*, he thought. *Don't ever forget.*

He shook the owner's hand.

"What's your name?" the owner asked.

"Jack, sir. Jack Dahl."

The old man's fingers slackened. His face twisted to juts and angles. He might have been in pain. *"Dahl."*

Jack didn't move. His insides went tipping sideways, tipping and breaking apart. A sudden feeling of loss thwacked like a mallet against the underside of his ribs—

"You Leland Dahl's boy?"

Jack just stood there, numbness seeping through him.

The owner yanked back his hand as though bitten. His eyes dug into Jack and went inside to raw, open places. "You are, ain't ya?"

Jack tried talking but his voice wouldn't work. On the wall, a mounted deer head watched him.

"I know you." The owner spat the words. He'd started quivering all over, and Jack thought he might fall. "I know your family."

Words now. Ripped from him. "Please. I'd work hard."

The owner shook his head. "I know you."

"Please. I need this."

"Get out of my store."

"I'm not like him."

"Boy. Your daddy's a meth dealer and a felon. Your ma's a drug addict slut. Why would anybody trust you?"

Jack stood there a second longer. Five seconds. Ten. Then he turned and walked out the door.

VI

I remember the color red.

The trees and the dark and the moon.

And the feel of my hand on the knife, while the warmth seeped through my fingers.

The light of the rising moon stretched out along the hills and cast shadowy shapes onto the road. Jack drove. Scarce houses loomed in the headlights and lost shape behind. The windshield wipers thwacked. Gray and drifting snow. *This isn't the end,* he thought. *It isn't. You can't lose heart. You just have to hold on.*

His eyes stung, and he wiped them with his sleeve.

When he turned into the driveway, he could see tire tracks carved into the fresh snow. A sheriff's truck by the barn. The windows dark. His throat closed. He looked toward the house, but nothing moved inside. No lights on. No smoke chugging from the chimney. He shut off the motor and threw open the door and tore toward the house.

"Matty? Matty!"

Halfway up the porch steps, he heard metal groan behind him. He turned. A man stood there in the shadows, with one hand on the open truck door and his breath frosting the air. Strong in build and big, over six feet tall, with hair aged gray and a face of stone. He wore a Stetson pulled down low over his eyes—Jack could hardly see them—and an open wool blazer over a dress shirt of starched blue cotton. On his hip, an M&P9 peeked out from the holster. Jack knew he was the law and that his last name was Doyle. Folks said he was good in a tangle and not a man to be messed with.

Doyle shut the door. Piled white powder sifted down off the window and dusted the ground. He came forward, one thumb tucked into his belt.

"Nobody's answerin'. I can tell you that."

Cold air raised goose bumps on Jack's skin. He didn't look at the house. Matty had to be in there. Had to be. "What do you want?"

Doyle took a few more steps, until he stood a couple feet from Jack. "DeeAnne from Services called. Said you might need checkin' on."

"We're good."

Doyle sniffed. He looked at the house and looked at Jack. "Whose name you shoutin'?"

"My brother's."

"And where's he?"

"At a friend's."

"A friend's."

"Yeah. I forgot. He went to a friend's place."

"What friend?"

Jack kept his eyes on Doyle. Snowflakes fell on his skin and melted. He said, "I don't know it's any of your business."

Doyle gave him a little smile. "I'd like to meet Matty. When he's not at a friend's."

Jack didn't speak. Doyle looked at the house again.

"Your ma around?"

"No."

"Well. Where's she at?"

"On a trip."

"You reckon she'll be back tonight?"

"Tomorrow, I think."

"Tomorrow."

Jack didn't answer. The needed thing was calmness.

"I got to talk with her before then."

"Whatever you've got to say," Jack said, "I'll tell her."

Doyle watched him. No expression. Snow bits gathered on the brim of his hat. "The bank put your place up for auction. Did your ma tell you? They're gonna force you out. You got two days."

Jack felt a wobble in his legs and sharp wounds scraping his throat. His head went woozy, and his ears started humming with loud noise. Everything in his view tilted. The barn and the trees shifted heights.

"You got somewhere you can go?" Doyle asked.

"We're fine."

They stood looking at each other in silence.

Doyle nodded. He lifted his head to the starlit sky, as though searching for something up there in the clouds. After a while he turned and gazed at Jack. Blue-gray eyes. Glistening like moon-stones in the dark.

"Son," he said. "If you need help, you oughta tell me."

Jack swallowed. He felt as if he was floating. He felt like a feather. He was cold and he shuddered and wondered if Mom was cold too, under all that snow.

"Comes a time most folks need a break," Doyle said.

Jack looked away. Branches rustled high in the tall old pine by the barn, and he saw an owl drop low, searching for something to snatch up, to tear bloody. He looked back at Doyle.

"Thanks for stoppin' by."

Doyle's eyes searched him a moment. Those eyes saw hidden things. Only God knew what.

He tipped his hat and turned and crossed the driveway to the police truck. Jack watched him get in. Watched the door shut and the engine start up and the lights flare bright. The truck wallowed through the snow and onto the roadway. The taillights continued on down the road until they disappeared into the waiting darkness.

He crashed up the porch steps and into the house. His throat was hurting. He threw the light switch, but the power was gone. The living room felt cold as a coffin, and he could see his own breath. In the black dark, he whispered Matty's name but heard nothing.

He lurched to the kitchen, holding out his hands in front of him, and found the cupboard above the sink. He opened it and fumbled for a flashlight and thumbed down the button. Dull yellow light soaked a hole in the dark. He could not see Matty. He held out the light.

A quilt from the sleeper sofa was lumped up against the wall under the kitchen table. Jack squatted and pulled the blanket back and saw a golden crown of hair. Then Matty looked up at him, his eyes big. Jack pulled him close. He held him and wrapped the quilt around him. "It's okay," he said. "It's okay. You're okay. I'm here."

Matty clung to him. He spoke not at all. After a while, he stopped shivering.

In the living room, he carried Matty to the stove and crouched on the cold floor, holding him. "I'm going to start a fire. I'll be right here, where you can see me." Matty wouldn't let go at first, but then he did. Jack rose and scrunched newspaper and put it in the stove's belly and formed a hut of good birch kindling over the paper. He lit a match. When the dry wood caught flame, he settled a big log on top and blew the fire bright. Flames lit up the walls and ceiling in flickering orange. He kept looking at Matty. Matty never took his eyes off Jack.

Jack went to the door and locked it.

With his teeth chattering, he dragged the sleeper sofa mattress in front of the stove and piled up blankets and pillows on top, making a cocoon to catch the fire's heat. He came around and picked Matty up and nestled him in the blankets. "I'm gonna get some food," he said. "Okay?"

Matty nodded.

He carried the flashlight to the cupboards and found three candles and lit them and placed them here and there on the counter. In the pantry, he got a can of beans and a can of peaches. From the high cupboard above the fridge came Mom's two best china bowls, the ones with the little flowers around the rim. Special-occasion stuff, passed down to her by Grandma Jensen. From the drawer he gathered two spoons and a can opener. He sat across from Matty, who studied his every move from within the den of blankets. With the can opener he nipped the peaches lid and turned the knob and poured the peaches into the bowls. He opened the peaches before the beans because Matty liked them best. The can of beans he put in the fire.

They ate the sweet fruit one slow bite at a time, light playing over the walls. The fire crackling. The house creaking as stiff places stretched and warmed. After the peaches, Jack fished the beans from the fire. They were nice and hot. When the bowls were empty he rose and tended the fire, and when he glanced back he saw Matty slumped in the blankets with his eyes closed and one foot free of the quilt. His pale skin glowed in the firelight. He had the look of an angel. Jack crouched and pulled the quilt over his foot and then just sat there, looking at him. *You do not need to tell him tonight. Let him have this night. Tomorrow you will tell him. Tomorrow you will have a plan. You will know what to do.*

He said this fiction to himself.

Outside the darkened glass of the living-room window, snow fell and fell in great flurries of white. Jack was tired and his hands were sore and his throat raw and his mind kept slipping, and somewhere out there in the dark he thought he heard singing. "Silent Night, Holy Night" and the song held many voices. Gleam of candle. A beacon. Hushed words and amen. Hallelujah. *Maybe they see us,* he thought. *Maybe they are looking.*

Snow fell and collected in heaps and there was no wind.

VII

The song that Jack heard was sung by many from afar. I wasn't there the first time, but later I went back and stood with them. I came closer. The house was cold. Jack slept in the blankets, his arm around Matty. His skin and hair lit up like a lantern in the fire's light. His face peaceful. I saw him so peaceful only that once. I knelt by him. I didn't touch him, but I watched him sleep. I see now why they don't permit such things.

I have never been nearer to anyone, and I have never been farther away.

Mom worked at the grocery store until after dark and then rode the bus to the stop and walked the rest of the way home. As she always did. She came into the house carrying a brown-paper sack. She looked at Jack. "I'm late again," she said.

"I saved you dinner."

She walked slowly. She smiled at him and at Matty on the couch, her face worn. "What did you make this time?"

"Mac 'n' cheese."

"My favorite."

She went into the kitchen and started pulling groceries from the sack. A loaf of bread. Ramen noodles. A package of M&M'S. Matty slid from the couch and toddled to the table. She opened the M&M'S and dropped one in his little hand. Carefully, she bent and kissed his head.

"What are my boys up to?" she asked.

Jack closed the book. "Just reading."

"Which one?"

"From the library."

When she saw the cover of the book, a shadow crossed her face. It was *White Fang*. She stood there looking at it. She said, "You did your homework?"

"Yes."

"I want you to do well."

"I know, Mom."

Jack left the book on the sofa and started putting the groceries away. "Sit. It's getting cold."

"Mama," Matty said.

She took a bite of mac 'n' cheese. When she bent to pour M&M'S into Matty's hand, she inhaled sharply and straightened, breathing hard for a moment. Her eyes watered. Jack could see the pain on her face. She opened her purse and took the pill container out of the little white prescription sack. Jack looked at her quickly.

"Does your back still hurt?" he asked.

She didn't look at him. "I think I'm just tired."

He got her a glass of water and sat at the table to watch her. The pill container. He kept staring at it. "Maybe you should stay home tomorrow."

She reached forward and ruffled his hair. "Don't worry."

"But maybe you should."

"I'll be okay."

"You can't stock the shelves, Mom. It's too heavy. You need to tell them."

She did not speak but dragged a hand over his and squeezed.

"I love you, Jack."

They sat in the living room. She and Matty on the couch reading *Goodnight Moon*, and Jack by the fire with *White Fang*. He tried to focus on the words but couldn't. He was doing the math in his head. Six days. She'd already missed that much work. Nine days the month before. He worried about the money, but mostly he worried about her. How wrung out she looked. How cheerless.

When he looked up, she was gazing at him intently.

"What?" he asked.

"I don't want you to read that book."

He closed it. "Okay."

"Please don't read it anymore."

"Okay."

"Promise me."

"Okay. I won't."

They sat in the quiet. All the unspoken things between them. He never should have brought the book home. He'd return it tomorrow.

Jack said, "I love you too."

"I didn't open the door."

Jack flinched awake. Outside the window the sky was black,

and in the stove the fire was down to embers. Matty sat bundled in the quilt, watching him.

"What?" Jack asked.

"When that sheriff came. I didn't open the door. Just like you said."

Jack nodded. "You did good."

"I was scared."

"I know. I'm sorry."

"Do you think Mom's okay on her trip?"

Jack blinked. "I'll bet she is."

Matty said nothing. Then he said, "The lights don't work."

"No."

"I tried them all. They don't work."

"No. They don't work."

"Will they work tomorrow?"

"No. Probably not."

Matty was silent. After a while he whispered, "I want to ask a question."

"Okay."

"Do you always tell the truth?"

"Not always. But it's good to tell the truth."

"Have you always told me the truth?"

In the smoldering glow, Mom's rocker made a shape on the wall. Jack shook his head. "No. I'm sorry."

"From now on, I want you to always tell me the truth. Will you?"

Creak of the house. Orange light.

"I will," Jack said. "I will always tell you the truth."

"Okay."

Matty lay down close to Jack and huddled into him and put his cheek on Jack's shoulder. His eyes drooped. He said, "I'm not tired."

He fell asleep.

The candles burned low and dimmed.

In the dark of the slow cold night, Jack dreamed of her as she'd once been. Standing in the front yard on green spring grass with roses flowering around her. Her cheeks pink and her hair clipped up in silver barrettes. Shears in her gloved hands for pruning. He stood on the porch, and she turned and smiled at him. A yellow summer dress. Her favorite color.

When he woke, he reached out in the dark for Matty and felt him there. Steady heartbeat. Jack lay in the quilts. Water leaked from his eyes, and he didn't make a sound. There was no song and there were no voices and no choirs of heaven singing. No grand amens or dawn of grace, and no one watching. No help to be had, and it was all a lie.

VIII

The second time I saw Jack, there were bandages on his hands. I don't remember noticing bandages the first time I saw him, but I remember them the second time. White tape and gauze. Blood dried in cracks. He wore a gray thermal. His hair was damp. I think about these things, but mostly I think about the look in his eyes. I don't know what to say about that look except that even now I can see it. No matter where I am. I can feel the look all over my skin. He was a boy alone in a house in the winter, and he had not been young for a very long time.

That is the look I remember.

When it was light enough to see, Jack rose and pulled on boots and gloves. He already wore his coat. He went outside to the woodpile, trudging through white up to his knees, and pried the axe from a stump and shook it to get off the snow. Winter stinging his lungs. He started coughing and had a hard time stopping. He should have worn a hat. He picked a dry log from the stack and stood it up and swung the axe so the blade sank deep. The wood splintered, and the blisters on his hands pulsed. He swung and chopped again and split a pile and carried the stove lengths inside and got a fire going, his head swimming. Matty still slept in the blankets.

He went back out and fished the shovel from the shed and chiseled a path from the door of the house to the Caprice and scooped snow away from the tires so they'd roll. Then he went in the house. The water from the kitchen sink was down to a trickle and cold as ice. He filled a pot and set it over the fire to warm.

He found Matty fresh clothes and woke him. Time to get ready for school. Matty stripped to his underwear and dressed in front of the stove while Jack got a towel from the kitchen and dipped it in the steaming pot of water. He washed Matty's face and neck and ears and then smoothed his unruly hair. He looked pretty good.

"I can do it myself," Matty said.

"I know."

Jack started coughing. His chest felt tight and his nose thick. Matty sat watching him. Jack opened a can of beans and gave it and a fork to Matty to eat in front of the fire. He thought he'd save the can of peaches. For what reason, he didn't know.

"What's six times six?" he asked.

Matty looked at him. "Thirty-six."

"Good. Nine times eight."

"I know these ones," he said, a look of reproach on his face. "I know to the twelves."

"Okay. Fourteen times three."

Matty closed his eyes. Calculating. "Forty-two."

Outside the window, the sky blued bitter and cloudless. Jack undressed and washed with the cloth and the pot of water and then bandaged his hands again. He got clean jeans and a gray thermal from the highboy and warmed up in front of the stove. He was buttoning the jeans when he heard something in the front yard—what sounded like an engine. He pulled the thermal over his head and said to Matty, "Get behind the couch."

Matty didn't move. He stood looking out the window. He spoke in a voice of sheer wonderment. "It's a girl."

When Jack looked, a girl was getting out of a blue car.

Not just a girl. Ava.

"Shit," he whispered. He crouched down, keeping his eyes on the window. She came toward the house, kicking her way through the drifts to the shoveled path. He motioned for Matty to get down, but Matty just stood there, looking out.

Matty smiled. Then he waved.

Her steps crunched on packed snow, then halted. Jack sank low. Waiting. Hushed silence. Strangely quiet. Then she knocked.

He slunk behind the couch. Matty grinned at the window.

"Get down," Jack hissed.

The next thing he knew, Matty had the door open. Jack straightened from behind the couch, flushing, and walked to the door. She stood no more than two feet from him. Her cheeks slapped red from the cold. On her head she wore a knit hat, and from it her hair scattered out in a flyaway mess. Her coat fell to just above her knees and was made of battered wool, a juniper green with tarnished brass buttons. It looked like some relic from World War II. These details he saw in a haze. She smelled like something warm: nutmeg or ginger.

"Hi," she said.

"Hi."

She took in a breath.

"I need my book," she said. "For school today."

Her hazel eyes watched him. Jack couldn't think. He tried to act casual but his heart was thumping. He looked down. Her combat boots were unlaced, and in the twelve or so inches between the laces and the bottom of her coat, he could see her bare legs. He looked up. She watched him.

"Maybe she should come in," Matty said. He stood beside Jack with his hands in his pockets.

Jack closed the door a little. No. Hell no. She could not come into this rathole house. "I don't have your book."

"Oh." She took a step back. "Okay."

"I left it at school," Jack said.

She watched him for a minute. Then she looked at Matty. She nodded. "Okay."

In the slight breeze, a strand of her hair lifted and blew across her cheek, her lips. Jack wanted to reach out. Tuck the strand behind her ear. What would that touch feel like? His hand almost lifted. He gripped the sides of his coat.

"We're in a hurry," he said.

Her cheeks reddened further. "Okay."

She turned and crunched off the porch and down the narrow path, her back straight, her wild hair streaming behind her, alight in the cold morning sun. Fresh snow sparkled around her. When the path ended, she got in the car and started it and backed out of the drive and headed up the road.

★   ★   ★

They left the living room a mess. Jack helped Matty into his coat and zipped him up and got his backpack. Matty wouldn't look at him.

"What?" Jack said.

Matty shook his head. Jack slid Matty's backpack over his shoulders.

"You could have let her in," Matty said.

Jack didn't answer. He found the stocking hat and pulled it over Matty's ears. Matty still wouldn't look at him.

"Why didn't you?" he asked.

"She told me to stay away from her."

"When?"

"At school."

"Why?"

"I don't know."

Matty stood there pondering this. He pulled his gloves from his coat pockets and worked them over his fingers. "Maybe she didn't mean it. Sometimes people say things they don't mean."

"Maybe."

"That's true," Matty said. "Isn't it?"

"Yes. That's true."

At last Matty looked at him. He nodded. He said, "I like her."

He went outside and waited for the bus.

An hour later it started to snow. Jack sat at the kitchen table, staring out the window. Pale flakes falling. The cold and the silence. He kept watching the window like she might reappear, but she didn't. He watched for a long time. Everything dulling to gray.

He rubbed his eyes and shoved at them with the heels of his hands.

With his eyes closed, he could see every detail of her. The curve of her lips. Her hair in the sun, her bare skin. Smell of spice. *You are all kinds of stupid*, he thought. *You could have been nice. You could have talked to her. You won't see her again.*

His chest felt hot, and he coughed and stood. *It's all right. You needed to get rid of her. Best thing. Besides, there's a lot of stuff you ain't ever gonna see again.*

He took to searching the house. In the kitchen, he found Mom's Tracfone. It didn't have any minutes, but he could buy more. He gathered matches and two candles and the tin of peaches. A roll of duct tape. He set them on the table. What else? Some forks and spoons, sturdy cups. Can opener. From the pantry the rest of the spuds. Can of string beans. Coffee. The fry pan would take up space, but they'd need it. He got the Tupperware bowl from the cupboard and dumped out the money next to the matches.

Thirteen dollars and thirty-six cents.

When he got to the living room, he emptied the highboy and sorted the good, warm clothes from the beat-up stuff. A sparse pile. He folded up a blanket and a quilt. Two pillows. He put it all on the table and climbed the stairs. Toothbrushes and soap from the bathroom. Bandages. A comb. The soap was near new and would last awhile.

He headed for the bedroom and stood there in front of the closed door with his hand on the knob. When he opened the door, she was hanging from the ceiling fan. Her eyes gaping. He turned and checked the dresser and came away with three dollars and some change. In the closet was a duffel bag. No guns. He'd pawned the pistol and rifle long ago. He searched the dresser again, but there was nothing else worth taking. On the carpet by the bed he spotted Dad's hunting knife and picked it up. Then he unfolded the letter on the nightstand and read the two words typed in bold across the top: PAROLE DENIED.

So this is why. This is why you did it.

He stayed there a minute, holding the letter. Then he opened the drawer and put the letter next to her heart-shaped locket and closed the drawer. Their wedding photo was sitting on the dresser in a silver frame. He didn't mean to do it, but he looked at the spot where she'd hung, and she wasn't there anymore.

He tramped across the snowy yard to the barn and tugged the door open on its rolling metal wheels. Frozen dirt floor. A tool cabinet with peeling red paint. He rifled through the aluminum drawers and, in the bottom one, his hand closed over cool metal. He withdrew it: a hammer. He stuck it in his back pocket. In the corner in the gloom, there was a rusted Coke machine next to an old bookcase and a puffy recliner couch. Flowered upholstery. The steel springs of the cushions exposed. *This is where he used to read to me.*

On the shelves the books were stiff from the cold and half lost in dust. He crouched and pulled out a paperback. He hadn't known it was still here. *This was my favorite book. I'd beg him to read it.* All those warm gentle nights a bunch of summers ago, back when everything was good. He thumbed through the pages. *Life lived on life. There were the eaters and the eaten. The law was: EAT OR BE EATEN.*

Bleak daylight fell through the barn door. Grim as his heart.
White Fang knew the law well.

Later that summer, Dad had slouched on the couch and snorted crank and dreamed up big plans. The moon was high when Jack last saw him come thumping into the house with jumpy eyes and a blue vinyl briefcase. Two buckles on the top. Between them, a little brass latch. Dad had paced the floor for a handful of slippery minutes and twitched at shadows like a rabbit in an open field until some thought spooked him and he took off into the dark. When he got back, the briefcase wasn't with him anymore. And then the cops came.

That briefcase could be anywhere.

In the kitchen, Jack spread out everything on the table and looked it over. He added three Hot Wheels. A Batman action figure and a deck of UNO cards—things Matty liked. He packed the duffel until it could hold no more and then looked to the window at the road. Somebody would be coming soon. A cruiser, or maybe Services. Probably anytime now.

He saved his backpack for last. He knew what was in there. He unzipped the pack and pulled out its contents: A folder with homework. His student ID card, some pencils, a syllabus. And Ava's calculus book. He laid the book on the table. The hot-air balloon on the cover. Her name on the inside. He took the folder and other items and threw them in the trash. He looked at her book again. Picked it up and felt the weight in his hands. Then he put her book in the backpack. He loaded the duffel and the backpack in the Caprice and drove out onto the road.

IX

There are no Starbucks here. No espressos. No cappuccinos or caramel macchiatos. In this place if we want coffee, we brew the pot with our own hands. We pour the cup. We drink it black.

If we have a problem, we fix it.

Question: If you had one chance to save everything that mattered to you, would you grab hold of it? Or would you let it get away?

When Jack pulled into the prison work camp, it was about two o'clock. He drove slowly along the row of buildings to a spot near the visitors' entrance and parked and shut off the engine. He sat and watched the snow land on the windshield. The cold and ashen sky. Finally he went in.

A correctional officer sat at the front desk, drinking coffee and talking on the phone. He kept talking and looking Jack over until he hung up. "You need something, chief?"

"I need to see an inmate."

"Who?"

"Leland Dahl."

The officer picked up his mug off the counter, sipped, and put it down again. He leaned back in his swivel chair. There was a radio on somewhere.

"Well. He ain't exactly one for visitors."

"He'll see me."

"He expectin' you?"

"No."

The officer took another sip. "You ain't on the preapproved list."

"I need to see him."

"How old are you?"

"Eighteen."

The officer studied him. He tilted his head a little, as though he'd had a thought about Jack. He slid a clipboard across the desk. "You gotta fill out this application, and I gotta see ID."

When Jack finished the application, he handed it over along with his driver's license. The officer inspected the application and gave a cursory glance at the ID.

"Jack Dahl. You family?"

"Yessir."

"And you're eighteen?"

"Yes."

"If you ain't eighteen, you gotta have an adult to supervise."

"Good thing I'm eighteen then, huh?"

"You visited before?"

"Nope."

"Well." He handed back Jack's license. "I gotta see if he wants to see you. Why don't you sit a minute."

Jack nodded and sat on a sofa opposite the desk. On the end table were a water dispenser and little cups for drinking. He watched the officer swivel around and pick up the phone and talk into it.

"Yessir. I got a visitor for Leland Dahl here. Uh-huh. Name's Jack Dahl."

The officer paused, listening. Jack waited.

"I think so. Uh-huh. Will do. You bet."

When the officer hung up the phone, he sat back in the chair and sipped on his coffee. Then he opened the desk drawer and got out a ring of keys and snapped them onto his belt.

"Chief," he said. "It's your lucky day."

The officer stood up out of his chair and called for another officer to come watch the desk. Then he pushed a button so the gate to the jail buzzed open. Jack rose from the couch and followed him through the metal detector and down a hallway to a visiting room, where the officer used his key ring to unlock the door. Fluorescent lights switched on overhead.

"Find yourself a spot," he said. "I'll be back with him."

Jack went in, and the officer shut the door. The visiting room was empty save for him. Cinder block walls painted white. Floor a discolored pale tile. Eight tables were scattered about the room. Cheap oak veneers. Plastic chairs on chrome legs. There wasn't anything on the tables. No magazines. Nothing.

He went to a table in the rear corner and sat with his back to the wall. The air stale. Faint smell of disinfectant. There was a small window by the door, but it was up high and was dirty and cobwebbed, so he couldn't see out. He clasped his hands on the table and looked at them. The white bandages. Red blotches soaking through. When he looked up, the door opened.

Leland Dahl stood in the doorway. He wore orange prison clothes, like hospital scrubs: a loose shirt stuffed down the front of ill-fitting pants. Too many years of meth in his blood had eaten him down to wire and bone. He stepped into the room and stood looking at Jack. Eyes bright. Sunken and carved in shadow. Jaw smoked by beard, long nose bent, dark hair greasy and aged gray and combed over to the side. He was tall, hunched, rachitic. He came forward and slouched in the chair across from Jack. "Well, well," he said. "Lookie who's here."

The officer stepped inside, shut the door, and folded his arms across his chest. He stood there, waiting. He was about twenty feet away.

Leland let out a low whistle. "Well. Look at you. All growed up."

Jack watched him from across the table. He didn't speak.

"How long's it been? Four years?"

"Seven."

"Seven years. Shit, I must be dreamin'."

Jack didn't answer.

Leland stretched big and slumped back in the chair, legs sprawled wide. "You look good, little man. Real good." He smiled. A single teardrop branded in jailhouse ink crinkled at the corner of his eye. He put his hand on the table and curled his fingers and drummed them in a hoofbeat rhythm. "How's your ma? How's she doin'?"

"She's not so good."

"Why's that?"

Jack leaned forward. He spoke low, so the officer couldn't hear. "She wrapped your belt around her neck and hanged herself from the ceiling fan."

Leland's hand froze on the table. His eyes blinked. Except for that, he didn't move a twitch. "You're lyin'."

"No."

"Who knows?"

"Nobody. Not yet."

"You buried her?"

Jack nodded.

"Where?"

"Does it really matter?"

Leland stared at him. His muscles coiled. He looked like something crouched and ready to bite. "Don't you, or don't *nobody*, come in here sayin' my wife is dead."

Jack's pulse began to beat at his temple. "Well, she is. But Matty and me ain't."

All this time, Jack had watched the officer, who now stepped nearer the table. Jack watched the movement of the man's eyes, how they scuttled to him and away. At the desk the officer had looked relaxed, but he didn't look that way anymore. He was still too far off to hear much, but a few more steps and he'd be close enough. Jack felt doom spread through him. Coming here was a dangerous thing. He knew it.

Leland said, "Where's Matt?"

"With me. But we're gonna lose the house. There's bills."

Leland sat with his arms outstretched, palms flat on the table.

His chest moving with his breath. He made a fist with his right hand and put it in his left, rubbed his fist, rubbed hard so the veins popped up purple on his knuckles. He put his hand to his mouth. "I can't do nothin' for you."

"We need money."

"I can't do nothin'."

"We've got nowhere to go."

"You gotta leave."

"No."

Leland looked away. In the yellow light, his face glistened with sweat. He jerked his fist from his mouth and shifted his weight forward and rapped his knuckles on the table. He didn't look back at the officer. He muttered to Jack, "Get outta here."

"Please."

"I don't want you involved in this."

"We're already involved."

There was anguish and, at the same time, a kind of loathing remorse in Leland's eyes. "Go," Leland said. "I won't say it twice."

"Did you even try to get parole?"

"*Boy.* You talk of stuff you don't understand."

The officer took a step closer.

"You could help," Jack said.

"Go. Dammit."

Jack blurted, "I saw the briefcase."

Leland's gaze, long and stricken, stopped Jack's words. He glanced over his shoulder at the officer and spoke sharply. "You're mistaken."

"I'm not."

Leland leaned toward Jack, angled close, and shook his head slightly. Back and forth.

"I saw the briefcase—"

Leland lurched from his chair and grabbed Jack by the head and slammed his face to the table. The world went dark in Jack's eyes and he clawed at the table, trying to stand, but Leland pushed his head down harder. Jack felt his front teeth sink through his lip and he tasted blood and heard ringing and clattering steps. Leland leaned his face down to Jack's and brushed his beard against Jack's cheek, slid his lips to Jack's ear, kissed once. "You know better than this. Don't you come back here. You hear? *Don't you come back—*"

A clatter, and the pressure let off.

Jack sat up. The pain came hot and hard and swelled over his face in pulsing echoes. Blood ran down his nose. He stood and staggered and sat again. The correctional officer had hauled Leland backward against a wall. An alarm was going off. Only one of Jack's nostrils worked.

Jack pulled himself up and swayed. He thought he was going to puke, but he didn't. Red spit drooled from his lips to the tile in a long string. He moved his tongue along the punctured meat inside his swollen mouth. His lip throbbed. Blood—all over the front of his shirt. He stumbled across the room to the door, the floor tipping under his feet, and then stopped, and in the pale light he saw Leland standing in the corner with his hands cuffed behind him. Breathing no harder than if he'd just woken from a nap.

"When you get outta here, don't look for us," Jack said. "Don't try to call. Don't look for Matty. We don't want you. You understand?"

The words came out slurred. Leland just stood there. He seemed oddly at peace.

"*Eat or be eaten*," Leland said, his voice quiet. Fierce. "You know the law."

Jack turned and went tottering into the hall and through the metal detector, cupping his hand under his mouth to catch the blood. Nobody stopped him. At the desk the officer stood and asked if he needed to sit. He shook his head and walked through the front doors to the Caprice and got in. He started the engine and drove out of the parking lot.

He pulled off the road near the Stardust Inn and put the car in park. The steering wheel was slick with blood. He wiped his hands on his jeans and looked at his shirt: soaked red. His nose was still bleeding. He lifted the front hem of his thermal and twisted it into a coil and stuck the coil into his nostril. Then he tipped his head back and swallowed the thick stuff running down his throat. He sat that way for a minute. A wave of darkness came over him, and he waited for it to pass.

When the bleeding slowed, he pulled the coil from his nose. He got the duffel from behind the seat and took out a clean shirt and the box of bandages and put them in his backpack. He could feel a cough in his lungs. Nausea. *Do not throw up.*

He shut off the engine and opened the car door and got out, holding the backpack in front of his shirt. He checked the street.

Gray daylight. The pavement wet with snow. Nobody coming. He started toward the Stardust.

A yellow cat crossed the street. It stopped. Then trotted away.

He waited until a couple approached the door and then slipped in behind them. He went down a dim hallway. Blood dripped from his nose onto the floral carpet. He found a housekeeping cart by one of the rooms and took a fistful of washcloths, a towel, and a spray bottle of bleach cleaner. He looked for aspirin or Tylenol. He didn't find any, but he did come across little sugar packets, for the coffee machines. He stuck a few in his pocket and searched the cart's other side. No medicine. He picked up a plastic cup and unzipped his backpack and put in everything. He roamed the halls until he found a bathroom. He leaned on the door and went inside.

Raw sunlight fell through a small window. He spat bloody dribble into the sink. He dumped out the backpack onto the counter and put Ava's calculus book back inside. He arranged the rest—shirt and bandages, washcloths, spray bottle, plastic cup—on the counter. He peeled off his bloodstained thermal and threw it in the garbage. After turning the faucet to cold, he wet the washcloths and set about cleaning his face. Fresh pain stunned him. His lip pulsed like a water pump. He swabbed blood from his neck and chest, then patted himself dry and put on the clean shirt. Wind rattled the windowpane. A vacuum turned on somewhere.

When he looked in the mirror, he saw his lip was still leaking blood. He leaned over the counter and studied the gashes. Deep, already swollen.

With a fresh cloth, he blotted the sweat from his eyes and then held the cloth to his lip. He poured the sugar packets into the plastic cup and filled it with water and drank. Refilled the cup and drank again. He changed the bandages on his hands. They hurt something bad. He stuffed the still-clean towel and the spray bottle in his backpack and slung it over his shoulder.

The door opened. A maid came in, carrying a bucket of cleaning products. She paused upon seeing him. She looked at the bloody washcloth.

"Sorry," Jack said.

She stood there, one hand holding the bucket by its handle. "Are you okay?"

Jack coughed. "Yes. I'm sorry."

He stepped forward to walk past her. She shook her head and put a finger to her lips. Jack stopped.

She stepped into the hall with the door resting on her hip and looked out. Footsteps. Jack caught the shape of a man passing by, so he slid out of sight. He listened. The man kept walking.

Silence.

She opened the door wider. She gestured to Jack with her hand. "Go."

"Thanks," Jack said. "Thank you."

She stared at him, frowning. "Do you need help?"

Jack swallowed. She looked like someone who cared for the people in her life. The look hurt him. He shook his head. "No."

He said thank you again and turned and walked down the empty hall and out the door. Wind from the north licked his face, and pain tingled in his nose. He got in the Caprice and started it. He opened his backpack and took out the hotel towel and the bleach cleaner. He sprayed the bleach on the steering wheel and the door handle. With the towel, he wiped off the blood until no more could be seen.

All of a sudden he felt a creeping fear that someone was waiting for him in the rear seat. He jerked around and looked, but there was no one.

No. He was alone.

Alone, and he knew it.

He checked the clock. Quarter past three. He drove onto the road. At the Texaco he stopped and pumped five bucks of gas and bought an airtime card for the Tracfone. Three dollars and sixty-four cents left. He got in the Caprice and headed toward Matty's school.

X

I think about the Ifs. The little choices along the way. Each choice leading to another. All of them pointing to an end.

If I hadn't dropped my calculus book.

If Jack hadn't picked it up.

If I'd stayed. That day, at his house. And not walked away.

There's a multitude of Ifs that I let myself think about. Some moments you long for, to live inside them, to never leave. Others you regret. You wish for a second chance. I make sure to remember them all. It's a fine romance, this slow dance with fate. A sweet torture. I don't forget. I never will.

But then there are other choices.

Some Ifs, they want their pound of flesh. They're hard to dance with. You drag them around with you. You carry them on your back.

I think about if Jack hadn't gone to that prison.

Some Ifs,

they break your knees.

* * *

Bardem crossed Henry's Fork and took Red Road north into the desert. Fresh snow covered the blacktop and stood in razorlike skifts atop wires strung between burnt-looking fence posts. When he got to Big Grassy Ridge, the sun was almost down. A cold blue dusk with shadows of the north hills falling across the dunes. Silent and barren. He slowed and pulled onto the shoulder and left the motor running. He watched the road.

In a minute or so, a cruiser came into view. On its sides were the words IDAHO DIVISION OF PRISONS. Bardem reached into the pocket of his shirt and took out a Ziploc bag of dried venison. He withdrew a piece from the bag and sat eating.

The cruiser rolled up alongside the Land Rover and parked. The correctional officer stepped out. He wore a green coat and a Smokey Bear belt buckle. Bardem shut down the Land Rover's engine and got out and walked around the vehicle to the officer. He ate a bite of venison. "Well?"

"It was him," the officer said.

"And?"

"He waltzed in about two o'clock. Asked to see Dahl."

"And what happened?"

"I put them in a room together. Listened to their conversation."

"I guess you want me to ask what you heard."

Bardem stood there casually, chewing. The officer looked away. The wind smelled of snow and had a snap that drew water to his eyes. He looked back. Bardem watched him.

"Do you have the money?" the officer asked.

"I don't know. Do you have something worth paying for?"

The officer shifted his weight. "I told you last week. Dahl didn't get parole."

"Dahl didn't get parole. And now you want paid for this?"

The officer swallowed. "I don't want a part of no trouble."

"Part of no trouble."

"Right."

"But you already are."

"What?"

"You already are part of some trouble. You knew what this was when you agreed to it. You can't know something inside yourself and then pretend you didn't. That's not the way things work."

The officer turned away. His nose ran, and he snorted. The sun was near gone. It pinked the clouds and lit the snow to gleaming, and overhead a lone hawk rode the wind above the white rutted ground. Bardem put the last strip of venison in his mouth and chewed. He wore no coat. It was bitterly cold, but he seemed not to notice.

"The kid talked about a briefcase," the officer said.

"What color?"

"He didn't say."

"Where is the case?"

"Uh. I don't know."

Bardem crumpled the empty Ziploc bag in his hand and put it in his pocket. "What do you know?"

"What do you mean?"

"I mean, did you hear anything else?"

"Well, Dahl got irate. Slammed the kid's face into a table. Then after, he said something real weird. Something like, *you know the law*."

Bardem cocked his head and gazed at the officer. His blue eyes tranquil. Like lake water. In the deep glowing dusk, his skin was the color of candles and his face wore an odd smile.

"Interesting," Bardem said.

"I followed the kid to the Stardust. Went inside, but he shook me. He's quick."

"Quick. Like you?"

"What?"

Bardem just stood there, watching him. "And now," he said, "you want me to pay you for this information?"

The officer looked out across the darkening plain. The bare scrub oak and the riprap of dead branches humped in snow. Desolate country for miles. "I think Dahl told him. Where the briefcase is."

"You do."

"I can show you where he lives."

"I know where he lives. Do you think I wouldn't know where he lives?"

The officer looked away. He didn't answer.

"You and I are the same kind of man," Bardem said, "to a point. Our paths are not so different. But somewhere along the way, you decided to snitch on your employer. How did you get to this place? I'll tell you. You are here because you allowed it. You see?"

The officer looked at his car, then inhaled and bowed his head.

"You made choices," Bardem said. "I think you understand."

"I can get you the briefcase."

"If you could get me the briefcase, you would have it."

"I can help you." The officer licked his lip. "I can hurt you too."

"What?"

"I can tell people."

Bardem studied the officer. Very quiet. He shook his head.

"No," he said. "No, you can't."

Bardem pulled a pistol from the waist of his jeans and shot the man.

The correctional officer fell backward and lay breathing in the snow. Bardem jiggled him with his boot and looked down at him.

"You threatened me," he said. "Why did you do that?"

He shoved the pistol into his belt and watched the officer jerk and shudder until he stopped moving. The dark blood spread. The blood was melting the snow all around him.

Bardem walked to the Land Rover and opened the door and got in. He started the engine. He turned the lights on and drove back toward town.

At the sporting goods store he bought a handheld police scanner and batteries. He picked up a police transmission just southwest of Saint Anthony, crossing over North Fork Bridge. He turned the dial, listening. They had not found the correctional officer yet.

He pulled up to the house shortly after dark and switched off the headlights. There was a mailbox with the name DAHL written on it in black marker. A hedge of dead roses. At the end of the drive were a house and a barn. Everything veiled in the evening fog. Beyond the hedge, a field of dead bracken. He turned into the drive and approached slowly through the snow. Clapboards with scaling paint. No movement. When he got out, he carried a shotgun.

He climbed the plywood porch steps and tapped his knuckles on the door and waited. Nothing. He switched off the shotgun's safety. Then he opened the door and went in.

In the living room, he stood and listened. The dark shapes and the quiet. Faint smell of rot. A rocking chair by the stove and a highboy with drawers ajar. Somewhere a clock ticked.

He walked upstairs and down the hall and looked in the bedroom and in the closet. A housecoat on a plastic hanger. It was cold in the room. There had been no fire for a while. He pushed open the bathroom door and then went down to the kitchen.

When he flipped the light switch, nothing happened. He switched on the shotgun's safety and set it on the Formica table.

He walked to the sink and tipped up the faucet and ran a drizzle of water over his hands. The pipes were near frozen. He patted his hands on a towel hanging from the refrigerator handle. From the cupboard he took out a plastic tumbler and filled it with tap water and stood drinking. Dull winter moonlight. The shadows of tree branches moving on the linoleum floor.

He set the half-full tumbler on the counter. He opened all the cupboards. Baking soda. Pyrex dishes. In the pantry, a can of sugar.

He sat at the table and read the mail lying there. Next to the mail was a little toy car. A green Ferrari. He picked up the car and studied it in the frail glow of the moon. He rolled the tires over the Formica, watching the little wheels turn. He put the car in his shirt pocket.

He picked up the shotgun and crossed to the living room and opened the front door. He stood under the eave, inspecting the night. His pale breath rising.

Darkness. Trees rustling in the wind.

From the sky, a single snowflake drifted down. He went across the yard to the Land Rover and got in. He put the shotgun on the passenger seat. Then he started the engine and backed out and drove with the headlights off down the pale serpentine road.

XI

Most people think there's right and wrong and good and bad, or at least some form of it. I said that once before. I don't know if it's true. I wish I did. But for him there's no right and wrong in this world, and that's the thing I'm getting at. His eyes aren't like yours. They don't see what you see. You can't look in those eyes and understand. I think sometimes I want to understand, but mostly I don't. I can't fathom him. It's a simple fact. And if you tried, I think you'd risk your soul.

I don't try. I never will.

People will tell you the devil's a liar. They say he was from the start. The father of lies and all that stuff. But I don't believe it. No. He tells the truth. You wouldn't think you could be fooled with the truth. But you can.

Living with the devil.

It is not an easy thing to do.

Ava stands in the dim hallway in her favorite nightgown. She holds a stuffed animal: a little monkey with brown fur. In front of her, the bathroom door is open just a sliver, and behind the sliver a shadow moves dark and softly quick, sliding across the morning light. She watches the shadow. She can hear him in there, can hear water running. She thinks about what to do, and then she decides. She walks to the door. Making her bare feet quiet on the shag carpet. The top of her head just reaches the knob. She peeks through the sliver.

Fresh rays of sunlight fall in slants from the window. Bardem stands in front of the mirror, filling the sink with water. His face is bloody. He holds a washcloth to his head, above his right eye. Blood on the cloth. Blood all over his shirt. He unbuttons the shirt with his free hand and takes it off and folds it lengthwise and drapes the shirt over the shower rod above the bathtub. He turns off the water.

Ava watches. She sees things about him.

His darkness.

How the air hushes all around him.

He removes the washcloth. His face is cut and bleeding bad. The swollen gash curves down his forehead and over his cheek. It looks like a snake. He sponges water into the wound. Blood pinks away and surges up, dark red.

She holds her monkey. He hasn't seen her.

He stands straight, naked to the waist, dabbing and swabbing until the bleeding slows. He opens the cupboard and gets out scissors and a little white packet and a clear bottle. His movements precise. He unscrews the bottle and tips its contents over the cut. Then he gets out a needle and thread. He threads the needle and pokes the point into the skin on his cheek and stitches the wound together. He knots and snips the ends. A light sheen forms on his forehead. Other than this, he does not seem to feel anything at all. He washes the blood from his face and stands looking in the mirror.

She takes a step backward.

His eyes fall upon the door.

He pulls it open and smiles. The stitches pucker. "Hello, little one."

Ava smiles cautiously. He bends toward her and picks her up and sits her on the counter to face him.

"It is important," he says, "to know what to do when you're hurt. You can't always rely on a doctor. Don't worry, my bird. I'll teach you these things. So you will know."

He takes a syringe from the cupboard and sinks the tip into a vial of liquid and fills the glass barrel. Then he presses the plunger with his thumb until a bead of liquid bubbles at the needle tip. He flicks the syringe with his finger and slides the needle into his bicep and slowly pushes the plunger down.

He tosses the syringe in the trash. He pats her leg.

"Sit and help me shave."

From the drawer he takes a jar of cream and a shaving brush and something made of smooth black wood, the handle about the length of his palm. He lays a clean white towel on the counter next to her and spreads his tools on it.

"Proper shaving," he says, "is an art."

He opens the jar and dips the brush in and strokes the cream along his jaw and cheeks, avoiding the stitches. Then his chin. Ava breathes softly: She breathes him in. He smells like wild things. When he finishes spreading the cream, he looks at her. "Do you want to hold my brush?"

Ava nods. She holds the brush in one hand. In her other hand, she clutches the monkey. The soft velvet fur. She touches her cheek to the fur and hopes the monkey will stay very still. The monkey watches Bardem. Watches him pick up the black wood. From the handle, he unfolds the long straight razor. The silver blade catches the sunlight and flashes off the mirror, a bright gleam in the glow of morning.

He does not look at her. He says, "You're a good girl. My little bird."

Ava's bare legs dangle over the counter's edge. The tiles are cold. She wants to jump down, but she doesn't move an inch. On Bardem's cheek, the wound seeps a pale mix of water and blood. He holds the razor to his jaw and pauses and then pulls the blade across his skin. Slow, exact. The sharp edge scrapes.

He looks at Ava in the mirror. Through the quiet air, his soft voice slips, making its way into her. "Do you want to know what happened to my face?"

Water trickles from the faucet. Flash of blade. *Scrape.*

Somewhere a dog is barking. Ava looks out the window. A little yellow butterfly appears at the glass. Wings the color of lemons tremble, paper-thin, and behind the wings the sky is soft and blue as a china plate. She holds her breath.

Bardem slides the razor across his cheek, just below the cut. He does not take his gaze from the mirror. "Most men think they could kill another man if they had to. They always think that. Men or women. Either one. But this is not so. No. When the moment comes, they don't have what it takes. They never do." He shakes his head. "They don't see the truth of themselves. They lack the will."

Ava watches the butterfly. It hovers along the glass against the sky and lands on the window. The wings slowly spread and close. She doesn't dare blink but then her eyes begin to hurt, and she blinks.

The butterfly is still there.

It is looking right at her.

Bardem cleans the blade and folds the razor and places the black handle on the towel. He takes the brush from Ava and puts it down, and then he lifts her chin, turns her face from side to side, inspects her.

"Here is the truth," he says. "There is only one."

Light as air, he runs his fingers down her neck to her chest and stops on the spot just over her heart. "What you put here will make you hurt."

Ava holds his gaze. In the soft melting light, she observes the gentleness of her father's eyes. The strange blueness. She sits very still in front of those eyes. Through her nightgown, she can feel his fingertips.

He drops his hand. "Your mother tried to kill me. With a knife from the kitchen drawer. See this cut? She shouldn't have done that." His voice is even. Colorless. "Because of what she did, I made her leave. She's gone now. Do you understand? She isn't coming back. Ever. She will never come back."

Sunlight flashes on the mirror. The sink of water and blood. Ava sits holding the monkey. Her feet dangle. Her toes feel tingly. Her legs. Her arms.

"Do you understand?"

Ava nods.

"Say yes."

"Yes."

Bardem watches her. Then he nods, and his lips smile a little. He looks in the mirror and runs the palm of his hand over his jaw. His chin. He does not seem to notice the stitches at all. Ava's insides knot. She wipes her eyes. *Don't cry.*

"All things you choose to hold in your heart," he says, "have the capacity for pain." He looks at her, looks hard. "Be careful what you choose."

Ava nods.

On the window, the butterfly lifts into the air and flaps away. Bright flutter, blue sky. Ava jumps down from the counter.

"I love you, my Ava," Bardem says. "Always remember. I love you and nothing else."

Ava goes to her bedroom and climbs into bed and pulls the covers up over her face. Tears leak down her cheeks, and she squeezes her eyes shut. Clenching her monkey. *Don't cry. Don't cry.* She hugs the monkey tight.

In a dream, Mom comes to Ava and sits on the bed and holds her hand. She leans forward and kisses Ava's hair. Quiet of the night and starlight at the window, between the billowing drapes. *Please don't leave me.*

In the morning, she is gone.

XII

Sometimes you block a thing that hurts. You lie to yourself and say it isn't there, but the whole time you know it is. It's like a piece of metal you've swallowed. It bothers you, but you've sort of gotten used to it. This thing inside you. You've been swallowing it for years.

They sat in the dark in the Caprice and looked at the house. The brick around the windows blackened from fire, and all the glass gone. Burnt porch. Wood rails twisted like charred matchsticks. Dead shrubs of hawthorn on either side. The front door propped open with a cinder block. A drift of snow blown in. Jack watched the windows for movement. Nothing. Cold and getting colder.

Jack inched the Caprice up the drive and around to the rear of the house. Old firewood lay stacked under the eave. It looked dry. He could see no tracks in the snow. Ancient trees of stripped oak to the west, and on the hillside, crops dead and flattened under clinging mounds of white. Big snowflakes floating down. Pale as bone in the moonlight. No other houses in any direction. No lights. Jack shut off the engine, and Matty tugged on his sleeve.

"What if somebody's in there?"

"It's abandoned. Nobody's here."

"The windows are black."

"Yeah. I think there was a fire."

"This house is scary."

"No. It's a good house."

"Why can't we go home?"

"I told you. We can't anymore. It isn't safe."

"Could we go someplace else?"

"We have to try here. It's gettin' cold."

Matty sat looking at the house.

"The fire was a long time ago," Jack said.

"There could be another fire."

"There won't be."

"Okay."

"Nobody's here."

Matty said again, softer: "Okay."

They got out of the Caprice and trudged up the back steps and into what looked to be the kitchen. Buckled floor underfoot. General Electric oven buried in soot, and along the wall the scorched remains of cabinetry. Smell of wet ash. The gritty taste in his mouth. *This house is like somebody's memory of a house*, Jack thought. *But not recent. They forgot it years ago.*

He looked at Matty. He stood there, shivering with his hands in his coat pockets. His breath a plume in the gray dark.

"Come on," Jack said. "Everything's all right."

The living room was mostly unburned, the air cleaner. There was a fireplace. An upright piano against the far wall and under the window a sofa crusted in silt. Flowered wallpaper peeling away from plaster. The ceiling waterstained. Jack went to the door and moved the cinder block away and kicked snow from the threshold and swung the door shut. The deadlatch looked rusted and dull, and he thought it wouldn't budge, but with some pushing the metal bolt slid into the strike plate. Scrape of steel in the groove. *Good*.

He looked out the window, toward the road. Dim moonlight shining down. Frozen sky and the gloom. No sound.

He went back through the kitchen and out to the car. Matty didn't want him to go, but he said he'd be fast. From the trunk he got the duffel, pillows, blankets. The hammer and the tarp. He piled it all on the living-room carpet. Darkness growing. If they could not cover the windows overnight, they would be real cold. They would be in trouble. They would probably freeze.

Matty watched him.

"It will be okay."

Matty nodded.

He coughed and tasted blood in his mouth. He touched his sleeve to his lip, and it came away red. Stitches were needed maybe. What to do about it? He picked up a blanket and wrapped it around Matty like a robe.

"Stay here."

He searched the bedrooms. Empty. The carpet dank and rotting. In the bathroom he opened the cupboard under the sink and found three dry bath towels, a glass tumbler, a can of Lysol. He carried the towels to the living room and put them on top of the duffel and headed to the garage and opened the door. Nothing. Cement floor splotched with oil stains. Nothing. The cough in his throat. What to do? Every minute colder.

In the living room, he walked the walls. There was a nice strong nail there lodged in the drywall. He pried it out with the claw of the hammer, his fingers numb with cold. He looked for more nails and came up with a row of three in the kitchen and pried those out too. Another a good half inch long from the bedroom. He stuck them in his pocket and picked up the towels. He draped one over the living-room window and measured with his eyes. If he used all three towels, it would do. After he nailed down the towels across the top, he looked at the other window. He would have to use the quilt. There was nothing else. He took it from the pile and hung it in place. He secured the bottom part against the wall with the cinder block. He opened the duffel and got out the duct tape and taped down the towel and blanket edges against the window casings. Matty stood wrapped in the blanket, watching everything. "What are you doing?"

"We need to keep out the cold."

"Should I help you?"

"No. You stay here."

Jack went out the back door and loaded his arms with split wood and carried the pieces inside and heaped the fireplace full. He struck one of the matches and opened the damper wide. Curls of smoke looped up the flue. The wood caught flame. He set a can of beans on the fire and brought in more logs and stacked them in the corner. In front of the hearth, he laid out the tarp over the carpet and made a nest on top with the blanket and the pillows. He put the duffel in the middle. His chest hurting. His lip. The cough in his throat.

He pushed the piano to the edge of the tarp to form a wall and hold in heat. He stood there in the glow of the fire. Outside the small pool of light, he could see darkness spreading. A black to choke him.

He looked at Matty.

Hiss of flame.

Matty went to the duffel and pulled out the deck of UNO cards. He sat cross-legged in the blanket nest and looked up at Jack. His face in the firelight. The cold air. "It's like a fort."

"Yes," Jack said. "Like a fort."

They played UNO and ate beans straight from the can, passing it back and forth between them. The old hearth warming. Faint fireshapes on the wall. Matty won three games, then set to building card houses while Jack brought in more wood. After they put away the cards, Jack covered Matty in the blanket and scrunched it around him and took off Matty's shoes and rubbed his feet over the socks. They had to sting from the cold, but Matty didn't complain. After a while he said, "Your lip is bleeding."

"Yeah. A little."

"Your face is all beat up."

"I got in a fight. It's over now."

"Who did you fight?"

"Just a guy. It doesn't matter."

"Why did he fight you?"

Jack coughed softly. He looked at the fire. It was dying, and its light didn't reach far.

"Did you make him mad about something?"

"We just fought. That's all."

"Does he know where you are?"

"No. He doesn't know where we are. Don't worry."

"I don't want him to come here."

"He won't."

"I don't want him to hurt you."

Jack didn't answer. Outside the door, he could hear the wind starting. Thin branches of the hawthorn scraping brick. A distant rustling. Trees. He tucked the blanket under Matty's feet. "Nobody's going to hurt me."

"Why?"

"I won't let them."

Matty was silent.

"Do you believe me?"

"I don't know."

"I won't let anyone hurt you either."

"Okay. I have a question."

"What?"

"I'm not going to school tomorrow. Am I?"

"No."

"Did you lock the door?"

"Yes. I locked it."

Matty lay there, looking at him. Studying him. Then he closed his eyes and kept them closed.

"Mom isn't on a trip," he said. "Is she?"

Jack swallowed. A spider crawled across the ceiling.

"No. She isn't on a trip."

In dreams he held the shovel and he dug. The cold handle biting his hands. The dark and the snow. When he got close to her, he dropped the shovel and fell to his knees. With his hands he pushed the snow and wet dirt away and uncovered her damp cheek. Plastic white of her skin, and her lips caked in black. Her yellow hair. Bit of rainbow blanket. When he woke he couldn't keep from getting up. The cough in his throat. The ash. He put wood on the fire, and then he just stood there watching Matty sleep. The fire crackling. He listened to the wind and he listened to the crackle and he listened to the thud of his heart.

"You should sleep," he told her.

"The house creaks," she said. "It keeps me awake."

"It's late."

She didn't answer.

"Come on. I'll take you upstairs."

"No."

She sat there on the kitchen counter in her nightgown, smoking a slender length of weed rolled in rice paper. Her knees drawn up over the kitchen sink and her hand across her skinny legs. Holding the joint with a wispy grace. Frail tendrils of smoke rising from the tip. She didn't turn toward him but kept looking out the open window into the dark. "I don't like this house."

"It's our home."

"Our home?"

"Yes."

She shut her eyes. "This is not a home."

"We can make it a home."

"No. We can't."

"We can make it good again."

She gazed into the dark, her pale-skin glowing in the moon-light. Almost cerulean. Her hair was tangled and unkempt. "We can't make it good. Nothing is good. Nothing ever will be."

"I can get help," he said. "I can take you to a doctor."

"You think I want help?"

"They have places you can go."

"I don't want help."

"What about Matty?"

"I'm all used up. There's nothing left for him. Or you."

"You're his mom."

She shook her head. "I am nobody's wife. I am nobody's mom."

"Matty needs you."

"I don't care."

"Please, Mom."

She looked at him then, her eyes mauve. At once clouded and lucid-bright from all the pills. "You know what I used to think? All those years? Before I learned better?"

"Shh, Mom. Please."

"Letters from your dad. He'd say he was coming home. That we'd all be together. Do you know how many times I believed him?"

He watched her, silent. *Ignore it. The twisting in your gut. Ignore it.*

She lifted the joint to her lips and drew in a slow breath. Exhaled the smoke. "I used to sleep to dream of him, but I don't dream like that anymore. In the dreams he came home and stayed, but now I know different. He is not coming home, and we are alone in this world, and no dream is going to change it. You know that, don't you? He's never coming home."

"He could get parole."

She shook her head, laughed.

"You have to keep hoping."

She shook her head.

"He's gone. But Matty's here. I'm here."

"You just don't get it. You think your love is strong enough to make me quit. But it isn't. I don't care. I *don't care*. Can't you see? I have a new family."

"You mean the pills."

"I mean the pills."

"You have to try, Mom. You're hurting yourself."

She shook her head.

"You're going to die."

"Oh yes, I am. And I hope for it. With all my heart."

"And what am I supposed to tell Matty?"

She smiled briefly. It was almost unbearable. "You live with your soul and you die with your soul. And my soul is dead. I'm already dead."

He tried to breathe.

Mom is sick. She just needs some help.

"You have to try, Mom. Lots of people who get addicted recover. Don't shake your head. I'll get a job to pay the bills, and we'll be okay. You'll see. We'll be happy again. Me and you and Matty."

She fixed her gaze on him. Whisper of wind. Shadows unfolding themselves from the darkness behind her. "You look like him," she said. "I hate you for it."

For a moment he stood there, shaking. This glass heart.

He left without looking back.

In the night he watched the fire and he watched Matty and he listened for cars on the road, but there were none. He lay awake. Coughing into the blanket. Listening to the wind. *This is not a safe place. You have to think about what to do. Someone will find you here. Someone will see the smoke.*

Just sleep. Don't think now.

Think in the morning. Go to sleep.

He lay there and watched the black sky. A few pale stars. He couldn't remember much anymore how she looked when she was alive. If only he'd turned back for one last look.

XIII

Sometimes I visit the moments and watch them backward, from end to begin-ning. As if I might find meaning somewhere in all of it, lost in the flow of inverted time. Stop and start. Push a button and hit rewind: Lying in the snow with the warmth gathering back into me. Running backward through trees, white cupped along branches, white that floats up in flakes to the sky . . . My hand ungripping Jack's, and behind me the devil following backward . . .

and

Heat of a fire and Jack lying on the ashen carpet, all the blood on his shirt unblotching. The cuts on his stubborn face unhealing, and his eye unbruising . . . the flames shrinking down by some miraculous force, until the lit match flares between my fingers . . .

and so on, and

Lockers and a crowded school and Luke Stoddard standing there, his white cheeks blooming to red. Here I can always hear Jack's voice: "You need good hands in football, don't you?" Math papers sweep together along the floor and gather into a book that rises from the polished concrete into my hands . . . a hot-air balloon on the cover . . .

And so on, and so on.

Stop and start. Rewind.

Some moments I speed up or slow down. And I ask myself how short it was, or how long, how wide and deep. I pull apart the minutes until there's no beginning or middle or end, but a circle, and all the minutes untangle into many marvelous moments seen at once. Where everything makes sense, and nothing hurts.

But you want the story in order.

From A to Z.

One to ten.

> *Beginning*
>> *to*
>>> *end.*

And I love you for that.

So. Here you go.

Doyle pulled onto Big Grassy Ridge alongside the deputy cruiser and parked and got out. Midge was already standing by the door of her truck, holding her black ledgerbook. Coat zipped to her chin and fur trapper hat over her ears. Faint shadows crossing the horizon. The sun coming up. Wind.

Doyle walked to the rear of the cruiser. "Damn."

Midge sniffed. "Yup."

The dead correctional officer was lying in the snow with his eyes open. His face frozen blue. He looked like he was gazing at something in the sky. Doyle crouched and studied the hole in the officer's cheek. "Looks like a .40 caliber. Close range."

Midge kicked a toe full of snow. "Got the call from Jake Willis, who was out huntin'. He saw the car."

"He see anybody else?"

"Not a soul."

Doyle put on gloves. He leaned on his bootheels and pushed the officer onto his side and inspected the back of his head. Stiff hair stuck to tissue. White skull. The bullet went clean through. He reached into the officer's hip pocket and pulled out a wallet. "Got a twenty here. Driver's license."

The officer's name was Frisby. Doyle had known him only slightly but thought he seemed decent enough. "Poor wife's gonna be heartbroke."

"Cute kids too. Three, I think."

"Hmm." Doyle tucked the wallet back into the officer's pocket. He stood and studied the boot tracks in the snow. Two pairs.

"What do you think he was doin' out here all this way?" Midge asked.

"Meetin' somebody's my guess."

Midge rose and pushed down her hat. Adjusted the earflaps. Her nose was turning red. Her coat looked too big. "Well," she said, "I wonder."

Doyle watched her. "You wonder what?"

"Well, I was just wonderin' about yesterday. I was meetin' a friend for lunch—she works at the prison—and I saw Frisby leave. He took off like a bat outta hell right after Dahl's kid left. Weird thing happened: kid got his face beat up."

"Dahl's boy came to see him?"

"Yup. He sure did."

"Well, how'd he get beat up?"

"Didn't see. Just caught a glimpse a him with blood all down his face."

"And Frisby was there?"

"Yeah. He was."

"Hmm."

"What you thinkin'?"

"Not sure. But somethin' don't add up."

Doyle walked along the edge of the bootprints. When he got to the tire tracks, he stopped and studied them. The cruiser made one set. The other belonged to a vehicle with wider wheels. Something four-wheel drive. "Will you get me a measurin' tape?"

Midge went to her truck and got a tape measure and brought it back. Doyle crouched and extended the tape across the track.

"You think this whole deal's got to do with the Dahl boy's visit?" Midge said.

"I got a suspicion."

He retracted the tape and eased himself up and stretched his back. He looked out over the desert. Hills dark in the grudging light. A bitter wind blowing from the north. He thought about dying alone out here. It bothered him.

"I reckon I ought to go out to this good officer's place before his wife sees this on the damn Internet." He handed her the tape. "You know where she lives?"

"Naw. But I can look it up."

"Well, don't worry. I'll find out. You get a report started. Send Hank over to pick up the body."

"Will do." She stood with the tape measure in one hand and the ledger in the other. "Doyle?"

He looked at her. She was just standing there in the wind.

"I got a bad feelin' 'bout this," she said.

"I believe that's called for."

"Do we have a plan?"

Doyle nodded. "We find Jack Dahl."

When he got to his truck, he took off his gloves. He reached into his jacket for his pillbox and dropped two heart pills into his palm. He put them in his mouth and swallowed.

Jack woke before sunrise. He lay in the makeshift fort and watched the gray dawn break. Leaden shadows moving in the cold and the dark of the house. Slow and pallid. Like the coming of some dull anemia. He coughed and reached out and touched Matty sleeping beside him. The thin ribs. Jack watched him sleeping. Oh, his chest. It hurt. He gathered the blankets about Matty and covered him good, and in the noiseless gloom he rose and pulled on his shoes and walked out to the yard. He stopped at the woodpile, and there he crouched over coughing. His lip throbbed. Blood misted the snow at his feet.

He stacked dry wood in his arms and then he just stood at the woodpile, his face to the chafing wind, and looked out over the yard. Darkened poles of trees. The road in the clearing and, beyond that, the dim white fields. Heavy sky. Farther along, he could make out houses here and there. Not close but not very far either. Wan light in the windows. There could be someone out there, watching.

Eyes to see. See the smoke, the tire tracks in the snow. He turned and carried the wood inside.

Stale dust of ash in the kitchen. The sooty taste on his lips. Blackened walls. *Look around you*, he thought. *Look at this place. You brought him here.*

He passed through the dark house to where Matty slept curled up against the piano, and he stifled a cough so as not to wake him. Quiet as he could, he piled the split logs in the cold hearth and then crouched and unfolded the hunting knife and scraped off wood shavings. With a little effort, he got a tuft of fire going. The small flame licked the dry wood and flared in the paltry light. Matty turned over in the blankets. He opened his eyes and whispered, "Hi."

"I'm right here."

"I know."

He lay watching Jack. He rubbed his eyes.

"What's wrong?"

"Nothing."

"Something is."

"I had a bad dream."

"What about?"

Matty shrugged. He looked almost ready to cry. Jack crawled to him and got under the blankets and held him. "Hey," he said. "Shhh, it's okay."

"It was a sad dream."

"You could tell me about it if you want."

Matty whispered, "We were back at our house, and we had this dog. His hair was yellow, and he would fetch things like a ball or sticks if you threw them, and he would lick your face, or you could shake his paw. He was a good dog." He stopped and drew a breath. "Then we left our house and we never went back, and we didn't take the dog with us. We left him there alone."

"That sounds sad."

"Yeah. It was."

"We didn't have a dog, though."

"I know. Just in the dream we did."

"Okay."

Matty didn't say anything. He lay huddled in the blankets, watching the fire. His face pale in the gaunt orange light. After a while he looked at Jack. "If we had a dog, we wouldn't leave it, would we?"

"No. We wouldn't leave it."

The fire warmed. Pop of flame. A glow of light on the ceiling. Jack held Matty until he fell back asleep, and then he rose out of the blankets and tended the fire. He couldn't rest. His throat hurt, and his swollen face. His heart. He walked into the kitchen, coughing.

Look at this place.

Any louder and the racking cough would wake Matty. He went outside. Wheezing and rasping. Then a long silence. The wind in the black stands of birch. He stood there holding his chest, and he lifted his face to the first raw light of day. *Where are you?* he thought. *Are you here? Do you see us here, in this place?*

He listened.

Nothing but the wind.

No, he thought. *You're not here. You never were.*

Doyle drove from Big Grassy Ridge to the Dahl place and climbed the porch steps and knocked at the door. He waited. No sound in the house. He knocked again. "This is Sheriff Doyle. Anybody home?"

He walked into the living room. The air was downright chilly. He flicked the light switch. Nothing. His shadow on the wall. Ugly feeling in his gut. *Don't think bad,* he thought. *Not yet.*

"Jack? Anybody here?"

He went to the kitchen and opened a cupboard and shut it. The refrigerator was dark inside. Upstairs, he looked in the bathroom. Empty drawers. *Yeah, well. You did this.*

He walked back into the kitchen and sat at the table. He put both arms on the Formica and leaned forward and bowed his head.

Bardem drove to the high school after the first bell rang. He turned into the parking lot and rolled down his window. Bright sun. The snowflakes drifting down in sparse frosty bits. He slowed to a stop. There were some boys eating pastries in the parking lot. Glazed doughnuts from Broulim's Supermarket. Three of them. Young, maybe fifteen. They stood around a Buick Skylark with their doughnut sacks on the car hood. Relaxed. Laughing. Bardem got out and approached them.

"Excuse me," he said. "I wonder if you could help me."

One of the boys took a bite of his doughnut. "Who're you?"

"I wonder if school is in session."

"Who wants to know?"

"Shut up, Blake," another boy said.

Blake looked at them, and then he looked at Bardem. He squinted a little, as though wanting to get a closer view of the man who stood there. He wiped his mouth on his sleeve.

"I'm looking for Jack Dahl," Bardem said.

"We ain't seen him."

"What does he drive?"

They looked at each other.

"Old Chevy," one said. "Red, I think."

"Do you know where he is?"

They shook their heads.

The sun shimmered on ice-topped pavement. Bardem stood there, gazing at them. "Do you know where you are?"

"What?"

"I said, do you know where you are?"

The boys looked at each other again.

"Every moment in this life is a choosing," Bardem said. "You're on a path, and with each choosing, you head farther down the path. You draw the destination. The shape of it. You see? The paths diverge in a yellow wood. You cannot travel both." He waited, watching them. "Today you're eating doughnuts in a parking lot. Where will you be tomorrow?"

The boys didn't move.

"Look, mister," Blake said. "We don't know what you mean."

Bardem smiled. "You're a bit stupid, aren't you?"

"Blake," one boy muttered. "Let's go."

Bardem stood with his arms at his sides, his fingers resting against his pressed jeans. Snow bits fell on his hair and gathered in clean white clumps.

Blake licked his lip. "We better go."

"That's good," Bardem said. He nodded. "Good choosing."

XIV

Maybe you think it's wrong. Me, guarding all these memories.

I don't care.

I will guard them.

Jack lay in the blankets and weighed what to do. The sun had been up for a couple of hours, but Matty still slept by the fire. He probably wouldn't get up for a while. Still, if he did, Jack knew he'd be scared. No, better to wait. *Wait until you've given him the phone. Until you've said goodbye.* In his head, Jack kept hearing Dad. What he'd said. *Eat or be eaten.* Why say that?

Yeah, so you read some books together. It doesn't matter. Not anymore.

Just forget, Jack.

All these memories.

He is gone, and you are here. You and Matty.

He pulled back the blankets and rose and searched the duffel and fished out a few toys. The little cars and Batman. He placed them in front of the fire for when Matty woke. Fresh clothes and a toothbrush. He laid the last dry log on the embers and watched it catch flame. Then he pulled on his boots and crossed the kitchen to the back door. Outside he filled the fry pan with clean snow. His cheeks hot. He could feel that he had a fever. How bad? He went in and put the fry pan in the hot outer coals of the fire. Matty still asleep. From the duffel he dug out a tin of peaches and coffee and spoons and set it all on top of the piano. Three potatoes and one can of beans left. The beans and can opener he put on the hearth, by the toys.

There had been no cars on the road in front of the house. Not in the night, and not in the morning either. No one passing by.

He'll be safe here for one day. You'll leave and be back by dark.

He made two trips to the woodpile and heaped a nice stack by the hearth. A few more would be enough. On the third trip he felt weak and stopped at the porch, light-headed. He turned and looked at the fields. The farmland: dead and white. The driveway, the road. Some coffee would help. Maybe a bite of peaches.

Come on, Jack. Just last the day.

You have to hold on.

The door squeaked behind him. Matty stood holding the knob, coat zipped to his chin, wild hair tangled, fidgeting from foot to foot.

"You brought Batman."

"I did."

"Are we having peaches?"

"Yes. We are."

Matty watched him a minute. "Are you okay?"

Jack smiled. The wounds stung in his mouth. "Yeah. I'm just getting wood."

"Can I help?"

"I'd like that."

Matty smiled. He looked at the sky. "It's gonna snow."

"I think you're right."

"We could make a snowman later."

"That sounds good."

Jack melted snow in the pan and made coffee. He poured a cup and handed it to Matty, who sat in front of the fire. "Have some," he said.

Matty took the cup in both hands and leaned his face into the dark heat. He tilted the cup and sipped. "It's really good."

They drank the coffee together, hot and strong. Then Jack peeled back the tab on the peaches. He gave the tin to Matty with a spoon. "Go ahead."

"You have some."

"I want you to have it."

Matty spooned a wedge into his mouth and handed the tin back. "Now you."

They took turns. Savoring each sweet bite. When the peaches were gone, Matty tipped the tin and drank the rich syrup and then licked the lid. Then he just sat quietly, cheeks flushed. His pale skin glowing in the firelight, almost incandescent: a lit match. Jack sat there with the taste of peaches like drenched sunlight fading in his mouth and something in his chest constricting tighter and tighter until he couldn't wait any longer. He stood and went to the backpack and took out the phone. Matty stared up at him, suddenly alert.

He walked to Matty and crouched. "Take it."

"You're going somewhere, aren't you?"

"Yes. I have to get food."

Matty looked at the beans and the potatoes. "Is that all we have?"

"Almost."

"Are we going to die?"

Jack sat by him. "No. Someday, I guess. But not now."

"Are you sick?"

"A little. But I'm going to get better."

"I could go with you."

"No. I need you to stay here."

"Why?"

"Someone needs to keep the fire going. It's an important job, short stuff. Can you do that?"

Matty looked at the fire. He didn't answer.

"There's enough wood for all day," Jack said. "And beans for lunch. I'll be home by dark."

"That's a long time."

"Yes. But you'll be okay."

"Will you be okay?"

"Yes. I will too."

"Are you sure?"

Jack nodded.

"And I'll be here."

"Yes."

"To keep the fire going."

"Yes."

Matty watched him, eyes bright. He looked as if he were being twisted by some tight, invisible grip. "Okay."

"I'm going to leave you this phone. For if you need it."

Matty's gaze held Jack's. "But I won't need it. Right?"

"I don't think so. But just in case."

"Who would I call?"

"Mrs. Browning. I put her number in. See? You just push the button. You tell her you're in the old Palmer house on Egin-Hamer Road. You only call if I'm not back by dark. You understand? Only if it turns dark."

"If I call Mrs. Browning, will she take me to Services?"

Jack's mouth felt dry. It hurt to swallow. Along the soot-stained plaster wall, a mouse scuttered, stopped. Watched him.

"I'll be back by dark," he said at last.

Matty took the phone from his hand and held it. "Okay."

At the high school, Doyle went to the main office where a woman sat at the reception desk, typing. She looked at him over her reading glasses. "Hello, Sheriff."

"Victoria. I'm lookin' for Jack Dahl."

She typed and squinted at her screen. "He's absent."

"Is there a teacher or somebody I could talk to about him?"

"Maybe Miguel Navarro." She buzzed an inner office. "Go on in."

Doyle walked into the office and closed the door, and the

man behind the desk stood. Doyle knew Navarro was the school counselor. He was tall and thin with a quiet soul and dark, shadowed eyes that didn't miss much. He'd been military years ago and limped from an old war injury, but he didn't talk about those days. That was fine with Doyle. Neither did he. Navarro held out his hand and smiled. "Sheriff."

They sat across from each other. Doyle in a hard curved chair on a metal frame and Navarro in a fake leather one at the desk. Light gleamed from the window, where icicles hung. A big motivational poster was pinned on the wall. It read: YOU RUN OUT OF CHANCES ONLY WHEN YOU STOP TAKING THEM. Navarro clasped his hands on the desktop. "What can I do for you, Sheriff?"

"I'm lookin' for Jack Dahl."

"He in law trouble of some kind?"

"Not that I know of."

"Have you tried his house?"

"Yes, I have. What can you tell me about the boy?"

Navarro picked up a pencil and tapped it on the desk. "He's got a younger brother. Matthew, I think. You checked the brother's school?"

"My deputy did. Nobody's seen him."

"And the mom?"

"Not hide nor hair of her, neither."

Navarro's smile faded. He studied Doyle. "You think he took off."

"I believe this boy's done flown the coop."

"You think he's got himself into some sort of danger. Don't you?"

"Yes. I do."

A fan kicked on somewhere. Papers on a bookshelf fluttered. Navarro looked out the window and let the pencil hang in his hand. "I tried to bring him in a couple years ago, but he wouldn't talk to me. He didn't give me any cause to drag him in either. Keeps himself out of trouble. DCFS dropped by, and I knew it was going south with the mom."

"Who are his friends?"

"I don't know of any. I don't believe he permits such things."

"What do you mean by that?"

Navarro shrugged. "He's a loner. Careful."

"I need to find him."

"Well. Then you've got a problem."

"Why do you say that?"

Navarro glanced from the window to Doyle. "I just mean he's smart."

"Oh?"

"On paper he's a mess—Cs and Ds across the board. But his test scores? His SAT was 1390. As a sophomore."

"I guess that means a lot, by the way you say it."

"If Jack Dahl don't want to be found, odds are good you won't find him."

Doyle tipped his head slightly. "I don't know. I'm pretty good at findin' things."

"I hope you are."

Doyle studied Navarro. His face, the shallowness of his breath. The smallest quiver of his hands. "You like him, don't you?"

Navarro blinked. "What makes you say that?"

"I can hear it in your voice."

"I like him."

Doyle nodded. "So do I."

He tipped his hat and left.

XV

What made you? How did you form? From where did your layers and your curves and your holes come? Your gentle and your savage places? The bright and the deep hallowed dark. The valleys and cliffs of your soul. The loud and the silent. For what does your heart beat?

I think about these things.

Jack would go see Uncle Red even though Red scared him. Red lived seven miles across town, but Jack drove the back roads to avoid being seen. Snow covered the blacktop, and clouds of fog huddled over the ground. He headed toward the river, carving a barren path. Wet gray flakes twisting and falling out of nothing. *What will you say? Think. You need to be ready.* Where the road forked, he turned into deeper unmarked snow.

Red's place sat back in the trees, down a narrow draw along the Snake River's edge. Cloudy vapor coming off the water near the house. A haggard shape in the haze. Weathered planks. Nails rusted and walls patched by black tar paper. The chimney pipe spilled a silky thread of ash and smoke. One of the windows was cracked open, and from it an electric cord snaked across the snow and vanished into the trees. In the side yard, deerskins stretched from saplings, where cuts of fresh meat dangled, venison left to age and bloom bone-deep flavor in the cold.

Dad had hunted with Red back in the day, when the freezers were full and the brothers were bound by secrets and blood. Red knew Dad better than anybody.

Jack shut off the engine and got out. Hush of quiet. The low rushing dash of river water on rocks and ice. Evergreens drooped with snow and beyond them, in the distance, was the jagged crest of the Tetons, monuments of stone rising up through the gloom with juts and angles and bleak shadowed parts untouched by sun. Inside the house a dog or two barked, and then Bev opened the front door.

"Now why're you out here in this crud?" Bev asked. "Supposed to snow all day."

"I need to talk to Red. He around?"

"Sure is. Come on in and get warm."

Bev was Red's wife number three, and Jack felt shy around her. She was a talked-about woman in town, made of curves and soft pillowy parts, with plump lips and blond hair she curled with hot rollers. Bev was given to astrology and reading palms. About a year ago she'd told Jack matter-of-factly that, in a dream, she saw him naked on a snowcapped mountaintop surrounded by the gods of Odin. She typically wore flowery kimono robes. Each spring she concocted healing elixirs of herbs and oils, and more often than not she told prophecies on weekend evenings while going fast on crank.

Bev held the door open for Jack while dogs came to wag tails and sniff until Bev shooed them outside. "We got coffee. Want some?"

"That'd be nice."

They sat at the kitchen table. A fire in the potbelly stove sent heat across the floor and walls. On the cast-iron stovetop, coffee steamed from a pot next to an empty pan, where eggs had fried. Washed garments hung on a clothesline strung from the room's corners. Socks and Bev's lace underthings looked near dry, but heavier coats and pants still dripped water. At the front door, a shotgun stood ready. Jack knew that if he looked to the rear door, there'd be another waiting there. Centered on the table sat an African violet atop a crocheted doily, and scattered around the violet were a pistol and a deck of tarot cards and an empty whiskey bottle. A mason jar of pot rested beside the whiskey.

"Red's out back smokin' deer for jerky," Bev said. "But I bet he heard you come up. He'll be in."

They sipped hot coffee. Shadows lay in the house's chill corners, and inside the windows, water beaded in droplets to trickle down glass. Fog the color of dishwater curled in wisps outside the dirty panes.

"How's your ma?" Bev asked.

The rear door opened. Uncle Red stood in the doorway holding a knife, the blade stained dark and glistening. He looked at Bev. "Coffee."

Bev scooted from her chair.

Red walked to the kitchen sink and ran the knife under the tap and rinsed his hands. He was dressed in a thick parka and field pants stuffed into Red Wing boots, and on his head he wore a scrap of black wool tied at the back like a scarf. He was fierce and redbearded, a veteran of old battles, his face hewn of bone and his long hair matted and his muscles lean. Red was Dad's elder and had been a fine meth chef years ago until a rival dealer laid hands on him with an axe. They'd meant to skin his scalp clean off, but in the end Red struck a deal. Folks didn't speak of that grisly skirmish. Red never cooked again, but some whispered that he still sold product to buyers who kept mouths shut. The axe had carved a savage swathe across his skull on the right side, and the hair there was mostly gone. He wore the black wool to cover the disfigurement.

Red put the knife on the table and sat. "You ain't at school. Why's that?"

"Doyle came by. That sheriff. He said the bank's gonna auction the house unless we pay what's owin'. I took Matty and moved us out."

"Huh. Where to?"

"That's my business."

Red's lip twitched and formed a line. "Where's your ma?"

"Dead. I buried her in the yard."

Bev dropped a spoon and it clattered to the floor. She bent to retrieve it. Red leaned back in his chair. He stared at Jack with a flat expression, his eyes dark as sable. "And what do you want from me?"

"I went to see Dad in prison. We got nothing, Red. I need the money he took. He wouldn't tell me where it is, but I need to find it."

"If he's tellin' or ain't tellin', that's his decision, boy. It ain't wise. You pokin' your damn stupid nose in his business."

Jack held Red's gaze but felt sick in his gut. Looking at Red was like looking at something clawed and yellow-eyed at too close a distance. An animal peering out through human eyeholes.

Bev said, "You could ask him, Red. You know he might say."

"A man don't ask what oughtn't be told."

"But he might—"

"Quiet, woman."

Jack broke in. "Then what about where he might have put it?"

"Didn't ask, don't know."

"It's not at the house."

"He ain't silly-ass-fool enough to put it there."

"Then where would he hide it?"

"That ain't for you to know. And what would you do with it, anyway? Head for Vegas? Run away and change your name?"

Jack thought of Matty. The sudden sting in his eyes, the tiredness and worry, enraged him. He looked to his lap, at his clenched hands. The bandages and spots where red showed through. "I'd use it smart."

"Not smart enough. *Nope.* Some buried things ought to stay buried."

"If you don't know, I'll ask somewhere else."

There was a long silence.

Red leaned toward Jack. He smelled of cooked meat and woodsmoke. A bitter tang of fire and heated flesh. "It *ain't* safe."

"I've got to try."

More silence. Red picked up the tarot cards from the table

and split the deck and drew back the halves, shuffled. "You'll ask somewhere else." He broke the deck, shuffled again. "Well, nephew, that's a real good way to end up dead, or wishin' you was."

Jack had been working his way to this moment, and now it was time. "What about that one he ran with? Named Bardem. I could ask there."

Red smacked the cards onto the table and diverted his hand to the knife. He raised it and pointed the tip at Jack, the bone handle a perfect fit in his grip. He paused, staring. Then he angled the knife lengthwise and bounced it gently on his flattened hand, once and twice, as though judging the weight. He ran a finger along the sharp edge of the blade, turned it over, sighed, pressed the skin of his thumb against the saw tooth, pricked up a slit of blood. "What do you know of Bardem?"

"I seen a picture of him once. Dad showed me. Said if I ever see him, run."

Jack watched Red's face spin through reactions: alarm, fear, brief distrust, then desolation.

"Since you ain't listenin'," he said at last.

Jack waited. Watching Red.

Red set the knife on the table. He motioned Bev toward the bedroom part of the house. "Go on."

Bev took two steps in the direction of the bedroom but then stopped and grabbed Jack's hand. "I see hard things for you up ahead," she said. "Be real careful—and you call if you need anythin'—"

Red raised his hand to smack her. "Go now, 'fore I do somethin' I regret."

Bev squeezed Jack's hand, then went toward the bedroom and pulled the door shut. The seconds lengthened.

Red spoke. "There's an old huntin' site where me and Leland used to hidey-hole up years ago. Up in the hills. Remote. A place nobody knows 'bout. If he was needin' to keep somethin' safe, I imagine he might keep it there."

"How far?"

"Hour maybe. Three at most, round-trip."

"You'll show me?"

"That's what I'm sayin'. You go on out and wait in the truck while I pack up."

Jack found that he had blood in his mouth from biting his torn lip. He didn't trust Red, and he felt the hazard, but the desperation was stronger. The worry. He looked down and caught the rise and fall of his diaphragm. The quickness of his breath.

Two hours. Three at most.

Plenty of time to be back before dark.

Red stood and picked up the knife and slid the blade into a sheath at his hip. The pistol he tucked into his coat pocket. "Time's wastin'. Wanna roll a joint for the drive?"

Jack savored the brief, dreamy comfort of the drive from Red's place to the hunting site. The steady rhythm of Red's truck over the road, snow bits falling, gray mist lifting, and the heater puffing out hot air. Pale colors of winter smoothed out in pearl and dove gray. He laid his head back against the truck seat and let his eyes close and wondered about Red. If Red thought the briefcase was hidden at the hunting site, he'd have searched there already.

Wouldn't he? Jack felt a sort of menace, but in the warm cloud of the truck a strange thing was happening in his head. He didn't care. He just didn't. He'd find the briefcase, or . . .

Or what?

His thoughts faltered.

Stop it, Jack. Red's not as bad as that.

Besides: There was value in knowing what Red would do.

The truck turned, and he opened his eyes. Red had left known roads and was now driving into woodsy hills Jack had never seen. They made the first tracks along the ridgeline. Tires spinning over rocks and sliding on deep powder curves. The tall, thin trees on the slopes watched like scraggy sentries. A smoky haze out there in the low valley. Finally Red pulled off at a bend in the road marked by a boulder and parked.

Red said, "It's about five hundred yards. Through them trees."

They got out. Cold air hit Jack's lungs and made him bend and cough until his chest was like fire. He looked up with watering eyes. The snow had stopped, and in these hills the sky was dazzlingly bright, the color of frozen sea and just as clear. Red broke a path through the snow without looking back, trudging one way and then another. Jack followed Red's footprints around tree trunks and under great dark branches, working to master the cough. Slow, even breathing. Not too deep.

He kept his gaze trained on Red's back. *Watch. You must watch him.*

This could all be a trick.

He felt for the folded hunting knife in his pocket.

The forest thickened. Great pine boughs and undergrowth.

Then they came upon a clearing. A camp trailer set against the trees, about twelve feet long. A horizontal strip of faded brown paint and the roof piled high with snow. The metal hitch rested on a log. Shape of a fire pit in the snow. At the side of the camper was an old wooden smokehouse and toolshed. A roll of orange twine hung from a hook. Red stopped and scanned the site, his breath whiffing from his mouth and floating toward the treetops.

"Check the camper. It won't be locked."

Red headed toward the shed. Jack watched him go until a gust of wind made him totter and almost fall. His legs were weak and his head felt tipsy. Fever, he guessed. He trudged to the camper and opened the door.

Coldness and damp. A mold smell. Linoleum floor, and on the bed a mattress stained dark. Rusted sink and a small stove and a dinette. Trash piled in a corner. Jack stepped inside and opened a cupboard. Salt and pepper. Bottle of ketchup. In a drawer lay some plastic silverware. A lighter. The blankets were rotting.

Mouse droppings. The smell was awful.

The briefcase wasn't there.

He sat at the dinette. What to be done, then? There was no one to give ideas. He bent over and laid his head in his arms on the tabletop. *Think.* What troubled him most was the dark silk that kept wavering in his head, concealing his sense of danger, making his brain dull . . . casting him over a black edge . . .

Something woke him. He jerked up and sat listening. The camper silent. He did not know how quickly sleep had come. How long? Minutes, maybe. The light outside was dim. Then he heard what sounded like a truck engine somewhere out on the road. Distant but getting louder. The motor slowed. Then whined to a halt.

He sank down and listened.

The camper filled with doubt.

He listened. The hunting site was far from the road, and the road was remote. Anyone coming wasn't here by accident. He argued to himself—unconvincingly—that someone had seen the truck and stopped to make sure everything was fine. A Good Samaritan.

But no. The truth was right there in front of him.

Red had called someone.

When he looked through the camper window, the first of them was already coming into view through the trees. One, two, three men. Two of them bearded. Carrying guns. One with an axe in his hand.

Jack lurched for the door and fell into a crouch in the snow outside. He made it two steps away from the camper before looking back to see one of their number advancing with the butt of a rifle raised.

Jack said, "You—" and the world tipped upside down in his view, and there was the glitter of sky while dark spots jumped before his eyes. Rolling over, he stood and staggered across the snow, ears ringing, then the gun struck again and he was down. He stumbled to get up but the world tilted, and he felt himself lying in the snow, lying crumpled, while the spots turned to fuzzy black circles, and there were boots and the mutter of voices uttering unknown words, and the black circles spread until he was inside them, and silence.

XVI

I was ten when my father gave me a book of poems. It was the nicest thing I've ever owned. The leather was all embossed with gold words. The paper thick. Decades old. I thought the pages inside held all the secrets of life. I read those secrets until the words faded and the paper thinned and frayed away in clots from the spine. My father always watched me read.

In stories, he said, we learn what's really true.

In that book I read "Invictus" for the first time. That poem by William Ernest Henley. He thanks the gods for his unconquerable soul and says that no matter what happens to him, he doesn't wince or feel afraid. Whatever hell or darkness he suffers, he doesn't bow his head.

Sometimes you read something and the whole world becomes very simple. You step out of yourself, and you see the truth clearly. And you think, What total shit.

He was alert before his eyes opened, listening to a murmur of words scatter above him. He opened an eye, found snow an inch or so from his face, obeyed an instinct that told him *lie still*. The pain in his head was sharp and stunning and pulsed in throbbing waves. His first thoughts came jumbled. Ungraspable.

Matty somewhere. In a house.

Call if I'm not back by dark.

An axe.

He'd had just enough time to feel panic when he was hefted to his knees. Bright sunlight. Only one eye would focus.

"So the little dog wakes."

Three tall men loomed over him, dark figures of menace, some wearing guns, their faces blurred by sunlight that came from behind them. Jack felt a powerful need to run to the truck or into the trees. *The truck—too far. The trees.* He squinted and saw the axe in the hands of one man, who smiled. A dental grill shone gold on his front teeth.

A voice spoke that sounded like Red.

"You shouldn't have come to me, Jack."

Jack aimed his good eye at Red. His head felt thick. He was cold and the sun was setting, and there was bitter wind coming down the rocky slopes.

"I warned you," Red said. "I warned you, and you wouldn't listen."

The ground swayed under Jack. The right side of his face was wet. He touched the swelling and tried to focus his blurry eye, but it was stretched tight and fattened half-shut. Blood trickled from a gash on his forehead, and his mouth dribbled spit. He bent over and vomited stringy wads of red saliva onto the snow.

Red, again: "They watch me, Jack. I couldn't do nothin' else."

He tried to focus his eye.

"Just do what they say," Red said. "Okay? You ain't gonna fight."

Jack wiped his lips. His mouth formed a response, but no sound came. He fumbled in his coat pocket for the knife.

"Are you looking for this?"

He looked up at this new, quiet voice. The man who sharpened into view stood with one arm raised, holding Jack's knife in his hand between finger and thumb. His boxed beard was aged gray, and he carried a semiautomatic rifle with a nylon strap over one shoulder. Collared shirt, a coat with western yokes on the front. Long straight nose and dark lashes. His eyes watching. His neck was tattooed with a spider, and he wore an old black top hat with a short crown. The man's gaze went inside Jack to the most secret parts and found out whatever it wanted.

He said, "Your father took something that belongs to me. And now you want to take it."

His voice gleamed in Jack's head like a raised hammer.

Jack looked to Red and said slurred words broken by swallows: "How can you—? If you knew—"

"I had to do it. They hurt me before—" Red stopped short and glanced at the hatted man nervously. Glancing back to Jack, he said, "Just tell 'em what you know, and they'll let you be."

The man tossed the folded knife to another, who caught it. This one wore a bandana tied over his nose and mouth like a mask. He looked young, maybe Jack's age, with a vivid gaze peering out from under a mop of black hair that curled in all directions. Their eyes connected and held for a second. Maybe less.

The boy slipped a canvas army pack from his shoulder and put the knife inside.

The knife was gone. Jack accepted this loss with a pang. He felt a swishing gurgle in his belly and turned aside to be sick again, but then wasn't. Everything moved in slow circles. The best thing he could do was ignore this leaden feeling in his heart and form a plan. If he just had time to think—

The hatted man squatted, grabbed Jack's chin, and tipped his head up, inspecting the blood and the puffy eye. He sniffed in a deep, grim breath and stood.

Red shook his head earnestly. "Why didn't you listen, Jack? Why?"

Jack spoke with his head down, the words wounded in shape but raked sharp with feeling. "I got a little brother. A *brother* . . . with nothin' to eat and no roof over his head. We left the house— left everything. Whatever happened with Dad . . . I don't need to know it. But I got a *brother* . . . and I mean to take care of him."

There was a long, electric silence.

"You visited your father," said the hatted man, "in prison."

"I thought he might tell"—Jack swallowed blood—"where it is . . ."

"And did he?"

"No . . . he didn't—"

Red: "I told you, he don't know."

"He's a liar, like his father."

"He ain't! I'll stand for 'im—"

The man with the axe came at Jack and kicked a boot into Jack's stomach and then his ribs. Jack's bowels coiled, went hot, and then he was curling up on the snow, moaning, and Red was shouting.

"This is over now! He's learned!"

"Kill him," said the hatted man.

The axe man lifted the axe into the air, and Jack flinched, prepared to duck under that silver blade—

Red made a rush and got between Jack and the other man, his right hand jammed into his parka. The man with the gold teeth stopped abruptly. He lowered the axe. Red turned on the hatted man.

"You're gonna do him?"

No one made a sound. Red watched the hatted man to see what he would do.

The hatted man strode within an arm's length of Red with no hesitation and looked directly into his eyes. "Explain yourself."

Red stared back. "What're you . . . ?" He licked his lips. He looked at Jack, his gaze lingering on the bruised head, the gash of open skin. "You scared him. That's enough. He won't ask no more questions."

"I decide what is enough."

"He's my blood."

"He is the son of a dog."

"This is a boy who ain't gonna tell."

"It's been decided."

"I'll go see Leland. Get 'im to talk."

"You've done that already."

Red spread his feet. "I won't let you do it."

The hatted man ran his gaze into Red. "You are here because

I spared you. I permit your existence. You will leave matters of my organization to me."

Red wiped his nose. The setting sun behind him blurred his figure to shadow, and the cold wind gusted through trees. His voice penetrated the air as he spoke.

"I ain't never been a good man. I cooked, and then I turned and sold for you, and I never looked back. I've lied and cheated and stole my whole way through life. *But I was a good brother.* What Leland done—I told him not to, and I never said boo after he done it, neither. He was told! But he did what he did anyway." Red reached up and tore the black wool from his head, revealing the old scar that jagged across his skull. "You see that? You took my head!" He stepped toward Jack through snow and looked at the others, his eyes big and wild. "This boy is my family. He's learned now, and he won't ask no more questions. Anyway, he's about all I got left, and you *ain't gonna* kill him."

Red's words were met with utter quiet.

Jack had been sinking into a black lustrous place, and when the dull light of awareness began creeping back, he could hear the men consulting in hushed voices. He sat up, aching. The goldtoothed man dropped the axe to the snow. Now he held a gun. Finger near the trigger and barrel held on Red, who raised his arms slowly.

The hatted man seemed uninterested by it all. He looked out across the frigid valley. "It's pretty out here," he said.

He pulled a pack of gum from inside his shirt pocket and drew out a stick and unwrapped it. He put the gum in his mouth and crouched and looked at Jack. Smell of peppermint.

"Are you afraid?"

Jack eyed him and did not truckle. "Yes."

The hatted man nodded. "You're brave," he said. "Even afraid, you're brave."

Birds watched from the trees without chirping. The man stood.

"All right. This is the best I will do." He regarded Jack, chewing the gum. "We let fate decide."

Red lowered his arms a bit. "What?"

"We leave him out here. If he lives, he gets to live."

Wind blew in the trees, cold. Red looked like a man who had just seen a premonition.

"Take his clothes," said the hatted man. "Tie him."

The boy in the bandana hauled Jack to his feet and dragged off his coat and shirt. His face was pale.

"Take off your pants."

Jack swayed on his feet. His breaths rising to the darkening sky. He bent and untied his boots and took them off.

"Not this!" Red shouted shrilly.

"Shut up, Red."

"He's learned—"

"Take them off."

Jack unbuttoned his jeans and pulled them off, one leg and then the other. The boy in the bandana mask took them and rolled them up with the coat and shirt. He stuffed these into his army pack. With twine from the shed, the hatted man tied Jack's hands behind his back. Then he tied Jack's feet at the ankles. Tight. Jack stood shaking in underwear and socks. The cold went through him like wind.

"Get on your knees," said the hatted man.

He dropped down, landing hard on the snow. His knees tingled in pricks and started to numb. He caught sight of his chest. Rise, fall. Rapid heartbeats visible just left of center.

Red muttered, his jaw tight, "It's near dark."

"Yes. But we did not kill him. This is what you asked."

"There are animals."

"The dog is in the mouth of the wolf. There is no going back."

"But—"

"You have won mercy for the moment," said the hatted man with finality. "It would not be wise to risk that further."

Red glanced at Jack. His arms were still raised, the pistol trained on him. He looked away.

"Give Ansel your gun," the hatted man said to Red.

Red took the pistol from his parka and gave it to the boy in the bandana mask. For a moment, Jack had nearly forgotten him, he was so quiet. Slender and still. Jack could see now, how much the boy looked like the hatted man . . .

"You will not return to this place," the man said to Red. "If you return, I will kill your wife. I will make you watch."

Red would not look at Jack. He nodded.

The hatted man bent down and brought his face to Jack's. He patted Jack's cheek. "It was good to be brave. That was good."

Then he stood. "Let's go."

Jack coughed up a string of blood. He mumbled, words lamed by the shivering from his body. "I—I will hurt you—for this."

The hatted man watched him. He shook his head doubtfully, as if a question had been asked. "No. I don't think you will."

He turned and walked a few steps toward the trees where beyond the trucks waited. Then he stopped. He did not look back.

"Ansel," he said. "Take his socks."

Ansel crouched near Jack and grabbed his socks and tugged them off. The bandana he wore fluttered in and out with his breath. His eyes met Jack's.

The last orange glow of the sun sank below the horizon and now the dark was nearly complete. Jack could hear Ansel's breathing in the gloom. Darkness and breathing. He felt a metal-cold shape fall into the palm of his hand. Unrecognizable and then at once familiar. His hand closed around it. The knife.

Jack's eyes adjusted to night, and the snowy landscape began to glow blue and light up the trees and above the stars turned brilliant. Ansel had already rejoined the others. They turned and walked into the trees, Red among them.

Red stopped and looked back and stared at Jack for a moment. Then the man nudged him with the pistol, and he went with them into the dark.

XVII

Don't worry.

All of this happened a long time ago.

Sometimes, none of it has happened yet.

Matty kept the fire going.

All day he watched, and when the flames got low he put on wood and poked the burning logs. He warmed the beans in the coals, and then he ate them. He built a house of UNO cards. The phone was in his coat pocket. He checked to make sure.

Afternoon died away. Spots of sunlight moving steadily through dust particles and over the dank carpet from holes burned into the roof. He flew Batman around the room and imagined foes for him to fight. He tried to catch a mouse but couldn't. The phone stayed there, in his pocket. He thought about what to do next, and then he walked to the big duffel bag and rifled through. When he found the calculus book, he opened the cover and looked at the name and the numbers written there. He sat in the fort of blankets and held the book.

He played with the toy cars. The dull sunlight was slanting onto the cracked plasterboard walls. The wind rattling down the chimney and shaking the roof. He'd used all the wood, and it was cold and he was hungry. It would be nice if he had a friend to play UNO with, but he didn't. He took the phone from his pocket and held it. He closed his eyes and listened to hear if there was anyone out there, on the road. No. Then he tried again.

He waited a long time. The sticks of sunlight had gone, and outside the small circle of embers, the house pooled with shadows. He walked to the door and opened it and stood looking down the dark road. No one was coming. He went inside and just sat in the blankets, the phone in his hand. Then he began to push the buttons.

When the men slipped out of view, Jack gripped the knife in his fingers and unfolded the blade. Behind his back his tied hands felt deadened, indelicate. Spasms sent him shaking uncontrollably, and his teeth chattered. The needed thing was calm. A plan.

Calm. Don't drop the knife.

He sawed at the twine. Hack, cut, tug. *Call if I'm not back by dark.* When the twine at his wrists broke, he set to freeing his ankles. Chest thudding. They'd be to the trucks in minutes. What to do? Try to stop them? Hide and let them leave? Soon the temperature would fall below zero. If they left, he'd probably die.

Stop them.

Hide.

Either choice was awful.

Twine snapped. He stood and abruptly fell in snow. Dizzy. He could not feel his legs. Weakened parts of him rushed away, like torrents of icy water beneath a frozen stream, surging downward to deep black. Mostly he was scared of this dullness in his head, making him simple. *Think.*

Stop them is better than hide, because you might live.

Stop them, then.

With a truck he could get to Matty.

A feral cry swept across the dark and shot him to his feet, wavering. A coyote or a wolf. He peered into the trees with his good eye, knife in hand, quivering. Black branches. Rustle of wind. His left wrist dripped blood from where he must have cut himself. How to stop them? How?

Draw them back. Maybe.

Check the camper.

Staggering, he crashed through snow on bare feet to the camp trailer and flung open the door. Cough and suck of air. In the unlit gloom, his fumbling hand found a kitchen drawer's handle and ripped it open. Rifling through, his fingers closed on what he wanted: the lighter. When he flipped a dial on the stove burner, the propane gas clicked once, clicked twice, and hissed on. Rancid smell of propane. At the bed he thrust the knife into the rotting mattress, slashed, pulled free a handful of the insides. It was dry, and it would burn. Lurching to the stove, he formed a wick a few inches long and laid it on the counter, trailing away from the burner. Knife: fold, tuck in waist of underwear. He pressed his fumbling thumb down on the lighter. *Get ready. You'll need to run.*

Out there in the night, an engine roared to life.

Gripping the lighter, he pressed and pressed again until a flame erupted. He lit the wick, pushed back from the stove, turned, stumbled for the door.

Three steps outside and the camper exploded. Jack was tossed through air, traveling sideways until he collided with the snow-covered ground. Air whooshed from his lungs upon landing. A great noise boomed and the dark sky burst open with orange flames, and his ears rang with buzzing noise. An instant later, the heat was on him.

He shot to his feet, burst forward, fell. Trying to grab breath. Loud sounds were suddenly distant. His body—gone. He could not feel it.

Stumbling up, he lurched toward the safety of trees with the heat beating on his skin and a column of fire rising up from the burning camper. At the tree line, he crouched down in the snow where tall cragged pines offered refuge. A dark lair. He squeezed under the twisted branches, scrabbled low, scraped skin, ensconced himself deep. The roar of the fire. Feet numb. Then he remembered and searched at his waist for the knife, unfolded it.

Calm, be calm.

A sooty, propane scent of rotten eggs spilled over the land. He wiped blood from his good eye and looked out. Great flames rose from the camper and bent with the wind, and smoke billowed above the treetops. He huddled down in the blackness.

Surely they would come back.

Out of curiosity, if nothing else.

Seconds passed. He watched the break in the tree line where Red and the men had left. Inhaling shallowly. Blackness. Wind.

Nothing.

He could not hear the truck engines.

Funny. He did not feel cold anymore—

Something whined close by. He jerked up, peered into dark. Listened.

Brisk pad of paws on snow. Then a whimper, lupine. Jack's chest began to ache. The knife was in his hand, the blade glinting. Firelight flickering through the trees. There, between the branches—he could see gray fur disturb the dark mold. Then a leg. Lean, with wiry tendons. Placed softly.

A wolf.

Light trembled among the pines, and the leg disappeared. *This isn't real*, Jack thought. *You're hurt. You're seeing things. That's all.*

But the padding drew nearer.

Until it stopped. Five yards away. Maybe less. Jack hunched lower. His spine tingling in pricks. His fingers gripped the knife.

You have lost it. You have lost it.

Just then came another noise: voices. Whispers drawn on the frozen air, sharp as scratches on slate.

So. They took the bait.

His grin split the wound on his lip, and he winced. From where he crouched, he peered out over the fire-splashed snow at the open clearing, perhaps forty yards away. Camper ablaze, burnt to a skeleton. Toolshed to the right. Trucks off to the left through the trees. Wolf, somewhere nearby. As he watched, the firelight blinked at him. There to the left, he could see figures. Two shadows blotched against the night.

Don't move.

They haven't seen you.

The figures divided. One along the tree line to the left. One headed right. Out in front of that shadow was the darker contour of a gun. He'd have to—

Suddenly Jack's head did something strange: He felt thinking gears unscrew, become loose and wonky, and the world undulated in his view until he closed his good eye and leaned his head against a tree trunk. Nausea. Reeling. A sense of whirl and tip. If the figure coming closer glimpsed human skin the gun would be fired.

He opened his eye. *Ready, then.* The trouble was running on legs he couldn't trust.

Now that the figure was nearer, Jack could see the gold flash of teeth. That dark length of the gun barrel. *Ready, then.*

The man stopped near the edge of the pines and scrutinized the thicket. Needled boughs. A dense black mass. Jack readied the knife, the quivering knife that glinted so brightly, that glimmered, dimmed, gleamed, dimmed again.

Now he'll see.

Something cracked behind him. Gingerly. Snap of twig or tree limb. The wolf? Jack's hair rose, and the man turned, trying to decipher the source of the sound in the darkness.

Now.

Jack jerked out from the branches, snagging skin, doing harm. Numb, bloody, wild. Bursting into the open, he charged, struck the man with a jolt that smacked them both to the snow. Jack jabbed with the knife, and the man grunted. The other one was shouting. Jack's legs straightened. Then he was running, the fire beating heat on his right side. Silent, except for a curious percussion of air, near his head. Someone shooting. He swerved into the trees. Lurching through snow. Toward the road. They were chasing behind. At least twenty yards back. Yelling, careening through forest.

The second bullet sheared a scrap of flesh from Jack's side. Again, the faint, airy noise. He spooked away like a horse, felt no pain, kept running. Veered left around a big tree and then ducked below the branch. He could see the truck.

One truck. Red's was gone.

He faltered over uneven ground and blundered to the truck. It was a Bronco. His pursuer was closing in behind him.

Open door. Get in. Key in ignition. Turn.

The engine started.

He switched the lights on. A smooth blackness beckoned in his head. Gripping the wheel, Jack put the truck in drive and smashed down on the gas pedal. The tires spat up snow.

Plink!

The bullet struck metal somewhere. Then he was speeding fast, pitching and swerving down the road and into a black maw.

131

XVIII

Start and stop. Rewind.

I imagine you're worried about Jack. Matty too. It's weird how some-times you don't know the moments that change your life, right when they happen. You only know when you look back.

Up next is the third time I see Jack. A long time ago, I said there'd be five.

The third of five.

Or maybe, for you, it's the second of five, or the fourth of ten.

Depending on which way you go.

Where you're at.

Or how many times you've been.

He wiped frozen stuff from his bad eye and tore down the snowy road and into the valley. Black sky. Unsteady passage of time. Seconds or hours. Shivering. Even with the heater cranked. He was starting to feel a fever.

Come on, Jack.

Just make it awhile longer.

A few miles from Matty, the engine made a whining sound and sputtered. Then it quit. Jack cranked the steering wheel to pull the Bronco off the roadway and onto the shoulder before it rolled to a stop. He turned off the ignition. In his mind he heard the bullet *plink*. So. It hit the fuel tank.

Headlights punched holes in the darkness ahead.

He looked in the rearview mirror, trying to listen. Drum of blood in his ears. No sound of trucks behind, no lights. He had no way of knowing if there was cell coverage up at the campsite. No way to know how quickly they might come after him. Had they called Red? Were they out there already, waiting to trap him? He had the knife in his hand, had not stopped gripping it. In the weak green glow of the dashboard, he could see the dark-smeared tip.

You've got to move, he thought.

He thumbed on the overhead light to brighten the cab. On the passenger seat lay his clothes. Coat. Shirt. Jeans. Boots. He blinked. Yes, they were there. Sitting on the seat like a miracle. He pulled everything on. Shuddering violently now. Mouth dry. Fold knife and tuck in coat. He searched the glove box and the floor under the seats, but there were no weapons.

No food. No sip of water.

His blood was all over the steering wheel.

Hurry.

He pushed open the Bronco door and touched his boots to the snow. When he stood, all his hurts stretched open to raise fresh pain throughout his body. He held on to the truck and counted slowly in his head until he marked a slight settling of the hurts.

Taste of sweat on his lips. Weak light from the cab. He looked into the cargo space behind the seats. Something lay there on top of a tarp.

The axe.

He lifted the latch to fold the seat forward and reached in and hauled the axe out. The agony took his breath. He waited, holding the side of the truck. Count to five. The old house where he'd left Matty lay east, through a field. Matty would still be there. He would. Jack wouldn't think anything else.

Call if I'm not back by dark.

He stumbled over the field, dragging the axe in one hand. Muddling along. Beneath the snow an uneven growth. Perhaps once a potato crop. He held out his other hand in front of him. The world kept shifting, until he closed his swollen eye. He could hardly see his hand before him. Distant lights of a home on that hill. Trees swishing in the wind to the south. Matty to the east. He fell to his knees.

The axe was too heavy. He let it drop from his grip and waited for the earth to come back under his legs. Presently the snow refocused, the dead crop beneath, the far-off lights of the home. A heavy kind of feeling in his body was to be worried about later.

Whisper of wind. Silence.

He concentrated. *Get up. Look behind you.*

Darkness.

Walk.

Slow going. He needed a drink.

Don't eat the snow. It'll just make you colder.

When he came upon the house where he'd left Matty, he

halted, wobbling. He squinted his eyes. There. Between those sags and wall slats. A pale fire might glow. *Dear God, please.* At the door, he heard a puzzling sound: a faint rise of melody.

A voice sang softly.

He fastened his hand on the knob. His throat hot. He stifled a cough.

At once the singing cut off, and he heard "Shh!"

Footsteps lurched, and the door opened. Warm air swelled out, and Matty stood in front of him. Bathed in fire, wrapped in one of the blankets. Talking, pulling his hand. Safe.

"I knew you'd get back. I knew it."

Jack smelled fried potatoes.

Matty put his arms around Jack and kept talking.

"I know you said to, but I didn't call Mrs. Browning. I'm sorry."

Jack risked no energy on answering. With every heartbeat came a feeling of shutting off. A black curtain falling. He stepped inside and stopped dead.

The girl from school stood by the fire, watching him. She looked struck speechless, as if she'd seen a horror.

Ava.

"I called her," Matty said. "From the math book."

Jack tried to process this.

Matty again: "Your face is hurt."

Jack lifted a hand to his forehead. Ava watched him, her expression a mask of wary alarm. On the hearth behind her sat a cooling pan of fried potatoes. Smell of butter. On the floor was a crate of food. Oranges, red apples, canned ham, macaroni and cheese. Cookies. Gallon-size jug of water, paper plates.

"You're bleeding," Matty said.

Jack glanced down at himself, dimly conscious of his filthy appearance. Blood blotched through the side of his coat. Dark cuts smudged his left wrist. He looked at Matty. "It's all right," he said.

Ava stared for a moment as though stunned. Then she walked to him and took his hand. "Come and sit."

He faltered forward a few steps and dropped to his backside on the blankets.

"Jack?" Matty asked, his voice a tremor.

She crouched and touched her hand to Jack's forehead. "You have a really high temperature. We have to cool you off."

"Water," he said.

She brought him a cup and tipped cool water to his lips as he jerked in swallows. Then she pulled off his coat and looked at the patch of blood seeping through his shirt, his gashed forehead. Her gaze slid to his. "You need a doctor."

"No," Jack said.

"I could drive you—"

"I said *no*."

The sound of Matty sniffling carried through the room.

"Get me cold water and a bowl," Ava said to Matty. "Be quick."

Matty did as she told. With great care, she peeled up Jack's shirt. Jack felt shreds of his own flesh break free from inside the fabric and he turned to be sick. She held his forehead while he vomited water into the bowl. When he finished, she helped him lie back onto the blankets. She held a cool cloth to his swollen forehead while he shook. He was getting blood all over.

"I'm sorry," Jack said.

"It's okay."

"You won't go anywhere?"

"No. I won't."

Jack's vision was tunneling. He could not keep his eyes open.

"Help me get his clothes off," Ava said. "Hurry."

The dreams came slow and sharp and warm with sweat. In Jack's head, he woke in the dark and could not find Matty. He sat up and pushed off the blanket and could not see him, and he said Matty's name and said it again, but nobody answered. No wind. The air so cold, it took his breath. He walked to the door and opened it to that black soundless night, and there in the snow he could see bootprints. The tracks went away from the house and off across a ridge of blue-lit snow until they disappeared into nothingness. *You didn't lock the door*, he thought. *You fell asleep, and you didn't lock the door. They came and took him, and you didn't keep him safe, and he is out there somewhere in the dark. He is in the cold.*

Well, then.

You better get up and go look for him.

He sat up and pushed off the blanket. Pain gushed through him. There was a bandage over his ribs. His clothes were gone. He looked around for them.

Ava sat by the fire, watching him. She stood and whispered, "Lie down."

"I gotta go."

Her cheeks glowed with color. "Oh. I can help you outside . . ."

He shook his head, embarrassed. "Not that. I gotta find Matty."

She came to his side and sat, laid a flat palm on his chest and pushed him back to the blanket. "It's okay. Lie down."

"My brother—"

"*Hush.* He's right next to you."

Then Jack felt him there. Curled up on his side, soft breath. Right there. Sleeping like a rock.

He closed his eye and tried to think of something to say to the girl who sat by him so sternly and saw him all bruised up and gashed. He could feel one eye swollen shut. He was soaked in sweat. He opened his good eye a little, and Ava lifted his head and put two pills on his tongue and brought a cup to his lips.

"Antibiotics. Swallow."

The room fell into a spin. He lay back into the blankets with Matty near while Ava faded off to a dim color, leaving the mind to drift. A new place would have to be found. Somewhere far. A safe place they wouldn't find. Pack up in the morning. Take the duffel. Matty's toys. Hammer, knife. Cooking things.

The girl will have to go.

"We'll find someplace nice," he said to Matty, or didn't. "You'll see."

He slept in and out of fever sweats, flinched in his sleep at flying axes aimed at the tender head. Red stood over him. Voice of the hatted man, who said it was good to be brave. Horrid cold . . . and then running on raw feet . . . a wolf snapping white teeth . . .

"You'll see. We might get a dog, even."

The girl came to him as still as darkness and gave him sips of sugar water. Heat flushed through him and when the water hit his stomach, those resentful muscles clenched tight to heave rebellion. She held him while he shivered. They might have found the truck and followed his bootprints through the snow.

"Lock the door," he said.

She said words back, but shallow sleep took hold and deepened while memories seeped from his veins to surface in his mind. Mom's body swayed from the ceiling fan, one foot kicked free of the slipper . . . *She is under all that snow . . . because she killed herself and you buried her, and there is nothing else to say about it.*

Wind whistled outside and fluttered towels nailed to window frames.

Night shaved off in chunks.

XIX

Let's be clear.
    I trust no one.
    I put nothing in my heart.

At early dawn, Jack woke to Ava changing his bandage. Washing where the bullet had torn his skin away. Her head bent, her worried eyes. Frowning in concentration. She wore the juniper coat unbuttoned and beneath was a shift of white, and her hair was wild. The light around her head like a crown. Wild tendrils aglow in the light of the fire. She looked at him. "The bleeding won't stop."

"I feel pretty good."

"You feel pretty good. Well, you look like shit."

This made him smile. She seemed angry. Or obstinate. Maybe both.

"You need stitches," she said. "Or something. I don't even know what."

He stopped smiling and shook his head, then winced when his bad eye throbbed. "I'm not goin' to a doctor."

She stared at him, defiant. Her hazel eyes radiant in the fire-light.

"And what will I do with Matty if you die?" she asked.

"I won't die."

She lifted her hands. They were smeared with his blood. "Really?"

"I won't."

"You have a fever."

"I can't go, Ava."

For several seconds she watched him, silent.

"Fine," she said at last. "You drink more water. You eat something. If you keep it down, you stay. If you don't, you go to a hospital. I'll drag you to the car myself."

He tried to answer back something smart, but instead his head started hurting again. Sleep caught him in a spiderweb grasp and pulled him down to enticing black, where time didn't have to be lived through.

The black thinned enough for a voice to float through. He could hear crunching. Then a hand wiggled his shoulder. His eyes opened to see Matty sitting beside him, cereal bowl in his cross-legged lap, lifting a plastic spoon. Lucky Charms.

"She brought milk," Matty said, chewing. "Cereal. She made pancakes for you. Do you want pancakes? I told her you like them, but only if there's syrup. She said there's no syrup, but she made them anyway. You want pancakes or cereal?"

Jack hauled himself into a sitting position. He sat there in the blanket fort. A bloodstain the size of his hand on the quilt below

141

him. In the hearth, the fire fed on a new log and water steamed from a pot. The box of Lucky Charms stood on the floor by Matty. Next to it was a plate of sliced apples. Pancakes. A cup of water.

"She said you have to eat this when you wake up."

Jack took the plastic cup and drank. He ate an apple chunk. He willed it down. He felt ragged. The bandage on his ribs was wet and the skin around discolored. Purple, green. He caught Matty staring at it.

"I'm all right," he said.

"You look bad."

"I'm not bad."

"Does it hurt?"

He nodded. "It hurts."

"What happened?"

"Just me being stupid," he said. "Will you get me some clothes?"

Jack thought about Ava peeling off his clothes. Then he tried not to think about it.

Matty put down his bowl and jumped up and went to a neat stack of clothes by the duffel and brought the stack to Jack. T-shirt, pajama bottoms, socks.

So. She'd gone through the duffel.

"Can you help me?" he asked Matty.

Matty shoved the pajamas up over each of Jack's legs and then Jack lifted himself off the blanket so Matty could pull them over his hips. He didn't trust his legs to stand. When they finished he sat with his head to his chest, inhaling slow breaths. One breath, two.

Half dressed. Quite the accomplishment.

All your life you wait, and you meet a girl finally, and you look like this?

He was about to ask where she was when the rear door opened and she came in through the kitchen, carrying a paper grocery bag. She looked at him, at the empty cup. Jack picked up a pancake and took a bite. His stomach protested, but he swallowed it down. She pulled the pot from the coals by its handle and set it off to the side. She didn't say a word to him.

"I'm eating," he said. "And drinking."

You won't throw up, he thought. *You won't throw up.*

She walked to him and crouched and slid her fingers over the inside of his wrist. The morning rays lighting rogue wisps of her hair. Her eyelashes. Her skin. His heartbeats beneath her fingers.

She scrutinized him for a moment. Frowning. Then she opened the grocery bag and laid a towel on the floor and put everything on the towel. Cotton swabs and tape and gauze. Pair of tweezers. A syringe, scissors. Needle and suture thread. A little glass vial. Bottle of Betadine. She examined it all with an air of purpose.

After a moment, she stood. "Let's get this over with."

Jack felt his insides go slippery, jump into his throat. "Where'd you get all that?"

"My father."

"Your father own a pharmacy or somethin'?"

She glanced away. "He keeps it on hand."

"What did you tell him?"

"Nothing." She spoke curtly. "He doesn't know I took it. I'm not stupid."

"And where does your father think you are?"

"He doesn't know anything. You let me worry about that."

They stared at each other.

Fire. Dry heat.

"What did Matty tell you, anyway?" Jack asked.

"Enough to know you need help."

She crossed her arms, her face fierce. She looked like she was being scraped by the edge of a sharpened blade.

"It's this, or you go to the doctor," she said. "Your choice."

All this time Matty had been listening, engrossed. "What's going on?"

Jack's head ached. At his side he could sense warm blood pulsing from damaged places just beneath his skin. This was crazy. Idiotic. Except, in some lucid part of his brain, he knew it had to be done.

Jack said to Ava, "I don't want him to watch."

"Watch what?" Matty asked.

Ava gathered the toy cars and brought them to Matty. She crouched and looked in his eyes. "Jack needs me to help him get better, but it's going to hurt a little. He doesn't want you to see that. So I think you should play with your cars over by the piano for a while. There's only one rule. While I'm helping Jack, you can't come over. Okay?"

Matty sat with his shoulders slumped. Then he inhaled deeply. He drew up his legs and clasped his knees. "You could say my name if you need me."

Jack nodded. "That's a good idea. If she says your name, you come over. But only if she says your name."

Matty's lip trembled. "But . . . I want to stay with you."

Jack felt his side dripping. The bandage. Soaked through. He turned and heaved up the little bit of water and apple and pancake. He couldn't even get to the bowl. He drooped back on the blankets, full of rage, of inexpressible frustration.

He spoke madly. "Do what you're told, dammit. Go."

Matty got up and turned away.

Jack's eyes began to burn. Blur.

Ava helped Matty to the other side of the piano and set him up. Plate of cookies and the cars and UNO cards. Jack could hear her reassure him. Then she went to the fire and got the pot of water and came back to sit beside Jack. She unscrewed the bottle of Betadine and washed her hands. Antiseptic smell. Then she removed the bandage. Carefully, without speaking, she began to lave water over the wound with a washcloth.

Pain, white-hot. Jack twisted on the blanket, moaned.

He heard Matty inhale.

Like a balloon released from a hand, he felt his body drift upward, become weightless, and he was lifting somehow, free of gravity, lifting from the dirty blankets and floating to a distant place.

XX

I once saw a deer get hit by three arrows and keep going. It took him a whole day to die. I followed him. I lost him for a while but then found him again, tracked him farther into the woods than I'd ever been. He was weaker by then, because of the arrows the hunter hit him with. Up close he was hurt worse than I first thought and covered in blood from the battle he'd fought. When he finally fell, I walked up and knelt by him. His hair was matted and warm and slick, and his ribs were rising and falling. Long ears and velvet antlers. He blinked and gazed at me. Dark lashes, his gentle brown eyes. I put my hand on his neck. I stayed there and looked in those eyes until the last of the light went away from them and his ribs were still. Then I got up and went home.

I think about that deer.

I see him all the time.

Ava pats the skin dry and studies the wound. Pale blood leaking from the torn flesh. Small pieces of cloth and dirt stuck in the tissue. A bit of rib bone peeking through. She takes the Betadine and tips the bottle over the gash. Jack doesn't move. She picks up the tweezers and sets to work, picking out dirt and bits of lint, swabbing the blood. Moving quickly. Thread the needle and stitch. Slow, even. Calm. *Just like he taught you.*

When she is done she dries the area and cuts open packets of gauze and lays them over the gash and secures them with tape. She strips the safety wrapper from the syringe and sinks the needle through the seal into the vial of amoxicillin and draws back the plunger until it is full. Then she slides the needle into the fattiest tissue around the wound that she can find and slowly depresses the plunger. Her hands do not shake.

With a cool cloth she wipes the sweat from his forehead and washes the blood from around the bandage. She cleans up the blankets as best she can. Then she just looks at him. His hair plastered to his forehead. Slim chest rising and falling, and his stomach split by the rungs of his ribs. The swollen eye looks a little better.

There is nothing else to be done. Let him sleep. Sleep is needed most. Liquids. What else? Check on Matty, check the door. Fill a cup of water for when he wakes. More antibiotics in four hours.

She disinfects her hands again and puts everything in the paper bag. She checks on Matty. The cars are sitting in his lap unplayed with, and the cookies are uneaten beside him. His eyes are red. He shoves at them with his hand.

"It's over," she says.

He nods.

She crouches beside him. "I'm sorry this happened."

"I know," he says.

"Want to play cars with me?"

"It's okay. I just want a little quiet time."

She gets him a glass of milk. She checks the fire. The door. She fills the cup. When she can think of no other task, she goes to Jack and just sits by him. She looks at him. Lying so still. Pale and swollen, bruised nearly everywhere. Now she begins to shake.

She slips her hand into his and squeezes. He doesn't respond.

It starts to snow. White snowflakes fall from the dark sky into the house, through the ceiling holes, glowing strangely in the waste, in the cold sunlight. Serene.

She sits with his hand in her lap.

Bardem parked under the cover of trees about five hundred yards from Llewyn Dahl's place and slid the window down. It was late morning. Frigid air rolling off the river. A slight wind. He propped his elbow on the window edge and glassed the house with a pair of 12× binoculars. Smoke at the chimney pipe. Truck in the yard. Most called Llewyn by the name Red.

Bardem slowly turned the wheel on the binoculars, focusing the barrels. The lenses narrowed on a second vehicle. A red Caprice.

He stepped out of the Land Rover and hooked the police scanner onto his belt. He slung the Winchester Model 70 bolt-action rifle over his shoulder with the leather sling. It carried his own refinements: a re-machined receiver belly, bolt face, new pins in the trigger, and bolt stop to remove play. A Leupold Mark 4 LR/T scope on steel rings. The rifle was chambered in .30-06 and would shoot less than a vertical minute of angle with 168 grain bullets at a thousand yards.

When he got to a stand of aspens, he squatted and studied the house through the binoculars. Front door, possible exit out the rear. Location of windows. A skinned deer twirled with a fatty glimmer from a side tree. Crossing the yard was a dog.

In his coat pocket, his cell phone quivered. He looked at the screen and pushed the button. "You were supposed to call last night."

"I'm sorry. I got caught up doing homework."

Bardem waited.

"Are you there?" Ava asked.

"Yes. I thought you might have more to say. A better explanation."

She didn't answer. Then she said, "I'm sorry."

"You don't have to say you're sorry. You have to do what you say you'll do."

"I know."

"You have rules because I want to keep you safe."

"I know."

Bardem looked through the binoculars. Snow had been shoveled off the porch that morning.

No movement.

"Sara asked if I can stay with her another night," Ava said. "Her mom's here. We're just doing homework and watching movies."

Bardem leaned back on his heels, studying the house. "Sara's mother is divorced?"

"Yes."

"Does Sara have brothers?"

"No. I told you already."

"I always want to know where you are."

"I know. I know how much you worry."

"You are my daughter."

He heard the engine before he saw the Ford F-150 rumble into view. Black, dealer plates. He huddled down, cradling the rifle at his waist, and glassed the truck as it passed. Two men in the cab.

"Okay," he said. "I want you to answer your phone if I call."

"I will."

He pressed the off button and glassed the truck as it rolled up to Red's house. The men got out. No Jack Dahl. They knocked at the door, and a blond woman let them in.

He turned the police scanner on low and sat listening. He ate an orange. An hour became two.

The transmission came through just as the front door of the house opened. Something about an abandoned vehicle. He reached down and turned up the volume. The vehicle was a four-wheel-drive truck. Blood found in the cab.

Coming out of the house were Red and three men. One of them younger. Black hair. Bardem lowered the bipod legs of the rifle from the forearm onto the ground, pointing the barrel at the figures in the distance. He lay behind the rifle, prone, and nestled the stock into the pocket of his shoulder. Sighting with the scope. Breathing softly, he pushed off the safety.

Jack Dahl was not with Red.

The first hollow point took a second to get there, and the sound took about twice as long. He inhaled softly and pulled the men back into the scope. They were standing, looking between them at the dead dog on the ground. Then they bolted for the house. The high *whang* of the rifleshot percussing back across the open snow. Bardem's second bullet tore through the old man's top hat and whiffed it off his head.

Bardem retraced his steps to the Land Rover and left.

Doyle pulled onto the snow-topped shoulder behind Midge's police unit and shut off the engine and got out. He walked along the edge of the road, studying the abandoned truck: a rebuilt Bronco with a lifted suspension and off-road tires. "Looks like we got ourselves a regular war wagon here."

"Yessir," said Midge. "A real road warrior. I ain't touched inside."

"You know this truck?"

"Never seen it 'fore today."

"Me either. Seems a memorable type."

"I'd say."

He nodded at the plates. "I guess you ran these."

"Yup. Plates don't match."

"Well. Let's have a look."

He put on gloves and opened the door on the driver's side and eyed the seat. Thick smears of blood, partly dried. The whole steering wheel was caked with it. Keys in the ignition. He reached into the truck and turned the key. The needle of the gas gauge pointed to empty. "Somebody had a bad day."

"A bad night too, is my guess."

He glanced at her.

"Folks who called it in live down the road," Midge said. "Figured they seen this truck here for about a day now."

"A day."

"That'd put it the day after Frisby turned up dead."

Doyle nodded. "That'd put it."

He folded the seat forward and checked the floor. A couple brass shells. Nine millimeters. Some .45 ACP casings under the seat. He closed the door. There was blood on the side of the truck. A dried thumbprint.

"You figure this's got to do with Frisby?" Midge asked.

"I don't figure anythin' yet."

A plastic blue tarp covered the cargo space in the rear. He pulled it back. There was a thin layer of whitish dust on the bed. Top to bottom. He ran his glove along the truck bed and held it to the sun.

"I do believe there's been some meth in the back of this truck."

Midge's eyebrows lifted. "How'd you know that?"

"I guess I'm figurin' now."

Midge wrote in her ledger and examined the truck bed. "Maybe what we're lookin' at here is a drug deal gone wrong. You think?"

"Maybe. Or maybe somethin' else."

That empty gas gauge bothered him. He squatted and looked at the tank. "Somebody shot at this truck. That's from a rifle, by the look of it."

"Shot truck might mean a shot driver," Midge said.

Doyle stood. He did not like the look of this mess.

"Where do you figure the driver went?" Midge asked.

"No idea. Coulda called someone for all we know."

He crouched by the driver's-side door and studied the ground. The new snow was perhaps three inches deep. No footprints left. He brushed at the snow with his fingertips and uncovered a patch stained crimson. He took a crouched step and found another splotch.

Midge had followed and stood behind him. "There might not've been a call."

"That's possible."

"The driver might've just walked away."

Doyle studied the snow. "If he did, I doubt he got far."

He straightened and turned slowly, scanning the frozen terrain. Barren fields. A stiff crop below the snow. He was thinking about Jack Dahl. He hoped that boy wasn't lying dead out there. He seemed like a good kid. The little brother too.

A wind came up, and Midge pushed her hat down. "Storm's comin'."

Doyle nodded. The sun was already setting. Soon it would be dark.

"You head back to town," he told Midge. "Get a map of all the houses in a ten-mile radius. We'll start at first light."

"Will do."

"And call Boise. Ask for the DEA," Doyle said. "We're gonna need help."

He got in his truck and watched Midge drive toward town. Then he just sat for a moment. Restless out here. Unsettled. He'd gotten this feeling before. Trying to figure out what might be headed toward him. Trying to head it off.

He reached over and opened the console and got the flashlight. Quiet except for the wind. He could smell the storm coming. He got out of the truck and put the flashlight in his hip pocket and looked across the countryside. *Okay. You're hurt. You're scared. And somebody's comin' for you. Where you gonna go?*

He buttoned up his coat.

Then he started walking.

XXI

If it looks like Jack's world is falling around him, just wait.

It's about to get worse.

Bardem sat parked with the window down, three miles away from the abandoned truck. With his binoculars, he watched the sheriff. Cold air blowing in off the hills. Snow starting. The sheriff looked to be searching the field.

He ate a little bag of dried apples. He drank coffee from a thermos. All this time, he watched the sheriff. The abandoned Bronco looked like something you would expect some drug runners to drive. He sat thinking.

If the Bronco was stolen. What would they do? Perhaps buy another vehicle.

Perhaps a new F-150.

When it was near dark, he swept the country with the binoculars. There were houses in every direction. Some obscured by trees. Rolling hills. He studied the land, and he studied the houses, and he judged the distance to each one.

The snow came down harder. The cold.

He checked on the sheriff one last time. No. The sheriff had not found anything yet. He probably wouldn't now. In the snow. In the dark.

He took the pistol off the passenger seat. Then he opened the door and set off toward the nearest house.

When Jack's eyes opened, it was dark except for dim orange light. Where was he? Where was Matty? What was this searing heat in his side? Above him, snow drifted in powdery skeins through charred holes in the roof. A great wind flapped the wall slats and shuttled down the chimney. It took him a moment to remember.

You're at the house. You're hurt.

He stared up at the hanging ceiling. Through the void, he could see black sky scattered with clouds and the gleaming lamps of stars. A distant world. Unreachable.

With his hand, he felt the bandage at his side. Damp. Matty lay sleeping in the blankets beside him. Fire from the hearth dressed his head in luster and etched the line of his cheek into sculptured marble. He held Batman in his hand.

Jack's chest tightened suddenly and ached, like a rubber band pulled too hard. He could not inhale—

He sat forward, sucking in breath.

Swell of dizziness.

She slept a few feet away, by the fire. Near his side. Curled on the dank carpet. Her battered coat tucked over her like a blanket. The little tattoo on her wrist. Black heart.

He swallowed. This heaviness in his chest. He lay down and looked up.

Just take some even breaths.

Stars glimmered.

His breathing calmed. He licked his dry lips. Then he turned his head to just look at her for a second, or for a minute, or for an hour. Her walnut hair. Her skin, her eyelashes. In the firelight he could see the curve of her breasts rising and falling under the thin material of her dress. His throat hurt.

He reached and pulled the coat up over her to make sure she was warm. The movement sent a chorus of pain through him. He lay back in the dark and looked up at the broken ceiling, coughing softly. He counted to ten.

He did this six times.

Come on, Jack.

Just breathe.

The pain sank down to a whisper.

Sometime later, the snow ceased and clouds drifted over the stars. No sound, save the low moan of the wind. Blow of snow off the roof and the house shuddering. Maybe some part of him wished he'd never made it back. That deepest part wished for it all to be over.

It'd be the best thing for Matty.

Best thing for everyone.

He lay there, breathing. Waiting for the sweet nothing of sleep.

Count the minutes. The slivers of time. Each sliver one more in the long slow end of something that, once lost, he feared he'd never find again. Each breath taken with a price.

A noise called him out of sleep. Soft whispers. The front door swung wide, and the man in the top hat stood in the opening. The night framed him from behind so his figure was just a shadow. His eyes landed on Jack. Lustrous, like wet obsidian. He raised the semiautomatic.

"If you want it to be over so bad," the man said, "I can help you with that."

He leveled the barrel at Matty and squeezed the trigger at Matty's head.

Jack threw off the blanket, inhaling, but his mind knew already: It was a dream.

No. Not a dream.

A warning.

They will find the truck.

They'll find the truck and then they'll find you. And they'll find Matty.

Faint canes of light slanted through the ceiling holes. Snow. The air cold. The fire out. *It must be almost dawn.* He sat forward.

Matty stood by him, balancing on one foot beside the blankets. He held very still and squinted at Jack.

"Look," he said. "Count how long I can balance."

Jack pushed back his hair and glanced about. Ava wasn't there.

He could see his breath.

Matty lifted his scrawny arms and teetered like a gymnast on a beam. He looked as if he could hear some invisible crowd cheer.

"Aren't I good, Jack?" he said.

"Yes. You are."

Matty smiled.

Jack bent his legs to stand, but hot coals of ache glowed in his side and stunned him. He ran his hand over the bandage gently, remembering the fever, the night, the dream. *They could find this place anytime.*

"We've got to go."

In the kitchen, a door slammed. Footsteps. Jack lurched to his feet and everything darkened, then cleared. Ava stood in the doorway, holding an armload of split wood.

"Ava, watch me balance," Matty said.

Jack did not know where to put his gaze. Ava's cheeks were red from the wind, and wet snowflakes glinted in her hair.

Think.

Not about her.

Where to go? Somewhere far. Take a bus, maybe.

"We need to leave," Jack said.

Ava looked at him intently for a moment. Then she walked to the hearth and dumped the wood. She turned to him, brushing dirt from her hands. She seemed to be waiting for him to speak.

Matty stopped balancing and stared at them both.

Jack hobbled across the room to the duffel and began stuffing things inside, unsteady on his legs. "Thanks for all your help, really, but we need to leave."

159

"Okay," she said. "Where?"

"Not you." He put the medicine in the duffel. The bandages. "Just us."

She folded her arms and watched him.

"You're here," she said. "So I'm guessing you can't go home. Or to a doctor."

He tried to not look at her. It was hard.

He went to the fireplace and packed the food. *Maybe the jug of water ought to be left. Nothing too heavy.*

"Get the blankets," he said to Matty.

Matty didn't move.

"What about family?" she asked.

The room fell into a slow spin. Jack needed to sit. He could see her, wrapped in the rainbow blanket. Hear the dead smack of the shovel striking frozen ground. *Don't think about that now. Don't. Pack. Leave.*

"I haven't seen a car," she said. "Are you planning to walk?"

Jack looked at Matty. "Hurry up."

Matty stood there. He was ready to cry.

Wind gushed and rattled the walls. Ava went to Matty and bent down beside him and folded a blanket. She looked at Jack.

"So where will you go?"

Jack stood. Feeling nothing inside these walls. His head hurt, his side. The bandage leaked tendrils of red. *Where will you go?* He didn't know. Where? How? Beyond this was the perfect certainty that the hatted man and his friends were looking for him. They knew who he was, and they knew what he wanted, and they would never stop looking for him—never.

There was no place to hide. Except maybe China.

"You can barely stand," she said.

He picked up the duffel, then put it down. Pain in his ribs.

Quiet.

Above them, the cold sun was rising. It shone through gaps and cracks in the roof to light up the room strangely. The wind puffing up snow, a sparkling white. Like some beast with bright-seeing eyes breathed down at the holes of the house. Hunched and translucent. Soundless.

Jack dragged his attention from the ceiling to look at Ava.

"The people who did this," he said. "They're coming. I don't know when, but they are. They think I know something. I think they want to teach me a lesson. Or something."

She searched his face and said nothing. Then she stood and got a cup and filled it with water. She handed it to him. "Drink."

He took the water.

"You should go to the police," she said.

He shook his head, and water splashed from the cup. "No."

"Why?"

Jack didn't answer.

Matty whispered, "It's a secret."

She paused. She said, "I'm good at keeping secrets."

Jack watched her. Those hazel eyes. Her intent face. He felt cagey, suspicious. And he liked her.

"I can't tell you," he said.

"You could," Matty pleaded. "You could—"

"No."

The quality of his own voice twisted Jack's insides.

Ava stared at him and then turned away.

Jack put out his hand abruptly—to touch her, to say something, explain—but she jerked backward and stumbled as though struck. She caught herself, turned, and went aimlessly to the fireplace.

With her back to him, she picked up a can of food. A cereal box. Her fingers gripped the sides.

He looked down. He set the cup on the piano.

"I'm sorry," he said.

Matty scowled at Jack, who spoke again, more gently.

"I'm sorry."

She didn't look at him. "I don't like to be touched is all."

Wind gusted and shook the roof. She turned toward him then, and sunlight gleamed from above and obscured her so he couldn't read her expression. When the light changed, he saw that her face had paled. She walked to the duffel and put the food inside and picked up the grocery bag. Her skin lit bright with sunlight. The heart on her wrist.

"Let's go, then," she said. "I'll take you wherever you want. I've got some money you can have."

Jack blinked. "Why are you helping us?"

"Because you need it."

He flushed at her bluntness. "Who are you, anyway?"

She hesitated. That look came into her eyes—the one he'd seen at school, a flash in deep water—and passed.

"I'm not your enemy," she said.

They watched each other.

I need your help.

That was Jack's thought. It was something he didn't want to admit.

Matty broke in: "We should go."

Jack did not look away from Ava. The cold air. Her eyes on him.

"Okay," he said. "Let's go."

XXII

People say you shouldn't look back. In the Bible, they told Lot's wife not to look back at where all those people and their homes had been. But she did look back.

I look back too.

What was I thinking then? When I jerked away?

I'm thinking of you, Jack.

You can't know who I am. If you did, you wouldn't trust me. You don't trust me now, even. I see that. You don't let anyone in, do you? I don't either. But if you knew . . . I think you would hate me.

You're hurt. I don't want you to get hurt worse.

Or Matty.

I want to help you.

But I want more than that.

A lot more.

The thing I want is justice. My heart beats with the want *of it. My chest aches with the need. I want Bardem to pay. I want him to fail. I want him to fall. I want to see him on the ground.*

Sometimes I feel the salt forming on me. I taste it on my lips. I am a pillar.

In the grudging light, Bardem came up out of the field and approached the house slowly. It had burned long ago. Blackened brick and the shape of a porch. The beams of the roof falling inward. He stopped and studied the driveway. The tire tracks in the snow were not more than a few hours old. Nothing moved. Finally he crossed to the porch and climbed the steps.

He pulled the pistol from his belt and opened the door and went in and closed the door behind him. He walked through the kitchen and into the living room. Snow sifting in from the roof. The ashen carpet was disturbed. To the left was a warped piano. At the hearth he put his hand over the coals.

He tucked the pistol in his belt. He picked up a gallon-size jug of water and spun off the cap with his thumb and sniffed. Then he put the jug down. He opened the grocery bag near the fireplace. Bloody bandages. Vials. A used syringe.

The ceiling creaked. He studied the room to make sure he'd seen everything. He walked around to the back of the piano and looked at the floor. The book was almost hidden behind the piano leg. He squatted and picked it up.

A schoolbook. Picture of a hot-air balloon.

He opened the cover.

He rose with the book and left.

There was something wrong with Jack's eyes. He looked out the car window and watched everything undulate—house, fence, barn, horse. Cat. Shimmer of snow. Each real thing rippled for a moment, glittered like a stone skipping on water, and then became solid again. Store. Traffic light.

Ava drove on vague roads he recognized but couldn't name. Matty sat in back. Dull pain tolled like a bell inside Jack. He held his side and put a hand on the armrest while a wave of sleepiness glowed over him.

"Give him something to eat," he heard Ava say.

Matty handed Jack a little bag of potato chips. Jack shut his eyes and took it by feel. Touched fingers to the bag. He'd open it later. Later.

"It's okay," Ava said. "He just needs some rest is all."

He let his head fall to the window. Who was she talking to? Her words came to him as if from the end of a tunnel.

Matty: "Is he going to get better?"

"Yes."

"You might just be saying that."

"No."

"He looks really bad."

"He isn't as bad as he looks."

Quiet. The car rolled along down the road.

"Someone was trying to kill him," Matty said, "weren't they?"

"I think so."

"They might try again if they find us."

"They won't find us."

"They might."

"They won't."

"Okay."

XXIII

The motel was one of those 1950s kind, with the office in the front and the rooms around to the side. Where you park right outside your door. The parking lot was pretty empty. I chose it for those reasons.

We got Jack into bed. He went straight to sleep. I closed the blinds. I locked the door. Turned on the lamp. I ran a bath for Matty and got him in. Then I went to the bed and sat by Jack. I just looked at him. His dirty hair and his swollen eye. The tiredness in his face. His slender hands. Something graceful about them. Gentle.

I'd gotten good at not caring about things.

Now I was caring.

I didn't like it.

Doyle pulled into headquarters just after seven in the morning and parked and went in. Midge looked up from the report she was typing out at the desk.

"You look tired as hell."

"Why, thank you, Midge."

She went to the coffee maker and poured a stream of what

looked like motor oil into a Styrofoam cup and set it on the counter in front of him. "Find anything?"

"At the old Palmer place. Somebody's been there, but they cleared out."

"Got any idea who?"

"Not for sure."

"Well," she said, "I got somethin' on the truck."

"What?"

"Officer in Boise come up on that old road warrior about a month ago. On the highway out there. Appeared to have a big tarp coverin' somethin' in the cargo space. Officer radioed he was gonna stop them and take a look. Passenger in the truck opened fire. Killed the officer dead."

Doyle took off his hat and hung it on a peg. "All right," he said.

"I think it's good to know just what we got here."

"It is."

"I called Boise. They'll arrive first thing in the morning."

"That's real good."

She pulled her coat from the back of the chair and put it on. "I done a map like you said. Got two deputies from Rexburg comin' over. We'll take a closer look now it's light."

"Hold up. I'll go out there with you."

"Nope. You drink that coffee."

"All right."

Halfway out the door, she turned. "Hey, Doyle?"

"What?"

"I hope whoever was drivin' that truck is back in Boise."

"I hope so too."

"I got a feelin' they ain't, though."

Doyle nodded. "So do I."

Doyle got a can of Coors at the gas station. When he got to the prison, he went through security and down the hall to an interrogation room and went in and closed the door. He sat in the chair across from Leland Dahl. A table between them. He set the Coors on the table. "Hello, Leland," he said.

Leland hunched casually in his chair, looking at Doyle. His eyes hooded, indifferent. He just sat there staring.

"When's the last time you saw your boy?" Doyle asked.

"Which one's that?"

"Let's say either one."

Leland shrugged. "Don't know."

"Okay. Maybe take a guess."

"It's been awhile."

"You ought not lie to me, Leland."

Leland appraised him. A dull expression in his eyes. Opaque. Like a drawn curtain. "Okay, I saw Jack. So what?"

"So Jack pays you a visit. *You.* A man he hasn't spoke to in years. Now, why would he do that? I can't think of any reason. Except one."

Leland stretched and picked up the Coors. He popped the tab and raised the can to his lips and sipped.

"Next thing I know," Doyle said, "I got a dead correctional officer and two missin' boys and a vehicle looks like a deer's been gutted in it. Now what are the chances of that all bein' a coincidence?"

The heater rattled on. Leland leaned back and tipped up the Coors and gulped, his throat chugging. He set the empty can on the table and wiped his mouth.

"Where are your boys?" Doyle asked.

"I don't know. Hey, you know a detective?"

"I think what you need to consider," Doyle said, "is how you got here in the first place. What you did and who you did it with."

Leland smiled without humor, saying nothing.

"You've got them boys involved with some very serious folks."

A noise like scorched laughter burst from Leland. "You're right about that."

"These folks will kill your boys, Leland. They won't quit."

"Yeah, well. Jack won't, neither. He'll fight."

"If you know where they are, you ought to tell me—"

Leland jerked forward in his chair and snatched up the empty beer can. He smashed it in his fist and dropped the can onto the table and banged a hand down to crunch the Coors flat. A crease of blood welled up from his palm. He made a fist and sat up straight. "I got nothin' left except those boys—but I *don't know* where they're at. And I wouldn't tell you if I did, neither."

Doyle looked at Leland, who stared back.

"Do you know what you've done?" Doyle asked.

Leland didn't answer. Then he nodded.

"Yeah. I know what I done. And what I'm gonna do."

When Leland returned to his cell, he sat on the edge of the bunk while an officer locked him in. For a long time, he just sat there.

Not moving. In his head fiddlers played sharp quick songs that rose in volume to fill the cell and scratch sounds higher and higher.

They're safe.

They're holed up.

Or they're out lying dead somewhere.

Buried in the snow.

Thrown in some dark hole.

A wave of jitters took him over. He stood, nerves jangling. The first thing he did was get a pencil from his desk. Then he reached over the bunk and pulled a book from where he kept it tucked between the wall and the bed's metal frame. *White Fang.* The cover with the wolf on it, and the pages dog-eared. He tore a page from the book and turned it sideways and scratched two words. What was needed and nothing more. He folded the page and put it in an envelope and filled out the address. He sealed the edge with a lick.

Somewhere an inmate laughed. A disembodied sound. Like ash drifting.

He shoved the envelope into the waist of his sweatpants and sat on the bunk. Then he began to pace. The cement slab. Plastic chair, steel toilet. Smell of sweat. He paced back and forth, clenching his hands.

He sat on the bunk.

He waited.

The racket of fiddles receded. The room and he were silent.

At six o'clock, the bell buzzed and the door unlocked. He rose and stood in front of the mirror above the toilet. With his fingers he combed his hair to the side. On his way to the chow hall, he fished the envelope from his pants and dropped it into the prisoners' outgoing mail.

It was dark when Jack woke. The motel room empty. He rose from the bed and went to the window and pulled apart the blinds. Lights in the street. Snow floating down in clumps under the raw glare of vapor lamps. The skyline low and shabby beneath a pewter sky. He looked for Ava's car. It wasn't there.

On the nightstand was a notepad. Matty's handwriting: *We went to get food. I hope you sleep good.*

He went into the bathroom and filled a plastic cup with water and drank. His mouth hurt when he swallowed. He filled the cup and drank again. Matty's clothes were on the floor. Ring of dirt in the bathtub. Batman sitting on the ledge.

He turned and saw himself in the mirror. The lumped eye, the gashed mouth. Dried vomit in his hair. *Well*, he thought. *You never were pretty anyway.*

They'd probably get back soon, but he could hurry. He sat on the side of the tub. After he rinsed out the dirt, he pushed down the plug and turned on the water. He left the door open a crack so he could hear any sounds outside. Then he undressed and gently peeled back the bandage. The floor went fuzzy. The wound was yellow and purple and swollen at the edges.

It looked like a bite. Like something out of a zombie movie.

He eased himself into the water. Sharp pinpricks tingled up his side. There was a strange weakness in his gut. He put a hand on the tub ledge.

It's all right. Just breathe through it. You deserve all this. Don't you?

When the tingling passed, he dipped a washcloth in the water and blotted the wound. Small pieces of dry blood came free and floated in the water. The color almost black. Like bits of soot. He bent and studied the deep ravine of broken skin, the rib bones peeking out from under the stitches.

Not good.

A new thought came to him: *There are stitches.*

Neat, even sutures.

Five of them.

So. She'd sewn him up.

He felt a rush of heat to his face. He'd been naked. He'd probably stunk to high heaven. What had she thought of him?

He washed all over and scrubbed his hair and rinsed. When he stood to climb out of the tub, the water was pink and swirled with blood, and a faint pink fluid still trickled from the damage at his side. He got a towel from above the toilet and patted down with one hand while holding on to the sink counter. His clothes stunk, so he wrapped the towel around his waist and held a clean washcloth to his side. For a moment he stood there. He couldn't seem to catch a deep breath. He filled the plastic cup with water and drank again.

A thought nagged at him.

Why is she helping you? Why?

No answer came to him.

He walked out of the bathroom, holding the washcloth to his wound. Favoring his sore ribs. He took a pair of sweatpants and a T-shirt from the duffel. He pulled the shirt over his head with one hand while the other kept the washcloth in place. Then he sat on the bed and watched the door.

The room darkened.

Silence.

It's been awhile. How long?

Somewhere a toilet flushed. A faucet turned on. Jack rose and looked through the window. Snow drifting down in the vapor light. No cars. Nothing.

They went to get food. That's all. They'll be back soon.

The washcloth was turning pink.

A queasy ache reached up through his stomach. Like when swimming and you go to put your feet down, but the water is deeper than you thought and you can't touch bottom. He sat on the bed. He thought he should lie down, but he didn't. Instead, he watched the door. He tried to breathe through his nose. Slow the breathing. *They'll come back.*

Ava will bring him back.

Unless she doesn't.

Then what?

Minutes wore down and dropped away. He watched the door. The odd sensation of time coming apart. A slow unravel.

XXIV

I took Matty to Big J's for a burger. And to get him out of the motel room. Let Jack sleep. That's what I hoped he would do—rest.

Here is what happened.

They order cheeseburgers and huckleberry milkshakes and eat french fries with fry sauce. Sitting in the booth with the meal between them. The big window behind them overlooks the dark and the street. Fall of snow. Soft light coming from the wall lamp. Heat and warmth. Smells of grease and sizzling beef. Ava watches Matty. He eats a fry slowly, dipping each bite in sauce. Still wrapped in his coat and hat.

He seems lost. He looks at her.

"Go ahead," she says. "Or it will get cold."

"These are good fries."

"Yes. They are."

"The shake looks good too."

"You should try it."

"Okay."

He sits there without moving.

"Are you okay?"

He nods.

"Are you sick?"

"No."

"What is it?"

He blinks at her. "Do you think we should save some?"

"Save some?"

He nods. "For later."

"You can eat it all. Here. You can put the sauce on your burger."

"Okay."

In the dim light of the lamp she watches him sitting, quiet. Gray circles under his eyes. He stares at the burger.

"What is it?" she asks.

"I was just thinking. We could take some to Jack."

Oh.

"We could do that," she says. "But when we finish, we're going to order him a burger and fries of his own. So you don't need to save yours."

"He likes huckleberry milkshakes."

"We'll get him a shake too."

He looks at all the food. "So it's okay."

"Yes. It's okay."

"Are you going to eat everything?"

"Yes." She eats a bite of her burger. "I am."

He picks up the plastic spoon and dips it into the milkshake and lifts the spoon to his mouth. "Wow, that's good."

In between bites of fries and hamburger, Matty talks about Batman. How he doesn't have any superpowers, but he's brave. Like Jack. When he finishes, he licks the milkshake spoon and tips the cup and drinks the last of the sweet huckleberry milk. Then he sits gazing out the window overlooking the street. Cowled in his hat and coat. He looks droopy. He looks like he might fall asleep. After a while, he says, "My mom's dead."

She watches him. Her stomach knotting. "I'm sorry."

"It's all right."

"I think mine is too," she says.

"You don't know?"

"I guess I know. In my heart."

He sits there, looking out the window at all the snow and the dark. He says, "The bad people are looking for Jack, aren't they?"

"Yes."

"Why do they want him?"

"I don't know."

"Do they want to kill him?"

"I don't know."

"They want to kill him."

"Yes."

He nods. Then he covers his face with his hands. "I don't know what to do."

"Listen to me."

He shakes his head. Then he lowers his hands and looks at her.

"I'll stay with you. I won't let anything happen."

He watches her, his face lit by the lamp. "Do you promise?"

"Yes."

Outside the motel door, a car engine turned off and a door opened. Jack stood.

Ava. Matty.

A wave of relief spread through him, so acute he had to bend and hold the edge of the bed.

"We got you a cheeseburger," Matty said when Ava opened the door.

Jack looked at Ava. Her battered coat buttoned up to her chin, her black-walnut hair. She met his gaze.

He sat on the bed.

Matty dropped a white paper sack in his lap. "And fries with fry sauce. And a milkshake with huckleberries." He put the milkshake on the dresser and slung off his coat and hat. "Did you get my note?"

"Yes," he said. "It was good."

Ava turned on the lamp. She looked at where Jack was holding the washcloth beneath his shirt.

"I took a bath," Jack said.

He could not believe the stupid things that came from his mouth.

"Isn't it great?" Matty said. "The water comes out hot forever."

Even from across the room, Jack could feel the heat of Ava's attention. He pretended not to. He opened the sack and pulled out the burger and took a bite.

"Thank you," he said to her. "For the food."

Matty turned on the television and sat on the floor with his toys. Ava locked the door. Then she got the grocery bag from the table and sat by him on the bed. "Are you okay?" she asked.

"I don't even know anymore."

But his stomach was waking up: The cheese and the beef. Ketchup. The burger, still hot. He finished it in seconds.

"Did you see anyone?" he asked her.

"No."

"No one followed you?"

"No."

"No? How do you know?"

"I know."

It was something in her stare that convinced him. He nodded and looked down. His hand, holding the now-red washcloth. What a mess he looked.

"We should patch you up," she said.

He stood, suddenly shy. "I feel pretty good. I'll go do it."

Her eyes were on his, that striking hazel. Full of uncertainty, of depths to fall into from a height. She handed him the bag. "Okay."

In the bathroom, he removed the cloth. The wound had almost stopped bleeding. He washed it again and bandaged it and swallowed the antibiotics. Then he looked in the mirror. The eye bruise had darkened, and his hair was a curling tangle. He turned on the faucet and ran his hand through the water and wet his hair down. He combed it with his fingers.

Well, this is the best you're gonna look.

He went back out. The wind was starting to gust outside, and the snow was falling harder. On the floor, Ava played with Matty. Jack got the milkshake from the dresser and sat on the bed and slurped a spoonful. Sweet, tart berries. The taste brought back pictures in his mind. Images of childhood, picking huckleberries with Mom and Dad in the woods. Matty, just a baby. Strapped in a harness on Dad's back. Mountain air, a drizzle of rain. The purple berries hanging from wet branches. Mom's voice, floating above the cool silence.

Happy.

He shut off the thought and finished the milkshake and fries, watching Matty and Ava play. Matty giggling. When had he heard that last? And her. On her hands and knees, she ran a toy car over the carpet. Still in her wool coat. Her voice clear and soft. Like a strand of song he'd never forget. Something deep in Jack moved. *All your life you wonder, what would it be like? And then it happens.* She glanced at him, as if feeling his stare, and he looked at the television. When she went back to playing with Matty, he resumed watching her. *Who is she?* He could not figure her out.

Her: A complexity of opposites. Of gentle and rough, of dark and light.

She sat up, frowning. "What are you doing?"

"What?"

"It's just . . . you keep looking at me."

He didn't know what to say, so he just shrugged and kept looking at her. His stomach was full and his side didn't hurt, and a warm golden haze flowed through him, making him brave.

She studied him.

"What?" he asked.

She almost smiled. "Nothing."

But she was looking at his hair.

"I know," he said. "I'm a mess."

Matty lay on the carpet and watched the television. Ava stood. Pink bloomed across her cheeks as she inhaled.

"I could cut it," she said.

"Okay."

She sat him in the chair by the lamp. The glowy light of the television permeated the room. She dampened a towel with warm water and rewet his hair with it. Her touch tentative. The way she looked at him.

"Are you ready?"

"Yes."

She stood in front of him with the scissors, considering his hair, mulling over her choices. Then she set about cutting. Her hands in his hair. Her fingers brushing his scalp, grazing his neck. It took some time, and he could tell she wanted to do it well. Her concentration. Without a word. His eyes felt hot and he looked down at his hands, blinking. It was so good—the way it felt—to be touched by her. Trust, risk, hope: It was too much. He lurched to his feet.

"What?" she asked.

He was shaking. "Nothing."

Her gaze unnerved him. He could hardly think. He had to sit.

"Should I finish?"

"I think so. Yes."

The room glowed. With gentle care, she resumed cutting. Everything transient in the light. Everything fleeting. When she finished, she washed his ears and neck with a fresh warm cloth. She walked him to the mirror to see. Then she saw his face.

"What's wrong?"

"Nothing. You did a good job."

"I'm sorry," she said.

"No, I like it." He fumbled for words. "I feel lucky. It's been a long time since I felt that way."

She regarded him, the freckles in her hazel eyes. Then she nodded. Something unspoken between them. A conversation.

On the carpet, Matty was already asleep. She flicked off the television. The room was quiet.

She took some blankets and a pillow from the closet and made them into a bed on the floor.

"You're tired," she said. Her solemn eyes. "Should you lie down?"

He felt exhaustion break over him. It made him dizzy. "I don't know."

"I think you should."

Jack got under the bedcovers. He watched her pick up Matty and tuck him into the makeshift bed. He just kept looking at her. This stillness in him. Did he dream this?

No. He did not.

He closed his eyes. From somewhere in his memory came a single word, from a song, or a prayer, some source he could not place: *hallelujah*. Seconds passed, a handful, while he lived in that brief space between awareness and sleep, the dark reach of it. Until he could keep it away no longer.

XXV

My sweet Jack: Let me photograph you on this night, in case this is the last time that we're exactly like we are at this moment. This reckless, fleeting glimpse of wonderland. This rapture of sight and touch and sound. Oh, my heart. The glory here, in this twinkling of minutes.

Let me photograph this one.

He woke in the frail blue dark, listening. Something he'd heard. A soft sound. He waited for his eyes to adjust. She was standing by the window, her shape. The light came from the radio clock. Blue numbers glowing from the nightstand. She pulled her dress over her head and stood there naked, her hair falling down her back. His pulse started to jump, and in the darkness she took one of his shirts and put it on. Then she turned.

He closed his eyes.

Feelings rolling over him. Ocean waves.

Shift of the bed. A rustle of sheets. She was there, getting under the covers. She curled on her side, facing away from him.

She thinks you're asleep.

So act asleep.

Stay perfectly still.

Instead, he turned and rested behind her like a spoon. His lungs, his head, his heart. He didn't touch her. He made sure to keep every part of himself a few inches away. Legs, knees. His chest not touching her back. His lips not quite on her hair. Smell of ginger. His body wide awake. The familiar warmth rushing up in him. To feel her there, to hear her breath. He closed his eyes and was imagining he could see her when she spoke, a whisper.

"Jack?"

"What?"

"Do you like me?"

He swallowed. Not moving. "Yes. I do—a lot."

She was quiet.

He waited, keeping very still in the blankets. The curve of her back before him. The bend of her knees to her waist. Each a detail to never forget.

Outside, wind whistled.

She was asleep. He thought so.

Then her whisper: "Would you still like me if I wasn't what you thought I was?"

"What do you mean?"

She didn't answer. He could feel her hesitation.

"Nothing," she said.

They lay there in the darkness. Her close to him. The faint light on the walls, inhale of breath. A sensation as though his soul might pull free of his body and go floating toward her. He didn't touch her. But, oh, he wanted to. In the bed, on the sheets, her slender body. Reach out, his mouth on hers. Taste her skin. Feel them both shaking. How he wanted to—he felt so greedy. She made him hungry. His hands, they could go down, find the edge of the shirt, and lift—

But he didn't.

He didn't.

Hurting her. He hated the thought.

His side was starting to ache. It made him tired. He thought she was still awake, and he lifted his head a little to see her face, to catch a glimpse of what she might be thinking, but he couldn't.

Would you still like me—words in his head—*if I wasn't what you thought I was?*

He whispered, "You don't trust anyone. Do you? I don't either. You see people. They're smiling. Going to classes or to the movies. Doing homework at the library or out at the store with friends." He tried to gather the right words. "You think, maybe you can be like that. One day. Maybe it can be like that."

He could hear her breathing. The quiet. Then her voice, hushed.

"Jack?"

"What?"

To his surprise, she rolled over to face him. Hair falling across her cheekbone, her eyes gleaming. A mirror to his.

"Thanks for not touching me."

For a heartbeat, she watched him. Then she shut her eyes.

He lay there in the small paradise, tinged in blue light.

It was all he could do.

In another minute, he was asleep.

XXVI

Chaos: things that are not random but seem to be.

The mail carrier left the post office at dawn with his bundle of parcels and letters and traveled the narrow, plowed strip of road through a haze of snowfall, delivering his bundles. Snow blowing sideways in big drifts. The temperature ten below zero. Wipers scraping. At noon he came to a place where the snow had blown across the road almost entirely, except for a single plowed lane. He followed the snowy trench of road along the river's frozen edge. Tires rolling, snow crunching softly. White flakes blowing. At the final mailbox, he unlatched the metal door and set the letter inside. The envelope wasn't made out to Red Dahl, but the address was right. He put up the metal door and drove on.

XXVII

I woke to the sound of wind. Gusting on the door, on the window. I got up and put on clothes and pulled on my coat and boots. I was going to sneak out. I had to.

I went to the bed and looked at Jack sleeping. His bruised face, his unruly hair.

All I can say is this: Some things you want so bad, it rips you up inside. It turns you inside out.

"Hi," Matty said.

Ava turned. Matty lay in his makeshift bed, looking at her.

"Hi," she whispered.

"What are you doing?"

"I have to go for a while."

"Where?"

She went and crouched beside him. "Home. I've been away too long."

He sat up. "I don't want you to go."

"I'll come back."

"When?"

"Tomorrow."

He was silent.

"I left some money on the table," she said. "For food."

"Okay."

"People will miss me if I don't go."

He sat there, studying her. Saying nothing. He drew up his legs and clasped his knees. "You could call my phone if you need me."

She nodded. "That's a good idea. And you could call me. If you need me."

"It's okay, Ava."

"It's okay?"

"I'll watch out for Jack."

They stared at each other.

"Don't go anywhere," she said.

"Okay."

"I don't want you to leave this room."

"Okay. I'll take care of him."

"Lock the door when I leave."

"Okay."

She watched him a moment longer. Then she straightened and walked to the window and parted the blinds. Snow drifting down, wind. The glass vibrating softly in its frame. No cars out there but her own. She opened the door and turned. "Matty?"

He was still looking at her.

She said, "Don't be afraid."

They each were silent: Ava afraid, and Matty untroubled. He started to play with the cars beside his blanket. She watched him a moment. Cold blowing in. Whirl of snow.

She stepped outside and closed the door.

She stood in the snow until the lock clicked.

XXVIII

Do you think you'd have chosen better? That you'd have altered the course? Alter what? What would you do at that reckonable moment? The end is coming, and soon your judgments will be sealed with dirt.

I know this: After all that happened, I still would make the same choice.

When Jack opened his eyes, Matty was standing right next to the bed, staring at him. "Want to watch a show, Jack?" he asked.

Jack yawned.

"There's a *Batman* marathon," Matty said.

Jack sat up. The other side of the bed was rumpled. Empty. He looked around. A commercial played on the television. Lucky Charms. *They're magically delicious!*

"Or we could play UNO," said Matty.

"Where's Ava?"

"We're supposed to stay here."

Jack rose and went to the window and parted the blinds. His

side burned vaguely. Tire tracks in the snow. Almost buried. No car. "Where did she go?"

"Home. She'll come back tomorrow."

Jack's heart started firing odd beats. "Did she say anything else?"

"She left money for food, and we're supposed to stay here."

Jack looked out at the day through the jumble of twisting snow and then let the blinds close. He walked to the armchair and sat. Matty sat beside him, on the arm of the chair. After a minute he put his head on Jack's shoulder.

They spent the morning eating cereal from the box and watching *Batman*. Side by side under the blankets. He'd planned to get up and take a shower, but sitting with Matty was justification enough to wait. The snow was less. The storm breaking. Anyone could be on the roads soon. Red. The dope dealers. Police. They slept a little, but Jack didn't really sleep. He thought he shouldn't have gone to see Red, but it was too late now. He shouldn't have let himself get hurt. He should have taken better care of Matty.

At noon he got up and showered and cleaned his wound with a washcloth and warm water while Matty watched television. He swallowed an antibiotic and got dressed and took deep breaths. In through the nose. Out. When he thought about taking care of Matty, he couldn't seem to take a breath deep enough to fill his lungs. Pounding in his head. He told himself to be fine.

Suck it up.

You're fine.

She'll come back tomorrow.

He went out and made the bed. His shirt lay folded on the

pillow—the one she'd worn. He lifted the shirt to his nose: smell of her, the subtle spice. He put it on.

He tidied things. Put away the cereal, picked up the dirty clothes. Then he sat in the chair by Matty. Batman and Robin were tied up, dangling over a pit of snapping crocodiles. Jack watched Matty watch TV, his tranquil face. He tried not to worry.

Come on, Jack. You just need to break through this.

Straighten out your mind.

Just keep going.

You'll be okay.

He sat like that for a while. Trying to make the worst seem better.

Time passed.

An hour.

Or two.

Maybe he should call Ava.

He knew he shouldn't call, but he looked for the Tracfone anyway. When he found it, he saw the text.

YOUR DAD WANTS TO TELL YOU SOMETHING.

His pulse started throbbing. He read the phone number.

It was from Bev.

"What?" Matty said.

Matty was looking at him.

It could be a trap. Of course it could.

But Bev is nice.

She wouldn't hurt you.

But Bev would do whatever Red said. No, the danger was Red.

What was the smart thing to do?

"Let's go for a walk," Jack said.

Matty looked at him. "I don't think we should go anywhere."

"We won't go far."

"Ava said stay here."

"We'll come back."

"You never do what I think."

Matty turned away. Jack pulled him close, but Matty's body stayed stiff.

"Listen to me," Jack said.

"What?"

"Bev sent a message. I think we should go see her."

"Why?"

"She wants to tell us something. Maybe something important."

"What if the bad guys are looking for you?"

"They might not even be out there anymore."

"Why can't we just wait?"

"We have to try. We can't just stay here."

Matty looked up at him. At last, he nodded.

"Get your coat," Jack said.

XXIX

Why did Jack leave that motel room? Why?

I don't know. Maybe he needed to act. To act, to move, to do. To not be acted upon.

It's like standing at the edge of a cliff.
You step back,
or you take a step forward.

They passed the motel entrance and Jack checked for the knife in his pocket, the metal shape of it. They set out up Barley Street and crossed an old iron bridge that spanned the river. At the street corner they stood watching. The stoplight flashing red. The fallen snow, soft underfoot. There was cold in the wind. They crossed the white intersection and headed along the street. Past Hunter's Drug & Hardware. Pink Petals Floral. The worn storefronts. He looked at Matty. His beanie pulled down over his ears, his small face tight with fear. His feet dragging. Jack took Matty's hand.

"Just stay close," he said.

"Okay."

"We'll be all right."

"What if something bad happens?"

Jack didn't answer.

"I'm sorry," Matty said.

"What for?"

"About what I said."

"What did you say?"

"How you never do what I think."

"Well, sometimes I don't listen very well. I'll do better."

"Okay."

Jack opened the door of Happy Hair & Nails, and they went in. The girl at the counter put down her nail file. She wore thick black eyeliner and a pink faux-fur sweater. She looked at Matty.

"Kid want a haircut?" she asked.

"We're looking for Bev," Jack said.

"Pedicures are two for twenty. Special today."

"Is Bev here?"

She scowled at him. "Bev's in the back."

They went between the rows of salon and pedicure chairs to the back of the store, where Bev told fortunes for paying customers. Jack parted the beaded curtain's fake gemstone strands, and they ducked through. Bev had decorated the storage room with flowery wallpaper and exotic pillows. Plush rugs that looked from faraway lands. Stage curtains hung from the rear wall, and a table draped in dark red velvet was centered upon the biggest rug. There was smoke in the air, and on the table sat a big bowl filled with loose incense. It burned on coals, to assist her divinations.

Coriander, hemp, fennel. A pungent smell. Spicy, bitter. The smoke stood unmoving in the still air.

Jack's eyes watered. Matty pinched his nose.

Bev pushed a button on her phone and put it on the table. "Come on in, kiddos. I been waitin' for you."

She stood in a cobalt-blue kimono and wore cat-eye glasses with diamond crystals and her hair rolled up in a high, wobbly bun. Two chopsticks poked through the mass of hair. Her lips she'd painted raspberry. "Don't be shy," she said. "I got cookies and tea."

Jack looked at her and looked away. "We can't stay."

"Sit. I don't bite."

They sat at the table. A candelabra chandelier hung from a chain that had been screwed into the ceiling. It cast wavery candle-light over the room. On the table, a dainty porcelain tea set stood with lemon wedges and homemade shortbread cookies cut into heart shapes. A small old-looking mirror of blackened glass rested beside the incense bowl. Tarot cards sat ready by the tea.

"Jack, I forget—you take it with honey or milk?"

"I don't really like tea."

"Try mine. I get it on Amazon. You want a smoke?"

"I'm good."

"I roll my own. No chemicals."

"No thanks."

"Matty, milk for you?"

He looked at Jack. "No thanks."

She poured them cups anyway.

They hunched over the drinks and sipped. Jack didn't favor

tea, and even with the honey the rose flavor had a tart bite that wrinkled his nose. A radio somewhere played soft nature sounds.

"I got your message," Jack said.

Bev nodded, thoughtful. On the table, her ornate phone sparkled in the candlelight. She reached for the incense bowl and blew lightly on the herbs and studied the rising smoke. A dark thread.

"We aren't here for a reading," Jack said. "I just want to know—"

"Hush."

With jeweled fingers, Bev pinched fresh incense from a nearby jar and sprinkled it over the coals. She closed her eyes and blew again. Burning seeds popped and flared. A sooty flame curled up.

Silence. Raindrops fell through a forest.

"My dad," Jack said. "What does he want to tell me?"

Bev lifted her head and looked across the table at Jack, the smoke swirling between them. "What you seek is not lost but only seems to be."

Jack stared. He blinked quickly, her words more than he could grasp. The smoke rose in a curl and died in the candlelight overhead.

"I don't know what that means," he said.

She watched him over the smoking bowl. Then she moved the incense aside and lifted the dark mirror. It fit in the palm of her hand, round in shape and framed in black pewter. The glass slightly convex, like an eye. She shifted the mirror in her palm gently, peering into the translucent glass. "Remove clouded thoughts from your minds."

Matty bit into his cookie.

"What about my dad?" Jack said.

Bev glanced at her phone. She set the mirror before Jack and leaned over it to grasp his hands across the table, her gaze radiant in the candlelight, tender. "Sweet Jack. How will you know who to trust?"

"What?"

"Men are beasts, Jack. And ghosts."

He pulled back his hands.

"They watch and wait," she said.

"Stop talking like that."

Matty shivered and scooted closer to Jack, bumping their chairs together. Jack looked at the mirror. He could see it—the eye—dimming and brightening in the candlelight. He felt weird all of a sudden, and he thought he glimpsed something there in the murky glass: a forest of towering pines blanketed in snow; the eyes of some wild animal shining, bright and unblinking, from deep in the woods—

He looked up, shaking. "My dad. I just want to know what he wanted—"

His voice ran high and broke off.

Bev stared into the mirror. She drew in a sudden breath, as if she'd been slapped. She lifted her gaze to Jack.

"He's here," she said.

Jack stood from the table, jolting it. The mirror quaked on the tablecloth, and a teacup fell over.

Bev's voice, piercing: "He won't hurt you, Jack. He just wants to talk—"

Jack grabbed Matty and turned and pushed him out through the beaded curtain, clutching his coat. There, at the counter, stood Red.

Jack was looking right into his eyes.

The face of bone. The disfigured head.

Jack shoved Matty back through the beads, sending Matty stumbling.

"Get up," Jack hissed. "Dammit, Matty. Go!"

The knife. He had it in his pocket.

"Wait," Red called. "Wait!"

Jack ducked between the beads. Bev stood beside the heavy curtain. There was a door. He grabbed Matty's hand.

"Run," he said. "Run."

They crashed out into the snow. By the time they got halfway down the alley, Red was already through the door behind them. Jack tightened his grasp on Matty's wrist, nearly pulling him off his feet. "Hurry," he said.

They tore into the street at a dead run. Jack looked back toward the alley but saw nothing. What direction to go? He slid on a patch of ice and fell, pulling Matty down with him. "Get up," he said. "Run."

Matty lay sprawled on the snow, terrified. Jack clutched his hand and pulled him up. Pain burst from his side, and he turned to look back. Coming toward him was Red—ten feet away. They both froze.

He unfolded the knife and held it pointed at Red. A heavy feeling in his body. This was the moment. The moment.

Red stood in the street. He looked at the knife.

"Don't move," Jack said. "You come a step closer and I'll put this knife in your throat."

Red didn't move. His head was bare, and his eyes ran into Jack's like a snake down a hole. He stood without moving. Snowflakes floated down, landed to melt on his scarred head.

With his free hand, Jack removed the motel key from his pocket. He slipped it into Matty's hand. "Go back to where we were, Matty. Wait for her. Do you understand?"

Matty nodded.

"No," Red said fervently. "You both stay here."

Matty just stood there, face pale. Looking at Jack.

Jack stepped in front of Matty and said to Red, "What do you want?"

"To help. That's all."

"Oh really?"

"I mean that, Jack. I done wrong, and I'm sorry."

"What do you want with us?"

"I got somethin' for you."

"I don't want nothin' from you."

Red looked at Matty.

"Don't look at him."

His gaze moved to Jack. He said nothing.

"Are those other men with you?"

"No. They been watchin' me. Thinkin' you might come back. But they left, Jack. I swear it."

"Where did they go?"

"Back to wherever they come from."

"I'll bet."

"They ain't comin' back. I broke ties with 'em. For good."

Jack almost laughed.

"I know I done wrong, Jack. But I'm tryin' to make it right."
Red put a hand to his coat.

"You keep your hands at your sides. Don't you take a step."

Red's hand dropped. "I don't know where you been, but I
think you ought to leave here. It's not safe for you no more."

Jack tightened his grip on the knife.

"It ain't me you got to fear, Jack. I ain't gonna hurt you. You
got no need to go flashin' that knife."

Jack glanced at Matty. He was standing with his hands covering
his face, looking out between his fingers. When Jack looked up,
Red had taken a step.

"You get back."

"They won't stop lookin' for you now."

"Yeah. I know."

Red didn't move. He looked up the street. "Think, Jack. Anybody can see you out here holdin' that knife."

"You think I won't kill you, but you're wrong."

"You won't."

"Try me and see."

"You ain't that man, Jack."

As Jack stood facing Red, he felt a tremble in the earth and
heard the jolting rush of a diesel engine. Blur of metal. The vehicle
struck Red from chest to knee with a crack; the world exploded
into a thousand pieces. Red traveled through the air, away from
the truck, turning over as he went. He landed forty feet into the

intersection. The truck slid sideways and stopped. Two men stood on the sidewalk, staring. In the intersection, the black truck circled around and sped up again.

Jack shoved Matty and sent him sprawling, out of the truck's path. He stumbled and dropped the knife. No time to find it.

The truck whooshed past.

He looked back. At the end of the street, the truck slowed. It stirred up the snow and idled in a billow of white. A Ford F-150. One figure in the cab.

The hatted man.

He pulled up Matty. "Run."

But Matty was looking at him, blank-faced. No expression at all. Jack picked him up and slung him over his shoulder. Pain. Awful. There were more people on the sidewalk. A woman with her cell phone. He was aware of the fading rumble of the F-150 as it turned to the north and rolled away.

Silence now. Snow falling.

He lumbered, wincing, into the intersection toward Red with Matty over his shoulder—his side howling—but he had to know.

He couldn't leave Red lying there alone unless he knew.

When he reached Red, he fell to his knees in the street and held on to Matty, who buried his face in Jack's shoulder.

"Hold me tight," Jack said. "Don't look."

Matty wrapped his legs around Jack's waist and locked them at the ankles. The pain nearly took Jack's breath.

Red's head was open, and pink stuff had spilled out onto the snow. His arm and a leg were bent at terrible angles. Jack took off his hat and covered Red's head with it, concealing the blur of matter and the blood. Jack didn't want people to see Red that way. Red never did like his flawed side to show.

He sat there for seconds. With Red. Too many seconds and not enough.

A north wind billowed and lifted Red's parka, blew it open. In the inside pocket, a white envelope fluttered. Bits of snow dampened the paper. Jack could read two words:

For Jack.

The silence now was complete.

Suddenly Bev bounded out of the salon, screaming.

"Red! Red! Oh no, Red! Not you—"

She ran into the street and crumpled.

Jack felt weak. He crouched and seized the envelope, the weight of Matty making blackness rush at his feet, and then he turned and staggered and started to run. Gripping Matty's knees to keep him upright.

"Hold on to me," he whispered to Matty, whose head stayed buried, who didn't answer. "We have to run."

In the distance, a siren wailed. He could hear shouting. Bev's screams. "Jack! Please—Jack! Stop!"

He kept running. He took a side street toward the motel. Holding on to Matty by the knees. *Don't fall. Hold him tight.* "Don't look back."

Halfway to the motel they came to the iron bridge, and Jack was starting to gasp. He hardly had breath. At the sound of tires crunching on snow he obeyed an instinct he didn't know he had and dropped down off the street and onto the riverbank. He listened

204

for the truck, but there was nothing. Even the siren had stopped. He stumbled for a few hundred yards, and the snow was deep. Finally he sank to his knees and pried Matty away from his body. Put him down in the snow. Shoved the envelope into his coat. The whole world pulsed slowly. Matty wouldn't walk. He was shivering, and Jack sat. Pulled him close. "It's okay," he said. "We'll just rest for a minute."

When they got to the intersection next to the motel, Jack stopped to watch the traffic before stepping off the curb and limping out into the road. Matty wanted to be carried, so that's what Jack did. He went along the side of the motel, keeping to the wall, doing his best to hurry. His eyes darted over the parking lot. Nothing. Outside their motel room, he took the key from Matty's pocket and slid it into the lock. He closed the door behind them and immediately locked it. He laid Matty on the bed, pulled off his coat and hat, and wrapped him in the blankets. Then he peeled off his own wet things. His shirt was spotted with blood. He went into the bathroom and got a towel and blotted at his side. The bandage was wet. He couldn't get his body to stop shaking. Vague thoughts. *Baths will have to wait. How will you listen for cars with the faucet running? How can you be sure he's safe in the other room? So far away?* He put on a new shirt and went to the bed, where Matty lay slumped against the headboard.

"Talk to me," Jack said.

Matty looked at him. Face empty.

"Are you hurt?"

Matty shook his head. Then he started to cry.

Jack sat by him. The death of Red hung over the room like vapor. These men would go further and further. They would never stop—never.

Jack gathered Matty close, held him through the sobs. Just so. He tried to think of something to say. What could he say? No words for this. He felt his incompetence bitterly and jabbed at his eyes and kissed Matty's head. Kissed again. *What if—? Can you imagine it? That beloved skull, crushed? That blessed head? What would you do?*

Hold him in your arms. Hug him. Life is gone. So quick.

XXX

INVICTUS

By William Ernest Henley

Out of the night that covers me,
Black as the pit from pole to pole,
I thank whatever gods may be
For my unconquerable soul.

In the fell clutch of circumstance
I have not winced nor cried aloud.
Under the bludgeonings of chance
My head is bloody, but unbowed.

Beyond this place of wrath and tears
Looms but the Horror of the shade,
And yet the menace of the years
Finds and shall find me unafraid.

It matters not how straight the gate,
How charged with punishments the scroll,
I am the master of my fate,
I am the captain of my soul.

I have one word for this poem: bullshit.

Doyle pulled up in front of Happy Hair & Nails and parked. The street was roped off with yellow tape, and Midge's cruiser sat in the intersection with its lights on. Somebody had put a sheet over the body lying there in the street. He stooped under the crime tape.

"It's just all-out war," Midge said.

"Did anybody see the truck?"

"It was a Ford. F-150. New. No plates."

He crouched and pulled back the sheet. "Dammit."

Midge looked away. "Dead bodies in the street. Who'd ever believe such a thing?"

Doyle covered Red and stood. "Bev saw the Dahl boys?"

"Yessir. They were on foot."

"They didn't go far, then."

He studied the shoe prints. Bloody impressions trailing away through the snow. The older boy had stepped in the damage left by Red. His gait had been odd, maybe injured. Or encumbered. After a few steps the smaller prints disappeared.

So he'd carried the little one.

Doyle raised the yellow tape for Midge to duck under. "There's nothing more to do here. You go on home."

He followed the bootprints, walking slowly. Scanning the snow for footprints. For blood. Those boys. He kept thinking of them. *Some things you remember*, he thought. *Like they happened yesterday.*

"Ma'am," he said under the porch light.

She stood there in her nightgown and bare feet, her hand falling slowly from the knob. No expression. She moved not at all. It was dark. Finally she said, "I knew you'd come."

"I'm sorry."

"He ain't got it."

"Got what?"

"I need to sit down."

When she looked, officers were already falling upon the barn from all sides. There were four, each advancing with a pistol in their hands. Starlight glinting off barrels. The door clapped open. A loud scuffle, and then the shot came like a rupture of yellow light.

"Oh God," she said.

She staggered out of the house and crumpled to the ground and buried her face in her arms in the dirt. Echo of gunfire. The riven night. Hot summer air. Doyle couldn't see any sign of Leland inside the house. He crouched beside her.

"Bobbi Jean."

"Oh God," she said.

An officer shoved the man out of the barn and into the night, sending him sprawling. Leland was quick. He dove and rolled, but the officer pulled him up instantly with the pistol at his chest. Leland stood with a shout and turned to see his wife, but she was on the dirt, sobbing.

"I'm beggin' you," she said into the dirt.

"I'm as sorry as I can be about this," Doyle said.

Bobbi Jean raised her crushed face to look at him. "Do you know what you've done to us? Do you? You don't get to say sorry."

Doyle lifted Bobbi Jean to her feet and brought her into the house while his men handcuffed Leland and pushed him into the back of the cruiser. Doyle closed the front door. It was dark in the house. Bobbi Jean wandered off and sat at the kitchen table and turned her face away. Shaking. She reached across her chest and held her palm against her heart. "Oh, Leland," she said.

"This isn't your fault," Doyle said.

She shook her head, sobbing softly.

"You didn't do anything wrong."

She shook her head.

Doyle didn't know what else to do. He went over and switched on a lamp.

"Dammit," he whispered.

Huddled against the wall in the shabby light was a boy, very thin, in pajamas. He was clutching something in his arms, shielding it with his hands: a small child. Wrapped in a blanket. The boy held the child close to him. He was frozen with fear.

For the love of God.

Doyle had thought maybe the boys were asleep, but now he had a sense that the older boy had been watching the whole time. *For God's sake.*

He walked over and squatted slowly. The small child was asleep. Swaddled in white. He looked at the boy. "Hi," he said. "What's your name?"

The boy didn't answer.

"It's okay," Doyle said. "I'm not going to hurt you."

The boy just hung on to his brother. "Who are you?" the boy asked finally.

"I'm a friend."

XXXI

I went to school. Then I went to the library to study. Sometimes you do things on autopilot. You go through motions with the mind turned off. Like when you see something coming from the corner of your eye, but you don't let yourself look at it fully. You're not ready to stare at it yet.

I knew he'd be waiting for me at home.

He was.

She turns off the road and approaches the house on the narrow drive that curves up between stone fencerows. Snow covers the posts and makes humps over the stone columns. It is almost dark. A long blue twilight with tree branches crossing the snow and wind making the branches whisper. She parks in front of the garage and gets out. The sidewalk between the garage and the house has been cleared, but no lights are on in the house. She sits and watches. The tall white house. Shutters across the front. Neat and well kept. He would not have it otherwise. She climbs the steps to the porch and stomps her boots on the knotted braid rug and goes in.

The foyer is cold. The floor of stone. The wood staircase ascends into dark.

He is not here.

The taut wires of her nerves relax a bit, and she opens the closet and hangs her coat and slings her bag of schoolwork onto the walnut bench. She crosses the foyer to the far side of the living room and walks in and runs her hand on the wall to switch on the overhead light. There is nothing. The power is out from the storm.

A lighter flicks. The flame erupts and hits the darkening glass of the window, where Bardem sits in silhouette. He lifts the flame to his lips and lights a cigarette. He gazes at her and says nothing.

She stands there, in the doorway. The whole room starts to whirl. Something in the way he looks at her makes her feel like she can't move. The room is colder with him in it. Sounds are louder. Minutes slow.

He flicks the lighter off. She can see the red ember of the Marlboro. The shadow of him. Smell of tobacco. He sits there, smoking. In the leather armchair. The fireplace with the great wood mantel and the dark hearth. He looks away from her. His thoughts seem elsewhere.

She finds her voice. "Is everything okay?"

He doesn't answer.

"The power is out."

Still nothing. He acts as if she isn't even there.

"You must be cold," she says.

"Do you know why I call you my bird?"

His voice is low and soft, a piece of velvet you might brush against your cheek, just to feel the lush texture on your skin.

"What?"

"Your heart. I always feel it racing. Like a little bird in a cage. From the first time I held you." He takes a drag on the cigarette. "I still remember: You were just a baby. I held you to my chest, and I could feel your heart beating. Right through my shirt. Fluttering, just like a bird's."

She crosses the room to the fireplace. Everything is humming. She stuffs the hearth with tinder and limbs of kindling wood and strikes a match. Smoke swirls up in a thread. Her thoughts spin. *He doesn't know anything. Where you've been. Who you were with.*

He doesn't know. He doesn't know.

He says, "You're a good girl."

The kindling catches fire. Flame shadows shift along the fine paper on the walls.

She turns. "Are you hungry?"

She knows this device of his. This cat and mouse.

To trick.

To catch or be caught.

"I'll make you some soup," she says. "Clam chowder?"

He leans back. Studying her. His face aglow in the fire. Those eyes. Serene.

"Tell me something," he says.

"What?"

"If you had one thing in the world that mattered to you, would you ever give it up?"

"I don't know what you mean."

"What would make you give it up?"

She stares at him.

"I'm talking about weakness," he says.

She watches him. Watches him study her in the capering light. She is undisturbed. In order. She puts her whole mind into it.

He smiles. "I thought you might want to say something. To convince me."

"Convince you of what?"

"Convince me of everything."

"I don't understand."

He lowers the cigarette to the tray on the side table, taps off the ashes. He looks at the fire. "We all come into this world untainted by experience. Pure. Without defect. Six trillion cells of impeccable biology. Molecules and protein. Then existence starts in. It's just life. The big game. Feel, hope, dream. The heart gets caught up. It begins to care. Dreams break, hopes shatter. Love is lost. That immaculate luster dims. There's the damage, Ava. The weakness. Life breaks the perfect mold we started from, and we dull, and we tarnish. We are all dark shells of that once lustrous start. There is no way around it." He pauses, clears his throat. "Except one."

She waits. She does not ask the question. What he wants her to ask.

Time is slow. Tick.

Tick.

He looks at her. The blue eyes clear as water. Halcyon. "You become impervious."

She flusters. "How do you do that?"

"Like anything else. You practice."

Wind gusts up and shakes the windows softly. The fire crackles.

A lamp turns on. The power has returned. He does not pull his gaze from her.

"I'm going to make you some soup."

"I've cut you off," he says. "Your money. Debit card, bank account. You don't have anything now. Except me."

Silence.

She turns and forces her feet to move until they arrive at the kitchen. She washes her hands at the sink and opens the cupboard and stares at the cans of clam chowder. Three rows of them, stacked neatly. She removes one and pries the lid off and heats the soup in a saucepan. Her hands tremble. She tries to stop them. He doesn't know anything. He's just a man. Not worse. Salt and pepper. The bowl on a plate. Saltine crackers, get a spoon. She brings it to him by the fire. Her hands steady.

"Your favorite."

"My little bird. Thank you."

"I'm tired. I think I'll go to bed."

She turns and walks to the foyer. His voice follows her.

"My bird. You're a good girl. Aren't you?"

She goes upstairs to the bathroom and locks the door. She is shaking. She is not low-key. Not in order. She washes her hands. Her wrist. The black heart. She scrubs, scratches. Rinses, soaps again. But it is not enough. Sometimes it isn't.

She checks the door to be sure. Then she takes off her clothes and steps in the shower. She turns the water to hot. So hot it stings her skin. She washes everything. Hair, face, arms, legs. Head to toe. She scrubs. To get off the dirt. Until the calm begins to come. Until she is sure that she is okay. Then she washes again.

She wraps herself in a towel and dries and puts on a pajama shirt and a pair of shorts. She doesn't lock the bedroom door. He will come in either way. He will wait until later. Come in and sit in the chair. She folds back the covers and lifts the pillow and there underneath lies her little monkey. Brown fur. One of the ears has come loose. She picks him up and crawls under the sheet and pulls the blankets around her.

She will go to sleep.

Go to sleep. Just close your eyes. You'll be all right.

He doesn't know anything.

Jack.

Sweet Jack.

Little Matty.

You will keep it together.

They need you.

She holds the monkey tight.

XXXII

I once told you that to understand the truth, you have to start at the beginning. But where is that, really?

The path to truth is crooked
and time itself a circle.
Come and see.

The earth is caked with new snow, and the slow pearly light of dawn covers everything. The sky, the frozen fields. The tree boughs frosted with tiny crystals at the tips. Ava is seven years old. For the first time, her father has taken her hunting.

He is teaching her. He is teaching her what life is about.

"Here is a nice spot—good line of sight," he says. "There'll be something on that hill."

He slings the long rifle from his shoulder and drops the canvas pack. He burrows down between the dark trunks of conifer trees, and she mimics his every movement. Great alpine limbs droop above. No tracks anywhere save their own. The known world is lost behind them. Across the field lies a white forest.

"You must hold the rifle steady to keep the sighting post straight. See?" Bardem shows her how to handle the gun. "Lie on your belly. See? Your body is most stable in this position. Your hand will rest here. Your grip will be light. Like a bad handshake. Wrist straight, fingers curled. Steady the butt against your shoulder. Like this."

She watches carefully. She tries to listen. To make him happy.

"Elbows down and in. Don't curl your finger around the trigger until you're ready to fire."

He hands her the rifle, and she follows each step precisely. Breathing softly. Controlled. The butt of the rifle in the pocket of her shoulder. She is being what he wants her to be.

"You must hold the rifle the same way each time," he says. "You will practice holding the same position. Steady. Solid. Stable. The same position each time, changing nothing. Accuracy is a function of consistency. Understand?"

She nods.

He watches her with great tenderness. He takes the rifle from her and lies beside her and turns her chin so that she is looking at him. He smiles. "Good work."

"What do we do now?"

"We wait."

They watch the glinting hillside and drink hot coffee straight from the thermos, their breath smoking. The shadow of the woods falls far across the field. Ava's belly warms. She sweats inside her coat. Her boots. The sun lifts higher, and everywhere the silent trees gleam. Like glitter inside a snow globe. Untouched.

"See there?" Bardem says.

She looks to where he points.

"Right out there," he says. "Someday that's where we'll build a house. A cabin. It will be a home. Just for us."

The spot is tranquil. She looks and imagines and hopes.

He rises and pulls a Marlboro and lighter from his jacket pocket and ignites the tip and smokes. He squats on his heels with his elbows on his knees, watching. He doesn't take his eyes from the tree line.

A breeze rustles pine needles and dies away. The sky is a blue vault.

As she lies there, looking out across the snow-mantled field and into the dark line of trees, a brief shape bounds through dappled sunlight. It disappears, and she perks up and squints. She thinks it's a trick of her mind until the shape emerges from the edge of the woods.

It's a deer. Lithe, graceful. A doe, she thinks. The deer halts in the fresh, pure snow and pricks her ears and raises her nose and listens. And Ava thinks: *What beauty there is in this world.*

Bardem lifts the rifle. He levels and shoots.

Rifleshot rolls across the field. Branches shudder, and snow sifts from trees. Air abruptly frays in two. In the distance, the deer falls and lands in the snow, jerking. Ava's heart feels as if it has stopped in her chest, but she doesn't make a sound. She clamps her eyes shut.

He squats by her. "Take the rifle."

She shakes her head.

"Take it. Do as I say."

"No."

He takes her hands and puts the rifle in them. "Look through the scope. Look through."

She is going to cry. Longing to run. To get away. To wash her hands, to be okay. Something black and something empty is about to swallow her up.

"Look," he says again.

She looks wordlessly. Through the eye of the scope. The deer is lying with the snow all around her stained pink. Bright. Like a snow cone.

"What you put in that circle is yours to take," he says. "You just have to take it. Do you understand?"

She nods.

"Say it."

"I understand."

"Good."

He takes the rifle and pulls her into his arms and holds her. Rocking slightly back and forth. He sweeps her tangled hair behind her ear.

"There, there," he says. "My little bird. It's okay."

XXXIII

People try to create order. Discipline. Rules. It gives them peace. A sense of regulation. Of strength. It makes them feel in control.

But life is chaos, reader. The sooner you learn this, the better.

Stay with me.

It's just a little while now.

When Matty stopped crying and began to breathe steadily, Jack laid him down on the bed and pulled the blankets around him. He got up and went to the window. The moonlight was slanting over the motel, and the parking lot was cloaked in shadow. The vapor lamps not yet lit. Somewhere Red lay broken on a metal slab. Jack went to the bathroom and twisted the handle of the tub faucet and squeezed shampoo into the water to make bubbles. The best thing to do was ignore this feeling of lead in the heart and get the mind to think. Rely on the head. What to do? He turned and walked to the bed. Matty lay there, watching him. "Come on," he said. "This will be the best bath you ever had."

Matty went to the bathtub and got undressed and stepped into the water and sat. Pale and skinny and naked. Holding his hands over his privates. Jack passed Batman to him. "What do you think?"

"This is the life."

"This is the life?"

"Yeah."

"Where did you hear that?"

Matty shrugged, bashful.

"Is it hot enough?"

He nodded.

Jack washed Matty's snarled hair and scrubbed him with a soapy washcloth and laved water over him. Knobby bones. Knees and shoulders. Spine. He drained the water and wrapped Matty in a towel and tousled his hair to dry it. Steam came off him like mist.

"Get on your PJs," Jack said.

"Okay."

"Are you hungry?"

Matty nodded.

In the bedroom, Jack took a chocolate chip granola bar and a fruit cup from the grocery bag and set Matty up at the table. Matty ate quietly. He kept looking at the door.

"What is it?"

He fidgeted.

"Tell me."

"Do you think the truck could be out there?"

"I don't think so."

"They won't be able to find us in here."

"No, they won't."

Matty took a bite of granola bar, chewed. "There were sirens."

"Yes."

"Do the police think the truck is the bad guys?"

"I think so."

"Because they ran over Red."

"Yes."

"And Red's dead now."

"Yes. He is."

"Like Mom."

Jack nodded. His eyes hurt. His throat.

"Are we going to die?"

"No. We're not."

"But we don't know."

"No. I guess not."

He ate a bite of pear from the fruit cup. "So we have to be smart."

"We have to be smart. Yes."

"So they don't find us."

"They won't. They won't find us."

"Can we stay here now, until Ava comes back?"

Jack hesitated. "I think so."

Matty finished the fruit and licked the cup and scrunched up the granola bar wrapper. He looked like he was thinking. "We're good guys," he said. "Is that right?"

Jack nodded.

"And we're smart to be here."

"Yes."

"Because we're together."

"Yes. Because we're together."

They lay next to each other in the bed, wearing pajamas and tucked under blankets. Matty said, "Will you sing a song?"

It was something he asked when he couldn't sleep.

"Okay. Which one?"

"You choose."

Jack thought of a song they used to sing. Sometimes he'd play it on his guitar and Matty'd sing. He figured Matty would like it. He began by humming the melody, and after a while he switched to singing softly. His voice wasn't that good, but Matty never cared. He sang slow and gentle, until Matty's eyes closed. For a while he kept singing. Matty always woke back up if he stopped too early. Later, after Matty was asleep, he kept hearing the tune in his head. The words.

I see trees of green, red roses, too
I see them bloom, for me and you.

He stared up at the darkness. The dull blue of the radio clock on the walls. That feeling in his chest—always there now—of not having quite enough breath.

He tried to think about morning. What to do. He wished he could take Matty to a library somewhere and read him a book or draw pictures on white sheets of paper, or maybe take him to see a matinee. Get popcorn and sodas. His eyes hurt, and he rubbed them with his arm. Overhead, the heater whirred into motion.

225

Hissing softly. He lay in the dark and the blue, and he wished for a more beautiful world than there was.

In the night, he made up stories in which Ava wasn't gone. She stood at the window, her shadow on the glass. She walked to him in just his shirt and pushed back the cover and slipped underneath and slid close to him. Her warm skin. The smell of her. He felt desire rising up, like famine. It would feel so good, to be touched by her. To be needed, to feel so needy. In the dream he pulled her to him. His hands on her hips and his nose in her hair. Both of them trembling. Both ready.

A little before dawn, he rose and left Matty sleeping and walked over to his coat on the chair and pulled the envelope from the pocket. He switched on the little lamp and sat and studied the handwriting. Scrawl of watersplotched words, slanting to the right. Abrupt letters. Sharp-edged. Just like him.

He tore open the envelope and unfolded the yellow paper inside. The page was ripped from a book: *White Fang*. It had a grainy texture. Two words were scratched lengthwise across the print in stark, angled letters. Words scratched deep and hard.

GO BACK.

XXXII

Where is the end and the start and the thing that causes the end that leads to the start? How do you tell where you were or tell the difference of where you are? Did everything lead to this moment? To this single grain of sand?

Ava gets ready, and then she waits. She sits on her bed. She listens. He will shower. Shave. Then he will make breakfast. Coffee. Eggs and bacon. Afterward, he will wash the dishes and utensils and dry each one and put them away in their correct places on the shelves. In the drawers. He will clean the marble counter with a microfiber towel.

Dishes clink. A cupboard closes.

She listens and waits.

And waits.

There. The front door closes. Seconds slip along, drop off. An engine starts. She moves to the wall by the window and shifts the curtains. Snow is dropping in fine cloud chunks from a cobalt sky. Below her, on the driveway, Bardem backs the Land Rover through the layers of white and shifts and heads away between snowflaked trees. She watches the flash of metal amid branches until the Land Rover disappears from view. She watches some more. Until she can no longer hear the engine. Until she is sure.

Silence.

Her blood. She feels it rushing. Rushing in quick, equal bursts.

In a satchel, she packs clothing. Going-away things. Toothbrush, shampoo, soap. Her little monkey. Needed things. She slings the satchel over her shoulder and heads downstairs to the foyer. At the end of the hallway, his bedroom door is closed. As always. She walks to the door and turns the knob. She pushes the door open and stands in the entrance. His smell breaches her nose. A subtle tang. Something musky. Feral.

She is not allowed in here.

At the door, she drops the satchel and walks to his dresser. She opens the top drawer. Inside are two pens and some paper. Envelopes. Tidy stacks. Nothing touching. She closes the drawer and opens the wardrobe. The shirts hang clean and pressed. Eight shirts. Button-front flannels, arranged by shade, from gray to black. In the dresser are socks. White briefs. Jeans folded.

Nothing is here. No sign of what he knows.

But he knows something. Oh yes, he does.

On top of the desk, a solemn row of books stands in order, arranged by author name. Hemingway, *For Whom the Bell Tolls*. Books of philosophy. Machiavelli and Nietzsche and Sun Tzu. *Thus Spoke Zarathustra*. A tome of Victorian poems. Leather bindings, elegant craftsmanship. Tall and mystical wonders held upright by bookends of dark burnished metal.

His altar.

This house is yours, bird. But not my room.

Go anywhere else. But not my room.

She turns. His bed is Spartan. Flat cotton; sharp, folded edges. Pillows neatly placed. On the nightstand sits a decanter of whiskey. An ashtray. His lighter.

Nothing.

There is nothing. Nothing here.

Under the bed. Beneath the desk. Behind the door. She looks in all these places. Nothing is here, nothing is here.

Blood. In her temple, jumping.

He could return at any moment.

I thought you might want to say something. To convince me.

Convince you of what?

Convince me of everything.

Seconds flutter along, flit away.

She heads for the door. And stops and turns.

There is no reason to do it—no good reason—but she does it anyway. She follows an intuition that says *look here* and goes to the side of the bed where he sleeps and lifts the pillow. Lying there is her calculus book. The hot-air balloon on the cover.

She opens the book. To be sure.

Yes, her name is there.

She steps back, a wild throb in her head—where puzzle pieces align, drop into place.

So. He knows.

Where you've been.

Who you've been with.

She takes no time to consider but instead strides to the neat row of books and flings them from the desk. The heavy bindings spill to the wood floor, break open. Thudding sounds jolt the air. She strikes the bookends and they knock over, thump to the floor, and tumble to vanish beneath the bed.

Silence again.

My bird. You're a good girl. Aren't you?

She stands, looking at the books. The battered covers. Broken spines.

Still silence.

From a scrape on her hand, blood drips.

She crouches on the wood and picks up *For Whom the Bell Tolls* and catches sight of her wrist. How quickly the small ink heart pulses, just above the vein.

The book trembles in her hand. She grips the pages inside and rips them from the spine. Next she fastens her hands around *The Prince*, splitting the binding apart and flinging the book's sections onto the bed. Not silent now. She can hear her fractured breath, the hurt sounds latching in her throat.

She stoops and seizes the books, gathers them in her arms, and piles them in the center of the white sheets. From the bedside table she grabs the decanter and pulls off the stopper and douses the books in whiskey, wetting Nietzsche and Sun Tzu. She flicks the lighter. Holds out the flame. Opens her hand.

Fire splashes across the bed.

She turns. With the heat on her back, she walks over and picks up the satchel. *When he sees the smoke, he'll return.* In the kitchen she washes her hands. Gently. Just once. She dries them on a towel. She walks through the stone foyer and out the front door, into the falling snow. The scent of scorched paper wisping behind her. Ashes curling in the cold air. When she gets to the car, she puts the satchel beside her, in the passenger seat.

Midway down the drive, she stops and looks in the rearview mirror. This stillness of blood in her veins. Except for a frail orange light in the windows of the house, the fire is unnoticeable. She sits and watches the house burn.

She continues down the drive, into the thick of the trees and onto the road.

Some eight hundred yards from the house, the firelight blinked across the binocular glass. Bardem turned the focusing wheel to sharpen the house. He adjusted the diopter rings. As he did so, the fire glimmered. He sat with the pistol in his lap. The shotgun and the rifle lay in the zippered bag beside him. He watched the house, forming conclusions. That she chose what she chose while knowing the consequence. The action and reaction that led to this desperate ground. He studied the car, which headed away from the house to vanish among the white trees.

He lowered the binoculars and sat there in the cold and the quiet with the engine idling. The gray sky hanging low on the horizon before him. Puffs of snow floating down.

Ahead of him in the distance, Ava turned onto the road.

He pulled from the shoulder and followed.

XXXI

I used to have this dream that something was following me. I don't know what it was, but I know it wanted to hurt me. I never did look back to see what the something looked like. But I know it was dark. Sort of indistinct. I think it was a person, but it was something worse too. Something more leeching. Like you could feel it reaching right into you to take what it wanted. I don't think I'd ever choose to turn and see it. I think you'd have to be willing to give yourself up to do that. You would. I won't ever turn to meet it.

The dream didn't make sense, in the way dreams don't. Sometimes the thing found me outside and followed me home at a distance. Sometimes it was at a store or at the library. Once it found me at school, but mostly it came to my bedroom at night. It waited by the side of my bed till I woke. Even in the dark, you can't help but feel it. You can't hide. And you can't get away. I know, because I'd try.

Always, it follows.

If you're afraid, it'll know. It'll know in a heartbeat. And then it follows faster. I think you can't let it catch you. And I won't let it. I never will. If you do, it will be too late.

★ ★ ★

Here is what happens.

Every time.

I start running. Down the street or across a park. Into a store. Anywhere. It follows. Other people might be there, in the dream, but no one else sees it. It wants me. Nobody else. I feel that. I run hard, but the something never gets farther away. It follows. I don't know what to do, and I get tired, so tired, until, at the end, I always run to my house. Because you should be safe at your house.

I run through the rooms. To the stairs. I run up the stairs. It follows. One set of stairs ends, and then another set appears. Weird stairs that turn and twist. I tear up them. Higher and higher. Until the stairs get narrower. More rickety. They creak. I can feel the something behind me. Closing in. I push faster. Racing, stumbling. It follows. I go up until I get to the very top, and suddenly I'm outside and the stairs just end on this ledge overlooking the night. Black sky. Stars. And it's high up. I jerk myself back from the ledge and just freeze there, swaying and looking out at all that dark—until I feel it there, right behind me. Until it's breathing right into my soul. And that's the moment I jump.

And then

I wake up.

I know this: Somewhere out there is a dark thing chasing us all.

Doyle turned into the Dunes Motel at a quarter past ten in the morning and parked by the front office and went in.

The woman at the desk wore her white hair in stiff curls held in place with a yellow scarf. She was smoking a cigarette and reading a Harlequin romance. When he tipped his Stetson, she glanced up with no great interest in what she saw and then returned to *Cowboy Commando*. He dinged the bell. She blew a whiff of smoke at him. "Hello, honey," she said. "You want a night? Or the hour rate?"

"I'm looking for some boys."

She squinted at him. "We're a moral establishment here."

Doyle stared at her. He looked around the squalid office. "Have a couple of boys checked in? One maybe seventeen. The other younger."

"Honey, I'm not at liberty to give out information about guests."

He put his badge on the counter. "How about now?"

She closed the Harlequin. She seemed unruffled. "Well, sir, I apologize."

"Has anyone checked in over the last forty-eight hours?"

She lifted the cigarette to her lips, inhaled. Blew a small ring of smoke. "A girl. Pretty one. Young."

"Was she with anyone?"

"I don't keep track."

"Maybe you can think about it right now and remember."

The clerk stood there, a pillar of menace in a scarf.

"These kids are in trouble," Doyle said. "They need help."

"I might've seen her with a little boy."

His phone rang. He silenced it. Looked at the screen.

Midge.

He pressed the answer button and listened. "Whose house?"

On the road, a fire truck rushed by, siren wailing. He swore softly. "Okay. Don't do anything. I'm on my way."

Jack cracked the blinds and peeked through, the hammer in one hand. Blood pounded in his ears. Endless snow. The sheriff's truck sat parked in front of the office. He watched the doors. Trying to think. The hammer clenched in his fist.

Can you do it?

If he comes here?

You lift and strike down. Do it quick and hard.

Hard.

He waited, trying to draw in air. Thirty seconds. A minute.

Lights flared in the distance and then on the road, a fire truck rushed past. The sheriff came out of the front office and got in his truck. He didn't look toward Jack's room. The motor went on. Then the lights. Jack watched it all without blinking.

The sheriff headed onto the road, following the fire truck. Jack waited. When it was out of sight, he let go of the blinds.

Utter quiet.

He went to the bed and dropped down to look underneath it. Matty lay on his stomach beneath the dusty wooden bed slats, his pale face in shadows. His chin on the carpet.

"Is he gone?"

"Yeah."

Matty crawled forward on his elbows and got up while Jack crouched there with the hammer still in his hand. He felt as if he were falling from a great height. Slipping through particles of air. Matty just sat, looking at him. He seemed in a haze.

Jack dropped the hammer and pulled Matty to him. Brushed the cobweb from his hair. *Hold him close. Like this.*

"I'm sorry," Jack said. "I'm sorry."

He held Matty, trying to breathe. Dragging air into his lungs. The effort of staying alive. He was getting stupid. It was stupid to stay here so long, and his head was not working right. *Concentrate*, he told himself. *You have to think better.*

Doyle. What you might have done to him.

What he might have done to you.

And then: *He is going to come back. And when he does it will be too late. Too late to think or do anything at all.*

"Who was it?" Matty asked.

"We have to go."

Matty just sat there, staring at the hammer.

"Come on," Jack said. "Pack everything. We have to go."

XXX

Once in school I learned about this Austrian physicist who told a story
about a cat. It was like a thought experiment or something. I don't know
why he used a cat, but I remember it was a cat. I like cats.

He said to imagine a box. It's a special kind of box, where you can't
see or hear anything inside it. Imagine someone comes and puts a cat in the
box, and that person sticks a bottle of poison in with the cat and closes the
lid. If the poison spills, the cat dies. There's no way it doesn't. And the bot-
tle has an equal chance of spilling or not spilling. The odds are dead even.

So what happens?

Simple, you say.

The poison spills and the cat dies,

Or the poison doesn't spill, and the cat stays alive.

You look at the box and wonder. Is the cat dead in there, or is it alive?

But you don't open the box.

You don't look.

You won't look.

★　★　★

Jack gathered clothes and stuffed them in the duffel and got the cereal from the drawer and what food was left and packed everything in the grocery bag. In the bathroom, he found Batman and the tape and the gauze and the bottle of antibiotics and brought them into the bedroom. All this time, Matty sat hunched by the bed. He hadn't moved. Jack went and crouched beside him. The panic never got too far from him now, would come at any time. The torn page in his coat pocket. Two words scrawled. GO BACK.

"We've got to go," Jack said.

Matty didn't answer.

"We can't just stay here. I need you to do what I say."

He was silent.

"Look at me. You have to get up."

"I don't want to go."

"I didn't ask if you wanted to. Get up."

But Matty would not.

The panic was reaching the edge of Jack now, and he tried to breathe it away. He went to the window and pulled up the blinds and scanned the parking lot, but there was no one. Shapes of snow falling incandescent in the light. The faint boot tracks were almost gone. But Doyle would be back.

So be it.

He took Batman from the duffel and sat beside Matty on the carpet and gave him the action figure. Matty took it wordlessly, and that was that. They sat in silence.

Jack said, "I should have been more careful."

Matty wouldn't look at him.

"Talk to me," Jack said.

Matty just sat there, head bowed, holding Batman between his knees. After a minute Matty said something, but Jack couldn't understand him.

"What?" he asked.

Matty looked up. His tired face. "I don't want to leave her."

They stared at each other.

"I don't want to leave her either."

His voice was thick. He spoke again.

"I don't want to leave her either—"

He swallowed, drew a breath. Ache in his throat. Words could not convey the dull pain of it. The raw glow from the window spilled over them. He studied Matty, the lines of his furrowed brow. The set jaw, stubborn. He choked back rage. *Will you live to see it? To see him become a man?*

"Come on, short stuff," Jack said.

Matty shifted. "She said to wait."

"We can't just wait."

"She told us not to go anywhere."

"I know, but—"

"But we did. And Red got run over."

They each fell quiet. Jack looked at the window, where snow pressed against the pane.

"Listen to me," he said. "You are my brother. My job is to take care of you. I will always do that. I will keep you safe. I will do whatever is needed. Do you understand?"

"He was the police."

Jack swallowed, said nothing.

"The police are the good guys. Right?"

"I keep messing up. I'm sorry."

But Matty wouldn't answer.

"I don't want to leave her either. But we can't stay in this place. We can't. I can't let anyone hurt you."

"Okay."

"You said we have to be smart. So they don't find us. Well, this is smart."

"Okay."

"I have to make sure no one hurts you."

"I don't want you to cry."

"I'm not."

"You look like you're going to."

"I won't."

"Okay."

Silence spun out. Sun dimmed and brightened again.

Matty was looking at him, his gaze clear, his small face wet in the vivid light. He got up and put on his coat and stocking hat. Holding Batman in his hand.

"Okay," Matty said. "Let's go."

They walked out through the motel door and headed south along a back road, hurrying. Trudging through snowdrifts under a granite sky. Jack had slung the duffel over his shoulder, and he carried the grocery bag clenched in one hand. Bright snow falling. Getting worse. He held Matty's hand and watched the road, but there was no one. Not even a snowplow. He heard an engine only once. They trudged along until they came to the bridge and then Jack had to stop. He leaned on the iron rail until he got his breath. The pain in his side was waking. His heart thudded, caroming against his chest. He did not like that thud. As though a dark pool pulsed.

Matty tugged his hand, and he looked around but there was nothing to see. No police car. No sheriff. *Okay*, Jack thought. *This is going okay. Good.*

They plodded along, with Jack moving slowly and Matty keeping close to him. Jack didn't know where he was going. He hadn't thought that far ahead. The road seemed to sway. *But it really isn't*, Jack thought. *See, Jack? You know the sway is just in your head. See? You're thinking straight. Good. You're doing okay.* He went on. Treading thoughts, deep water. Each heart thud darker black.

On Main Street, he stopped again while snowflakes dazzled about the tumult of sky and danced in all directions. Air currents traveled over the snow. Cars here, noise. Stores open. *The sway is just in your head.* Matty tugged on his hand, urgently, and Jack blinked. He could see Matty standing there, looking at him from an incomprehensible distance. Glowing in the cold.

A car slowed and pulled alongside them. Someone stopping. He turned and started to tell Matty to run, but then he didn't. He just stood in the street and waited. Holding Matty's hand.

The window slid down.

Ava leaned over from the driver's side and looked at him with her lovely eyes.

"Get in," she said.

Jack cleared his throat and muttered, "Hi."

Matty smiled at her—a smile that was scared, tired. Relieved.

"What are you doing?" she asked.

Jack tried to answer and couldn't find words.

"Walking," Matty said.

"Get in the car," she said again.

Matty opened the rear door and got in.

Jack just stood there, inhaling the snowflakes. The dark pool in his chest pulsed, and he knew that he needed to sit. He looked at Ava. He wanted to sit by her. For as long as he could.

He opened the passenger door. Got in.

She pulled onto the road. Jack leaned his head on the seat and watched what passed before him. Storefronts, the branches of trees. A park. His eye fell on Ava's wrist. With every breath came a sharp longing.

"The heart on your wrist," he asked. "What does it mean?"

She stared at him and then looked away. "A lot of things."

"I like it," Matty said.

"What happened?" she asked.

He shrugged, feeling obstinate. Feeling tired. "A lot of things."

Cozy heat hushed from the fan while car tires crunched the snow. Hum of the engine. He let his eyes close.

Her voice: "Where do you want to go?"

For a long minute he considered the question.

"Somewhere far," he said.

Her response was casual: "Okay."

But Jack heard it in her voice. The pact made with him. Earnest.

A vow.

He gave himself a moment longer, eyes closed, to ponder the brief world inside the car. This small sanctum. Warmth, peace.

Sufficient to maintain. Everything outside the sweeping counter opposite. The storm. Dispassionate, coldly coming.

He turned his head and watched her, the little heart on her wrist fading in and out of focus.

If he could stop the clock hand. If.

"First there's something I have to do."

XXIX

Sometimes even now I catch the sense of him. Flash of memory. The way he moves. His smell, the gentle solidness of his voice. The way he doesn't talk too loud. The way he takes what he is given and never acts like he knows more than you.

You could love someone like that.

Anyone with a heart could.

When Doyle turned onto the tree-lined driveway, he saw a long, black cloud pluming above the trees. Thick haze of smoke. He reached the house and got out.

He covered his mouth.

Smells stained the air: burning paper, aluminum. Sewer gas. Red embers. He stood in the blur of blue-and-red lights, looking across the fire trucks at the house. Stalks of exposed walls smoldering in the cold air. Shapes of household items. A blackened bed. An armchair.

Midge came forward. Grime covered her uniform. Her whole

face was sooty. Around her neck she wore a pink scarf, darkly smudged.

"Sheriff," she said. "We've got a heck of a mess here."

"Anyone inside?"

"No, sir. He's got two vehicles registered. No sign of either."

"Hmm."

"House was empty till just a month ago. You know who bought it?"

"I do know, Midge."

"You think we got a meth operation here?"

"No, Mr. Bardem is above all that. This man is something different."

They stood watching the firefighters spray water at what remained of the porch. Steam came off the wood like smoke.

"It's a curious thing," Doyle said, "this house burnin' down."

"I hear you. They ain't been here two weeks."

He glanced at her. "What do you mean 'they'?"

"I mean Bardem and his girl," Midge explained.

"Girlfriend?"

"Nope. Daughter."

"How'd I not know this?"

"I don't know, sir. They just moved in."

Doyle kept looking at the house. He went over and over it all in his mind. "We have got ourselves two missin' boys and the burnt-down house of a very serious customer: a known associate of these boys' daddy, who helped himself to a whole lot of drug money. Money nobody ever found. And here just yesterday there's a girl got a motel room over at Dunes. And she was seen with a little boy. What are the chances of all that?"

"Not good, I don't think."

They stared at each other. The house whined softly as it cooled.

"Get a description out on both vehicles," Doyle said. "Call everyone. Tell them you don't know what these folks will do. You tell them."

"Yessir."

"Do we have the Bardem girl's name?"

"Not yet."

"Get it. I want her name. Then send these deputies out to every hotel and motel within fifty miles. Bus stops. Check those. Cell phones. I want numbers."

Damn fool mistake not to check that motel room. They're likely gone now.

Doyle watched Midge set off toward the house, shouting instructions to the other officers, her filthy pink scarf flapping in the wind. He'd make a sheriff of that one yet. Then he got in the cruiser and backed around and headed toward the Dunes Motel.

He wanted to help those boys.

He could stop what was coming.

Surely he could.

XXVIII

Here we are, you and I. Trapped in the circle of time.
   All that is straight lies.
   There is no end.

After they checked into the Sunshine Motel in Rexburg, they drove around the rear of the building and carried the duffel and the bags up metal stairs to a room on the second floor. Matty climbing the snowy steps in front of Jack. Ava following. Matty wanted to carry the duffel, but it was too heavy so Jack took it from him. Jack stood looking into the room. Cheap furniture. Wood laminate. Two double beds. The bathroom door stood open. Above the tub was a sliding window that looked big enough to fit through. Matty watched him. He felt sweaty. He felt about to fall over. *Come on Jack*, he told himself. *You just need to hang on.*

   Fill, lungs. Beat, heart.

"Is this a good place, Jack?" Matty asked.

"I think so."

"I'm kinda scared."

"We're okay. This is good."

He dropped the duffel on one of the double beds and went back to the door and switched on the overhead light. Brown walls. Lace curtains at the window, stained yellow from cigarette smoke. A fetid smell. He got Matty out of his coat and shoes and sat him on the bed and pulled the cheap chenille bedspread around his shoulders. He set the duffel on the carpet and shucked off his own coat. Spot of dried blood on his shirt. Matty kept asking him how he was feeling.

"It's all right," Jack said, sitting beside him. "It doesn't hurt."

Ava stood in the open door under the white light. Snowflakes glittered on her hair and melted. Jack lay back on the bed and took her in. Her eyes, her cheeks aglow with hectic color. If he looked long enough, he could memorize it all, so no detail would be lost. He did not know how soon he slept.

She sorts through the first-aid supplies, but there isn't much left. Two bandages and the disinfectant. Ibuprofen. The antibiotic: one capsule. She tips it into her hand and goes to the bed and looks down at Jack's face, the bruises still blue and discolored. His lips are dry. She touches his forehead. He feels clammy. Hot. She fills a plastic cup with water and puts the capsule on his tongue and lifts his head to help him drink. She pulls off his boots. Matty lies beside him. She turns and sits on the opposite bed. *You have to think,* she says to herself. *You have to be smart. So you can help them. No matter what.*

And why does it matter to you? So much?

I don't know, she thinks. *I don't know.*

So quiet. She examines her hands, her dirty coat.

The voice of Bardem: *You're a good girl. Aren't you?*

Hours pass. She watches the brothers sleep. Matty, with his untamed hair and ears that stick out. The purple shadows beneath his eyes. Jack, curled up around him. His face, for once, so peaceful.

She reaches for his hand and holds it. She thinks: *I don't want to hurt you.*

XXVII

Maybe it's odd to you why I cared so much. It was odd to me too. All I can say is sometimes you live your whole life for a thing that reveals who you are.

There is no why.

When Jack woke, he hardly knew where he was. He pushed back the blanket and jerked up. Gray dusk. Ava was watching him.

"Hi," she said.

He looked around. Beds, television, curtains. The motel room. Wind outside. Matty slept beside him. "Did I sleep?"

"Yes. How do you feel?"

"I feel weird."

"Weird how?"

"Just weird. But I think I'm better."

"Are you thirsty?"

He shifted his legs over the bedside and turned to face her. She sat on the opposite bed, biting her lip. Waiting to see what he would say. The sweat on his forehead was cool now. He felt less tired. All at once his mind was clear and urgent. "Do you want to leave here?"

"What?"

"Do you want to leave here? This place. With me."

She hesitated. But she looked resolute. As if she were going to say yes.

"And go where?" she asked.

"I don't know. Anywhere."

She blinked at him. Her hair lit up in the twilight with tendrils of black walnut, of gold. She didn't answer.

He glanced away, embarrassed. "I'm sorry—"

"We don't really know each other."

She said this in a whisper.

Somberly, she watched him.

On the beds, they each waited. Neither sure what to say. Jack tried to see through her eyes, to see what she knew. If she could see how he was. *What* he was. He turned up his palms and examined them. They were worn down to the quick, the skin raw from the shovel.

Digging. So long ago.

"My mom was on opioids," he said. "Getting worse every day. About a week ago I came home from school and she'd hanged herself in her bedroom. I didn't call the police or anything. I buried her in our backyard."

His words struck a silence between them. She stared at him with her striking gaze—that fine shade of amber green—and he stared back.

"I'm sorry," she said.

"I get it if you don't like me now."

"I like you."

The truth of it was there in her voice. She watched him, intent.

"I mean," she said, "you don't really know me."

Her eyes flashed with something then. What? Whatever it was disappeared in an instant. A quick luster in the dimness. Water in the dark catching sudden furtive light.

She looked away so her hair hid her face.

Jack almost couldn't bear the distance of her. He wanted her closer.

Could she hear his heart, hitting against his ribs?

He said, "I know enough."

The gloaming light. The wail and hiss of wind at the motel door.

He got up and reached for his coat. From the pocket, he drew the folded book page. Crumpled, scraggy, thin. And heavy with significance.

He sat beside her on the bed. He didn't touch her.

"My dad's in prison," he said. "They booked him on robbery, but everyone knows he stole from a place that was laundering drug money. They had him on camera, but they never found the money. People say he hid it. People say he did a lot of things. They say he killed a man, but I don't believe that part, and nobody ever proved it either. I don't think he did it. He did some bad things, but he wasn't a bad man."

Jack pushed a hand through his hair. He felt a perilous need to speak, to tell her everything, but to say these secrets was a terrible thing.

"When I was a kid, he used to read to me. Before everything fell apart. We went to the library, or sometimes he'd take me to this bookstore where I could pick any book I wanted for a quarter. He bought my favorite book there: *White Fang*. I was just a kid, but I begged him to read it to me. He did too. That summer before they took him. He read it over and over. He told me everything I ever needed to know was in that book. He said, 'The wild lingers in you, Jack.'"

For a moment, he became inarticulate in his effort to express himself. His heart. What dark lived there.

"I went to see him in prison," he said. "I asked about the money he stole. Where it was. I had to take care of Matty."

He searched her face in the twilight for some sign of aversion or disgust, but there was none. He went on: "He wouldn't tell me where he hid it."

She waited, watching him.

For a few heartbeats, he watched her too.

The things she made him feel. As though he were enough.

"He gave me a clue, though," Jack said. "I didn't know it at the time. Then he sent me this."

He unfolded the page and showed her.

Quiet: The room was made of it.

"Go back," Ava said softly.

She said the two words like a question. Or like the words of a spell.

The page in Jack's hand trembled, and he folded it closed. "Dad would read *White Fang* to me out in our barn. He had this spot with a couch and a Coke machine. We sat on the couch, and he read to me."

Recognition dawned on her face. She looked as if she was being scraped by the winds of a storm. "You want to go back."

His voice rose on a peak of feeling.

"The money's there."

On the other bed, Matty stirred. Jack stood—something inside him screwing tighter and tighter—and went to Matty and sat on the bed and tucked the blanket around him. He could feel the heat of Ava's attention on his back. He glanced at her briefly, half afraid, as if a longer look might result in a burn. He didn't know what to say, so he didn't say anything.

Silence.

"The police would have looked," she said.

"They did. They tore the house apart. The barn too. But they didn't find it."

She shook her head.

"It's there," he said. "I know it."

Silence, all the deeper. It was the kind of silence that lovers share in a disagreement. Unspoken words between them.

She leaned forward. Her lips seemed to lift toward his face as she inhaled. The smell of her, very close, a bloom of warmth in the cold. If he could lean toward her, in a gentle way, and kiss her. The thought rolled through him like rapture.

Careful, Jack. This girl will break your heart.

On the bed, Matty shifted again. His eyelids fluttered, and then the air filled with the measured breathing of his sleep.

Ava stood, her stature determined. When she managed to speak, her voice sounded odd. As if some taut string had reached its limit and torn free of her body. "We should leave here, Jack."

He shut his eyes.

"Let's just go," she said. "Somewhere far."

"I have to do this first."

"Why?"

His breaths were choking him. Even with his eyes closed, he could see Matty, lying there twined in the blankets, his hair matted from the stocking hat. The deck of UNO cards in his coat pocket.

"We can't just leave," he said, hoarse. "We don't even have food."

"These people are dangerous."

He dragged his gaze up to hers. "I know."

But she wasn't looking at him now. Her expression was faraway, lost to something else. *What are you thinking, Ava? Why won't you tell me?*

He put a hand to his lips and wiped them. "We don't have anything. I have three dollars and sixty-four cents."

"What if the money isn't there?"

"It's there."

She met his stare. She didn't speak—just shook her head.

If he could take her hand, pull her down to sit next to him.

"I have to do this," he said.

"They'll catch you."

"They won't."

The fading light. Matty's even breathing. Ava crossed her arms and looked away from him. "They'll hurt you."

"No."

"They will."

"I'll be careful."

"How's that worked for you so far?" She smiled at him softly. It was not a smile like he'd ever seen—at once wise and sad and full of fear. It made Jack shiver. In the dusky light, the heart on her wrist shone black.

Wind. The room sighed, creaked.

Jack examined his hands, his bloody shirt. He knew. All the danger he was willing to risk. For Matty. And now for Ava. Her face in the burgeoning dark. Her voice a petition. *Please*, he thought. *Don't let go of me.*

He inhaled and spoke slowly.

"He's my brother. I have to keep him safe." He looked at her, holding her eyes with his own. "I have to keep us safe."

Out there, in the gusts beyond the lace-covered window, a darkening curtain of snow descends. Wind starts to moan.

Dread.

It slides through Ava like eels. She stifles a shudder. Jack does not know the danger, doesn't understand.

I have to tell him, she thinks.

And I cannot tell him.

Jack gazes up at her. He is wounded and pale. Lean to the point of sickness.

She looks at Matty's sleeping face. Listens to his breathing, soft and even. Jack's breaths clatter in and out. He is almost obscured in the gloom.

Seconds slip by, drop away.

Jack leans forward, swimming into view. "I'll be okay."

"You don't know."

"I do. I believe it."

His eyes are unrelenting. Ava can almost hear the gears of stubbornness whirring inside the machinery of his brain. She argues with herself unconvincingly.

Tell him.

Who you are.

Now, no matter what.

What to say: *You don't understand, Jack. He'll make you hurt. He'll take what matters most. He'll do it with a smile, and then he'll smoke a cigarette.*

She says, "I don't want you to go."

"I know. I'm sorry. But I have to."

For a heartbeat, she says nothing. She tries to tell herself, *It will be okay.*

Bullshit.

"It will be all right," he says. "You'll see. You have to believe it. Just don't give up on me. Okay?"

Silence again.

But not really. Wind is slashing out there, and the cold presses down on the room like a slab. The shrinking light, the smell of dust.

She means to tell him. To change his mind. But his face is there in the dark. Sweet, quiet Jack. A thing she doesn't dare hope for. As she looks at him, the dread subsides. Something about Jack is comforting. Responsible. He is gentle, he is strong. She trusts him.

Wait, then.

Tell him everything. After. When you're back.

Safe.

She sits by him on the bed. She is quiet, and so is he.

Each begins to hope.

"Okay," she says. "When do we leave?"

XXVI

I've got these memories.

   Sometimes these memories have me.

Jack tried to convince Ava to stay, but she wouldn't hear it. She sat on the bed, regarding him, unshakable. There was no persuading her. Finally he gave up. He rose in the dull light and went through the duffel. Getting inside the house would be the first hard part. *Take the back roads. Park the car and hike in from the south—not from the front. Then the barn. Find the briefcase. The money.* A flashlight would be of use, but there wasn't one. *So. Take the candle. The matches. Leave the can opener.*

   Could be someone'll be watching.

   Yup. So get in and out.

   Fast.

   Take the hammer.

He thought about making more of a plan, but there was no good plan to think of and after a few minutes he just sat in the chair. He didn't dare talk to Ava. He was about to get up when Matty woke.

"It's dark," Matty said.

Jack turned on the lamp. "Yeah. You fell asleep."

Matty sat forward and looked at Ava. Then at Jack. "What's happening?"

"Nothing."

Jack said this too quickly.

Matty pushed the blanket from his shoulders and looked at the duffel sitting on the table. He didn't say anything. Jack stood and went to the window. Howl of wind. Snow blowing. Ava's eyes were on him, and after a minute, he said, "There won't be many people out tonight."

"Because of the cold," Matty said.

"Yeah. Because of the cold."

"It's so cold, I just farted snowflakes."

"You farted snowflakes?"

"A kid at school said that once."

Ava laughed. It was a soft sound, warm. Like the sun in winter. "You're funny."

Matty started laughing, and then Jack did too. Something deep in him churned. If he could capture this moment. Grab on to it.

Matty said, "We should probably stay here. Because of the storm."

Jack looked at Matty's face.

"So why are you packing the duffel?" Matty asked.

"Just so we're ready. When we need it."

"How long can we stay here?"

"I don't know."

"That means not very long."

"No. Not very long."

He could hear the weirdness in his voice. Matty twined the bedspread in his fingers and looked away.

Ava stood up. "I'm going to the bathroom." She looked at Jack, her expression like a weight. "Tell him."

She went into the bathroom and shut the door.

Jack sat on the bed by Matty. For a minute they watched the snow swirling beyond the windowpane.

"I'm sorry," Jack said.

"You don't tell me a lot of things, but I still know."

"I know."

"You think you're protecting me. But I'm the one who has to be brave."

"You're right."

"Are you going to leave?"

"Yes. But it won't be for long."

"In the dark?"

"Yes. In the dark."

"Ava too?"

"I think so."

"How soon will you be back?"

"We'll be back before morning. Before you even wake up."

"I'm awake now."

"I know."

"I want to go with you."

"I know. But you have to stay here."

Matty bent over and scrubbed at his eyes. He wouldn't look at Jack. "When we were walking on the road, you were acting really scary."

"I know. I'm sorry."

"Are you getting better?"

"Yes."

"Are you just saying that?"

"No."

At last, Matty looked up at him. His hair curled and messy, gilded in lamplight. "Okay."

"You'll be all right."

"It's okay. We don't have to talk about it anymore."

Jack got up and brought Matty a carton of grape juice. They sat on the bed, side by side, with their backs against the headboard. Jack looped his arm around Matty. His chest an open wound. *You have to do this, Jack. You have to. There is no other way.*

"Can we watch TV for a while?" Matty asked.

"Yeah. We can."

Jack turned on the television and found an episode of *X-Men*. "Is this good?"

"Yeah. This is really good."

Matty sat sipping the juice. Wolverine growled and popped out his claws.

"Wow," Matty said.

★   ★   ★

Jack's stitches need another dressing, so he steps into the bathroom to take a shower. Ava gets out cereal and a fruit snack for Matty and sets it on the nightstand. In case he gets hungry. She pulls her hair into a ponytail and puts on her boots and her coat. What else? On her phone she searches for contact information for the county sheriff's office. She writes the number down on the little pad of paper by the food. Matty watches her, saying nothing. He's getting sleepy again. She lays out his pajamas and turns away while he changes into them.

"Don't look," he says.

"I won't."

"I'll know if you do." His earnest voice. "I sense danger. Like Spider-Man."

"I won't look."

In the bathroom, the shower water drums down.

"Okay. You can see."

"Okay."

He stands shivering. "I'm kind of cold."

"Let's get you some socks."

She sits him on the bed and helps him pull on socks.

"Better?"

"Yes."

Outside the window, vague shapes move. Shadows of snow falling. Skewing down in the wind. Almost too dark to see.

She shows him the pad of paper. "This is for you. I want you to call this number if we aren't back by morning. Okay?"

"But you'll be back."

"Yes. But just in case we aren't."

"I'm not supposed to call people."

"That's true. But this time it's okay."

"Who does the number call?"

"Someone who'll come and help you."

"A good person?"

"Yes."

He clamps his hands in his armpits and squints at her. At last he says, "Okay."

"And you keep the door locked."

"Okay."

"You have the Tracfone."

"Yeah."

"If anyone comes, you hide under the bed."

He nods. "I'm not stupid."

In the bathroom, the shower turns off.

"Let's get you into bed," she says.

She pulls back the blanket, and he wiggles between the sheets. His mop of hair almost conceals his eyes. "I want to ask you something."

"Okay."

"If you go, you will always come back," he says. "Is that right?"

"I'm not going anywhere yet."

"I know. But when you do?"

She tucks his hair behind an ear. She can't trust her voice.

He is quiet, waiting.

She looks at him, looks deep. "Yes. I will always come back."

"No matter what."

"No matter what."

Across the street, Bardem sipped his coffee and watched the motel. It was near one o'clock in the morning, and no cars were on the road. Frost iced the windshield. Starless night. Quiet. When the motel door on the second floor opened, he put the thermos in the console and sat forward.

Jack stepped out of the doorway first. Then Ava.

They walked downstairs to the rear of the building, where Bardem knew her car was parked. He waited. Chill air coming in. One minute. Two. At the rear parking lot, headlights appeared. He raised the binoculars and watched Ava's car pull onto the street, heading west.

The little boy was not with them.

He thought about that for a minute.

He opened the glove box and took out the Hot Wheels car. He studied the toy in the dull glow of the Land Rover's dash. A green Ferrari. He rolled the tires over the dashboard, watching the little wheels spin.

Sigh of wind. Snow.

For a moment he gazed at the motel door on the second floor. Then he dropped the toy into his shirt pocket.

He put the Land Rover into drive and crawled onto the road, heading east. His breaths puffing white in the cold. A couple hundred yards past Nuzzles Animal Shelter, he pulled off the road and stopped. There was a chain padlocked around the shelter gate, and the windows were dark. He got out and opened the tailgate. The bolt cutters in the toolbox were heavy-duty and would snip through a half inch of steel.

In the cold and the snow, he walked back along the shoulder of the road with the bolt cutters. The dark cloaked him. He wore it like a coat. Above the door of the shelter a sign read: LET LOVE WIN. ADOPT A PET TODAY.

XXV

Even now, I cannot stop thinking of Matty, who stared with such trust in his face. Whose eyes said, You told me you would always come back.

Matty slept for a while. When he woke in the night, Jack and Ava were still gone. The bathroom light was on. He lay in bed for a long time, and then he got up and walked to the motel window and parted the curtain. There were lights outside above the doors, and snow floated down through the yellow gloom. No one was coming. When he finished looking he went back to bed and turned on the television and flipped through the channels.

Over the Garden Wall was on Cartoon Network. He liked this one—Wirt sounded like Jack. He watched for almost an hour, the pad of paper in his hand. The one with the telephone number. Sometimes he watched snowflakes stick against the window. No one came.

But they'd be back.

Jack said by morning.

He was just starting to doze when now in the room he heard

a noise he didn't like. A noise that sounded spooky. He could hear the old Woodsman warning Wirt and Greg about the Beast. He opened his eyes. The TV lit the room a creepy green and scary music played. He sat up. He turned off the televison.

Quiet.

Dull bathroom light.

The snow-covered window was dark.

The hairs on Matty's skin rose, and he imagined there was something out there in the snow. But that was dumb—there were no things with claws, hungry for boy meat. Everyone said so, and most important, *Jack* said so—

He heard a whimper.

Somewhere outside.

He wormed under the covers and listened until his breathing steadied. He listened.

Quiet again.

But not all the way. Cold drafts whistled out there. On metal. Along the second-floor balcony.

He didn't move.

So. That was the sound, probably.

Stupid!

There are no real Beasts.

To prove it, he jerked himself out of the covers and looked around. Television, bed, window, door. Scary shadows. He sat forward and waited.

Nothing.

What to do? He could hide under the bed, but he didn't. He

took hold of the Tracfone and clutched it in his lap. He just sat there, the paper pad in his hand.

Still silence.

He began to laugh a little. *What an a-hole! Afraid of the dark.*
What a baby.

A whine set him on his feet. Outside the door.

He crept to the window and peered out. The snow made no sound as it fell through the yellow light and into darkness—

"Ohh-oh!" The air sucked out of him.

There were eyes out there.

Shiny brown eyes—nice eyes. Big and warm.

It's an animal, he thought.

He pulled the chair from the desk and got it in front of the door. He stood on the chair with his heartbeats booming and put his face to the peephole. He could see movement. A pale paw in the dark. Now another. Two ears.

A puppy.

He blinked and looked again. The puppy waited in front of the door.

There was a puppy outside. The light wasn't good, but it was enough to be sure. It was really a puppy, crying out in the cold. Soft honey fur and floppy ears. A black nose that sniffed. It was still pretty small—he could tell. He watched it stand there. Head tilting down and kind eyes looking up. A sad face.

It was skinny. It looked like it needed to eat.

He looked at the bolt on the door, and he looked at the puppy. It might run away any minute.

He got off the chair and scooted it back. Then he went to the nightstand and put down the paper pad and brought a box of Cheerios to the door. He poured some cereal into his palm. Then he unbolted the door. He opened it slowly.

Snowflakes swirled inward. Cold.

The puppy quivered, studying him.

Matty dropped to his knees and held out his hand. "Hi. Are you hungry?"

He was just a few feet away. The puppy put its nose down toward him.

Don't move.

Just keep your hand out.

Now just wait. It's scared. It's making sure.

The puppy took a step and licked his fingers. It was the best thing ever. Matty patted the soft fur. "How'd you get out here?"

He scooted backward while the puppy snuffled cereal from his hand, a little at a time, until he and the puppy were all the way inside the motel room. Carefully, he turned to block the doorway so it couldn't get out, and he sat cross-legged on the carpet. He cuddled the puppy's neck. The cold was blowing in, but he hardly noticed. He could see the dog was a boy.

"Are you lost, boy? Huh?"

He felt more than saw the movement behind him. He turned. The man who strode into view and stood in the doorway looking at him wore a fancy pair of boots. He carried a shotgun against his shoulder and had a black zipped bag in one hand. A scar zigzagged across his cheek. His eyes looked calm, untroubled.

"Hello, Matty," he said.

270

Matty's blood started to pump. He straightened.

"I'm not supposed to open the door," he said.

The man cocked his head and gazed at him. "Wise advice. But the door is open."

The puppy gnarled gently and shrank behind Matty's legs.

"I saw . . . I saw this dog," Matty said.

The man didn't answer. He just stood there, holding the bag. The shotgun. Then he came in. He closed the door slowly. Slid the bolt.

Matty looked at the Tracfone on the bed and at the man again. "I need to call my brother."

"No. You don't."

Spill of light from the bathroom. Matty backed toward it. He could go in there and lock the door. Above the tub was a window.

The man nodded toward the bed. "Sit."

The dog whined. Sad eyes.

Matty sat, and the man pulled the chair to the bed and sat opposite him, the shotgun across his lap. "If you shout, I'll hurt the dog."

Matty trembled.

"Your brother has been bad," the man said.

Oh, how that hurt Matty's stomach.

The man slouched casually. "Open your hand."

Matty looked at the window. Dark, snow. He hoped Jack was far away. Ava.

"You need to open your hand," the man said.

Matty put out his hand. The man set the little green Ferrari in his palm. "There. See? It's a car."

Matty gripped his fingers around the rough surface of the wheels. The metal. He was ready to run—*would* run for the door in a second or two, once he could think correctly—

"Look at it."

He glanced down.

"Is that yours?"

Matty nodded.

"I want to hear you answer."

"Yes."

"Well, it's a toy. Nothing special. But it's yours. Isn't it? You see the problem. I took something that is yours. People do that now. They take all sorts of things. Things that aren't theirs. It's just a toy car, they say. As if this means it doesn't matter. But it does matter. Don't you think? It is important, if you earned the thing or not. If you deserve it. And then one day there's an accounting. And nothing is ever the same."

He opened the black bag and drew out three zip ties and a pair of scissors and duct tape. He laid it all in a row on the nightstand. "Your brother took something of mine."

The puppy lay down at Matty's feet. It licked his ankle and put its nose on his socks.

"Do you want to know what he took?"

Matty didn't answer.

"He takes a lot of things, your brother. Things he hasn't earned. He's like his father. Don't you think? They take things they haven't earned."

Still Matty just sat there.

"No? Well. That's okay, Matty. That's fine."

The man stood and picked up the shotgun and the zip ties and looked down at him. "You're kind of freaking out, aren't you?"

Matty sat watching him in frozen terror.

At his feet, the puppy growled.

The man smiled. The odd peacefulness in his gaze. "It's just a toy car. That's true."

Bardem tied the boy and taped his mouth. By now the boy was shuddering with cold. Bardem wrapped him in a blanket and picked him up and slung him over his shoulder and set off down the motel stairs. There was a heavy-duty aluminum dry box with a watertight shell in the trunk of the Land Rover. It was altered to fit his needs, insulated to hold in warmth, with little holes drilled into the lid. He stuffed the boy inside with the blanket and closed the lid and clipped down the metal latches.

Then he went back into the motel room and waited.

XXIV

It is all chaos, reader.

The whens and whys and hows.

The sooner you learn this, the better.

They sat in the car, watching the house, but everything was dark. Bleak night, deserted road. No one came or went. There were no close neighbors. Jack got the duffel and moved everything to the backpack so he could carry it on his shoulders. Free hands—better. He chanced several glances at Ava and felt his chest ache. He didn't know what the ache was about, but he thought it was something about goodness or grace. About trust. Things he'd not thought about in a long time.

"What now?" Ava asked.

"We'll just have to go see."

"Do you think somebody is in there?"

"No. It looks quiet."

"Quiet doesn't mean there's nobody."

"Maybe. Do you want to stay here?"

She stared at him in the dark, her face grave. "No."

"I'll be fine."

"I'm going with you."

They got out. Snow covered the north field and made mounds over the dead scrub. They broke their own trail through the new tufts of snow, booting a path a foot deep. The distance perhaps a mile. Approaching the barn from the side. The night sky black and hunching. Flecks of lonely starlight shining down. The weathered wood a pale shape. In the hushed cold, they squatted and watched. No light anywhere. No tracks in the drive.

In a tree, an owl stared down at them. A white coat of feathers. Its yellow eyes shining.

No one.

No one is here.

Jack got the hammer from the pack and went around to the back of the barn. Crunch of snow beneath feet. The latch on the rear window was weak. Gray wood. When pulled, the shutter scraped open. They stood listening.

Nothing.

The wind in the naked stand of trees.

"Stay close to me," he whispered. "Okay?"

"We could still leave."

"It's going to be okay. Come on."

He pushed her up and through the window, then hoisted himself over and dropped beside her onto the dirt floor. Cold and wood. Exposed joists. To the left was a large hook, hanging by rope from a metal pulley. Shape of a shovel. The corners dark. All of it was veiled in gloom, too hard to see. Jack shoved the hammer into his belt and opened the backpack and took out a candle and some matches. Pain was stitching in his side.

They stood breathing.

White plumes of air. Smell of decay.

Jack struck the match. The rack of elk horns above the door bent in shadowy beams and curved to black antler points. On the plank wall, he could see part of a picture in an old frame. Summertime. Mom was standing in front of a lake, holding Matty, smiling. Matty was just a baby. Jack a boy at her side, clutching her hand. *We went fishing that day.* Jack scorned the sudden leaping in his chest and swung the candle out into the darkness. In the corner was the Coke machine. The floral couch. Bookcase.

He listened.

Nothing. A distant scratching of branches.

Wind.

They crossed the barn, their shadows reaching over the dirt. Jack would have time later to think about all the hurts rising up in him. Here was the M&M'S machine that he would beg to have quarters for. The cast-iron woodstove. *On stormy nights when the electricity was out, we'd sit here on the couch, in front of the stove. Me and Dad. He taught me to read.* Shadows capered over the wood. The cops, when they came, had cut the couch cushions open with a knife and searched inside. Overturned the bookcase. Upended the Coke machine. Opened the stove and dug through the ashes.

Jack held out the candle to the left and crouched by the bookcase. Sparse flickering, paper spines in disrepair. Novels. A stained picture book. Ava stood beside him watching. *My shelf is the bottom one. Here is the copy of* Hatchet. *Worn and dog-eared.* The Giver. A Wrinkle in Time.

He pulled free the last book on the row and turned the pages. Yellowed and shabby. *White Fang knew the law well: to oppress the weak and obey the strong.* He closed the book and put it in his pocket.

"Jack," Ava whispered.

"Shh," he said.

The briefcase was here.

Had to be.

He stacked the books on the floor, half expecting to find some secret hiding spot. Moved the couch. Nothing. Cold dirt. He looked up and scanned the timber joists, but there wasn't an attic or a door. Behind the Coke machine were just wooden planks. He went over the room again. Moving books. Checking the stove. How much time passed, he didn't know.

"Let's leave," Ava said. "Let's just go."

He looked at her, standing with her hands clenched. Watching him. She spoke gently. "It's just money."

"No." He was choking. "No, it's not. It's not."

How to explain? It's not money.

It's food. It's shoes for Matty. A place to live.

Red died for it.

I don't want them to win.

Wax dripped from the candle to splotch on the floor. Twinge of pain. He bent over, holding his side. A smell there. It occurred to him that he'd taken the clues of *White Fang* dangerously to heart. Now he could see the lie of it.

There was no briefcase here in this sepulchre of dust. No castle in the air. He said to himself what he hadn't let himself say before. *You want death*, he said. *You wish for it.*

That, at least, is not a lie.

He dropped to his heels and picked up a book from the floor. He put it back and leaned against the shelf. Heat in his eyes. Melted wax searing his hand. Some rage running through him. *Life lived on life. There were the eaters and the eaten.*

Ava bent and pulled at his hand. "We need to go."

He was about to get up when he realized he was sitting on dirt. Frozen dirt.

He got up and crossed the barn to get the shovel, then carried it back. He handed the candle to Ava. "Hold this. Don't let it go out."

With his throat stinging, Jack dug the sharp edge of the shovel into the dirt. Gripping the shaft. He put his boot on the steel step and struck with all his weight. The shovel jerked from his hands and clattered across the dirt. He nearly fell.

"Jack," Ava said. "The ground is frozen."

"This floor looks like dirt everywhere," he said, "but it's not. I remember when we built it." He picked up the shovel. "I think the briefcase might be buried. I have to try."

"Okay."

"I have to keep trying."

He had a thought and turned to the door, and there he picked up the ice axe. He handed her the shovel. "If you don't want to dig, it's okay."

"I'll dig."

He tried where the couch had been first. He raised the ice axe and began to chop the hard earth. Lift, slash. Dig. He dug and kept digging. Smack of the axe striking dirt. The memories claiming him. The shovel, the axe. *She is under the snow. A few feet away.*

Dig.

But there was nothing. He pushed the bookcase away from the wall. Cold burning his skin. Pain in his side. Dig. *You have to keep going.*

After a while, he stood in a hole maybe a couple of feet deep. He looked at Ava. She'd stopped and was holding the shovel.

"It's okay," she said. "Let's just rest a minute."

He sat on the rim of the hole. Darkness closing in. The broken floor. Black earth. There in the hole he saw pale plywood. He held the candle closer.

A wooden lid.

He shoved the dirt away and dug again until he exposed the top of a crate. He jammed the claw of the hammer under the lid and pried the nails up. Chunks of earth fell in. He took the candle from Ava and put it close.

"Look," he said.

He reached in and gripped the handle and dragged out the briefcase.

She stared, her eyes wide.

Blue vinyl covered in grime. Two buckles. A brass latch.

Jack's head felt light. This ragged heart. He was about to get up when, behind them, he heard metal scrape. Very softly.

Then the barn door opened.

Coming through the door was one of the drug runners. The boy with the vivid eyes. The bandana around his neck. They all froze.

At that moment, Jack realized that the boy would not be alone. He would turn around. He would call for the others. And when he did, they would come, and it would all be over, and they would die. Too late to get back to Matty. Too late to do anything.

"Don't turn around," Jack said, gripping the hammer. "Just keep coming in."

Ansel didn't move. A pistol was tucked in his belt. Ava was walking backward toward the window and holding the candle. Flickering light. The briefcase stood there on the dirt. Jack picked it up. "Close the door," he said. "Don't turn around."

Ansel just gazed at Jack. Those dark eyes. His curling hair.

"Take the gun out of your belt and drop it," Jack said.

He didn't. He shook his head and glanced at the briefcase.

"Don't look at that," Jack said. The distance between them was no more than ten feet. "Look at me. Why are you here?"

Ansel looked at Ava. "Your candle. I saw the light."

She snuffed the candle.

Blackness.

He heard Ava draw in breath.

Jack stepped out of the hole, keeping his eye on the door. Hint of starlight. Ansel's shadow—he hadn't moved. "Are they with you?"

"Inside the house. We've been watching it in case you came back."

Jack moved toward the window. Carrying the briefcase. His veins pulsing. *You are so stupid. What have you done?*

Ava boosted herself through the window and landed outside in the snow. Jack turned and met the boy's gaze. Everything cold and quiet. Something about him so still. Steady. Like a mountain.

"They don't know yet," Ansel said. "Soon they will."

They stood staring at each other.

Jack swung the briefcase through the window and hefted himself up and jumped down. Pain, his stomach rolling. He fell. In the branches, the owl spread silvery wings and lifted into the air.

Jack staggered up.

The briefcase.

He had the briefcase.

"Hurry," Ava said.

He felt something whiff past the air near his head and crash into the tree behind him. The shot was a faint snap, muffled in the dark of the night. He turned in time to see the small flash of a second pistol shot. "Run."

But Ava was staring in terror, and when he looked, he saw them coming from the house across the snow. He could make out two men. Gold teeth. Black top hat.

Jack gripped Ava's hand.

"Hide," he said. "Hide."

★ ★ ★

They tore through the snow and into the field behind the barn. Ava slipped, and he dragged her up. He looked back. They were partly concealed by the trees, but he knew they'd be spotted in minutes. Maybe less.

He had the case in his hand.

They crashed through a stand of white birch and descended into a dark trough. Jack tugged Ava to the ground and covered a cough with his arm. An itch in his lungs. They could hear hushed talking and then just silence, the more sinister. No way to get to the car. If they found the footprints in the snow . . .

Jack pulled Ava to him. "Let's just wait," he whispered.

Quiet. They lay in the snow, trying to listen. Shivering. Jack was wet with sweat. His side bleeding again. He concentrated to stifle a cough and knew he couldn't run far. He lifted his chin, squinting to see. Full dark. A scrape of dead branches. How long could he run?

"Are they coming?" she whispered.

"I don't know."

In the biting cold, he got to his knees. He could hear only his heart. He looked toward the house but could see nothing. The hammer was still in his hand. If they found the footprints . . . "Listen to me," he said. "If they find us, you are going to run. Don't look back. Do you understand?"

"Why?"

"Just say you will."

She lay watching him. Snow clumped in her hair, her lips tinged blue. "No. I won't."

"You have to."

"I won't leave you."

They lay there for a long time, but they were freezing, and finally he crawled up. There was only the night and the snow. Dreary field, shadows of blue. Shape of the house beyond. The barn. He thought of Matty at the motel. Alone. "We can't just stay here," he said. "We have to move."

He gripped the case, and they staggered out from the ditch. A moment later they stumbled through the standing birch. Slipping and lurching. At the edge of the field, they stopped to listen. Hot pang in his side. He stood looking at the broken ends of branches. Bootprints.

Stillness.

They blundered on, cutting a perimeter around the field. Gray light breaking. He had to pause to get his breath. They crouched, watching. Seeing nothing.

They'd left, then.

Or. They were lying in ambush.

He mumbled. "Let's wait awhile and see."

Ava said something. Maybe asked a question.

It was hard to stand. So cold. Blood moving slower. He thought of Matty. He tried to decide what to do, but his head swam. All this thought of running. He couldn't run. "We just have to get to the car," he said.

Ava took the case from him. "Get up, Jack. You have to stand up."

"If they find us, they'll kill us."

"I know."

She led him across the snow. Foot tracks everywhere. When they got to the car, she opened the door and pushed him into the passenger seat and hurried around and got in. Lugging the briefcase into the back. The house stood in the distance. Shrouded in the grudging dawn. He began to think they had a chance.

She started the engine and he turned, looking for a sign of them, but other than the tracks he saw nothing. Snowflakes began falling, and she turned the wipers on. Jack's eyes kept lolling shut. How long could a person go without sleep? *I'm coming, Matty. Hold on.*

His eyes were half closed when headlights flared over the car from behind. Jack winced as dizzying lights shone on them. He shielded his eyes and wrenched about to look out the back window.

It was the F-150.

Ava didn't look at him. She kept her head straight and hit the gas.

XXIII

You can't just tell people they're the master of their fate and then let them believe it. They'll think they've done something wrong their entire life.

They sped along the back road and headed south to Rexburg. The F-150 slowly closing the distance behind them. The Ford was fast but Ava knew the roads better. On the highway they lost ground. When they exited at Sage Junction, Jack watched the yellow beams of the F-150 headlights pass along the edge of the rear window. Yards behind, gaining fast. Scrape of wipers. *This is the end*. He turned around.

"Turn here."

Ava switched off the lights and jerked the wheel to the left, hard. The back end of the car fishtailed and threatened to swerve right, but Ava turned into the slide, riding the gas pedal until the car righted itself. Jack looked back and watched the truck attempt the same hard turn, but it skidded across the intersection and slammed into the bus stop kiosk. There was a screech of metal. Steam erupted from the crumpled hood. He could see one of their party getting out. Ava cut into an alley while Jack watched behind them. One second, two. No one followed.

She glanced at him. "Let's go get Matty."

They drove along the row of buildings to the end of the block and then turned and came back. The motel sat there in the dull light like some last destination at the brink of the world. Snow shifting down. A gray veil. Brief moan of wind, and then quiet. Finally they drove around to the side parking lot and stopped.

He opened the door. The motel was blocks from the intersection where the truck had crashed, and he feared the men would be on the streets searching in minutes. "I'll go in," he said. "If they come, you have to leave. Okay? You have to leave."

She nodded, watching him. Cold. Tired. Afraid.

He got out and crossed the parking lot. Long shadows. Glow of streetlamp in the distance. His breath shallow, rough. He climbed the metal stairs to the second story and walked past the rooms. Cold silence. No lights coming through the lace curtains. The TV off. At the door, he stopped to think. *He'll be asleep. Just pick him up and carry him. Gently, so he doesn't wake.* He slid the key into the lock and opened the door.

Darkness. An earthy smell. Odd. Like shaving oil. A column of light landed on the bed—the empty bed. Next he heard a whimper. Very soft. Someone was there. At the back of the room.

He thought, *What have you done?*

Sitting in a chair against the wall was a man, his head bowed. Dark hair and wingtip boots. A shotgun across his knees.

Matty. Where is Matty?

Jack took two steps inside and closed the door. Pulse of his blood. He felt unsteady. A sense of sliding on thin ice. The man moved not at all. He didn't even look up. He might have been taking a nap.

"Where's my brother?"

The man didn't answer.

Seconds passed. Jack stood there. The whole room was wavering. A voltage charge in the air. The man, ten feet away. Calm, his hands resting on the shotgun receiver. He seemed undisturbed. As if he didn't notice Jack at all. *Do something*, Jack thought. *Where is Matty? Where is Matty?*

"Where is my brother?"

The man didn't answer.

Jack stepped back and snapped on the light. He felt off-balance. He didn't dare to even blink. The shotgun was a Humpback Browning Auto-5. The forearm compact for a fast swing.

"Look at me," Jack said.

The man lifted his head and gazed at Jack, his eyes blue. A deep scar snaked across his face. And Jack realized who the man was, and he thought: *You are going to die.*

The room swayed.

"I know you," Jack said.

Bardem leaned back and watched him.

Solar flares flashed at the edges of Jack's eyelids. The overhead light glared down. Everything too bright. He could hear his own irregular breath. Underneath the bed, a dog eyed him. Muzzle on paws. It was trembling. *Find Matty, get Matty, get him, get him somewhere safe. Figure out a way.*

A glass of water sat on the end table. Bardem reached for the glass. He took a sip and set the glass down.

"If you know me," he said, "then you know you ought to tread lightly."

"What do you want?"

"You have something that is mine."

"Where is my brother?"

"That is not the question. It's the answer."

Jack stood there, looking into Bardem's gaze. Stillness: Those eyes were made of it. The stillness of a forest. Of a cat blinking in the night.

"I know your question," Jack said.

"Oh?"

"Where is the briefcase?"

Bardem cocked his head. "You think you're very smart. Don't you? You think you have a cause. Is that why you did all of this? Now look at you. You have lost the thing you care about most."

Jack put a hand on the wall. The veins in him starting to shiver.

"You know," Bardem said, "I'm here to help."

"Help."

"Yes. Help you see what is most important."

"I think I can do that myself."

"Do you, really?"

The dog whined. Jack felt a spasm. *Find Matty* find him—

"Your situation does not look good," said Bardem. "Don't you think?"

"I think I have something you want."

Bardem leaned forward, resting his chin against his knuckles. "You disappoint me, Jack. I expected more from you."

"Where's my brother?"

"He is somewhere cold. He is getting colder."

Air, humming. Jack stood there, holding the wall. His insides felt sweaty. Outside the door, he heard something: voice of a man. Soft. A creak on the metal stairs. Then he heard the long, sharp honk of a horn. Ava.

Jack said, "Tell me where Matty is."

Bardem's hand slid to the shotgun grip. He seemed troubled by nothing at all. "I'll give you one day. You will bring me the briefcase. You will lay it before me. If you don't, I will kill your brother. Do you understand?"

"How do I find you?"

"Ask Ava. She'll know."

Silence, complete. Jack's lips formed the word. *Ava.*

"You should move," Bardem said.

Jack snapped off the light and stepped away from the door as it swung open. In the sudden dullness, the man with the gold teeth launched into the room with a gun. Bardem shot twice, so fast it sounded like one long gunshot. Part of the man spread across the wall.

Jack's ears were ringing, he could barely stand. Blood on his coat. Part of the doorframe hung loose off the drywall, and blood dripped from the splintered plywood. He backed out through the doorway and took one last look at Bardem standing there looking back at him in the weak light. Then Jack turned and reeled away, past the rooms and down the stairs.

★ ★ ★

By the time he lurched onto the sidewalk, he was starting to hear beyond the ringing. *Find Matty.* He couldn't think that far yet. *Ask Ava. She'll know.* Starting across the walk, he saw the F-150 parked on the street. Something tugged on his coat, at the shoulder. The pistol shot was just a quick muzzle flash in the pink morning light. He turned and set off at a dead run. Sliding on ice. He didn't know where he was going. When he was halfway across the street, all of the glass in the store window in front of him shattered into pieces. He spun around. The hatted man stepped out from the cover of the truck and opened fire.

The deep heavy *choom* of the shotgun sounded like a cough rattling off buildings. The hatted man fell down instantly. Blood everywhere. Spattered on the snow. Jack didn't even see where the shot came from. He looked up. Bardem was on the balcony of the motel, above him. His elbows resting on the rail, his eyes watching. The shotgun in his hand. He tipped his head at Jack, and then he went back into the motel room.

Jack stood, teetering. A tang of gunpowder hung in the cold air. Everywhere silent. *Go,* he told himself. *Don't you stand there. You go find Matty.*

He turned and loped down the street, his bootprints red in the snow behind him. When he got to the parking lot, he could see Ava waiting in the car. He opened the door and got in.

"Drive," he said.

XXII

When you lay eyes on him, you see. The devil is just a man.

When Bardem came down the steps and out of the motel, he had the shotgun slung over his shoulder and the zippered bag in his hand. There were lights on in some of the rooms now, and a woman in the front office peeked through the door. He walked to the parking lot and went toward the black truck. This was blocks from the Madison County Sheriff's Office—there would be lawmen soon.

When he got to the man who he'd shot from the balcony, Bardem stood over him, looking down. The top hat had blown off his head, and he was lying facedown in a pool of blood, still holding a pistol in his hand. He was shot in the neck and chest, and some parts were missing. Bardem squatted and rifled through the man's clothes and came away with an UZI clip and several .300 Winchester Magnum cartridges. He dropped the clip in the snow and slipped the cartridges into the pocket of his coat. Then his eye moved to the truck.

He stepped to the truck's side and jerked open the door and looked in. A boy sat huddled in the back of the cab, watching him. Maybe sixteen. A bandana around his neck. The boy looked away. A canvas army pack was on the seat. A can of Mountain Dew.

"Were you with this man?"

The boy nodded.

"Don't nod. I want you to answer me."

"Yes."

Bardem glanced toward the street and heard the low cry of a police siren. A new day was waning all about. He looked at the boy.

"I'll tell you what," he said. "I'll count. Jumping jacks. I'll do five."

The boy looked into his eyes, bewildered.

Bardem pulled a lever to fold the seat forward. "Well, it's a chance. Isn't it?"

The boy didn't move.

"You need to run," Bardem said. "I can't wait for you."

The boy got out from the truck. Bardem could see the dread in his eyes. He set the zippered bag on the front seat of the truck and stepped away and began jumping. Spreading his legs and touching his hands overhead. Landing gently with his arms at his sides. "One," he said.

The boy started running.

The form of the jacks was poor, because the shotgun kept jostling. By the time Bardem got to five, the boy had crossed the parking lot and was almost at the street corner. Bardem unslung the shotgun and stood there, leveling the barrel. He fired as the boy rounded the corner. Bits of brick wall exploded, showering the snow.

He lowered the gun. "Well done," he said. "Good running."

He looked up the street once more. There was a pandemonium of sirens coming. He picked up the zippered bag and walked to where he'd left his vehicle. After he opened the trunk, he stuck the shotgun inside. He patted the top of the heavy-gauge aluminum box with his palm. Then he closed the trunk.

He wiped his boots in the snow to get the blood off. When he got in the Land Rover, he cleaned his face and hands with a sanitary wipe from the console. Then he left.

XXI

The men in the F-150 came. They watched Jack climb the motel stairs and pass by each room. They watched him stop and open the door. They watched him go inside.

I saw all of these things.

I didn't leave.

I tried to warn him.

They drove north along Route 20 toward Ashton. Riding in silence. Snowflakes hitting the windshield. After a while Ava whispered, "Where's Matty?"

Jack didn't look at her.

"Are you hurt?"

He didn't answer. He laid his head back onto the seat, looking at the road. Trying to take breaths. His coat was covered in gore—his hands streaked with it.

"Talk to me," she said.

He turned his face on the headrest and gazed at her. A separateness engulfing him. As if he looked at her through several feet of water. Gleam of light, sharp cold. Blood driven by heartbeats throbbing in his chest. *You cannot bear the truth.*

"You're his daughter."

She looked at him. Just looked.

"You're his fucking daughter," he said.

She hit the brakes and turned off the highway onto a deserted plowed road. Fallen barn. Snow deep in the side ditches. She sped over jarring ruts and across a field and slid to a stop at the top of a ridge. A grim white plain stretched for miles.

Dead bracken. Wind moving in currents over the road.

She looked at him. Angry, afraid. "Where's Matty?"

"Don't you know?"

She shook her head, confused. "I don't know—"

"Tell me where he is."

She stared at him. Her volutions of hair snarled in kinks and twists. Her gaze fierce. Her eyes brimming. "I don't know what you mean."

"Don't lie, Ava. Not to me."

The car idled. She was about to cry. It meant nothing to him.

"Say something," he said. "Tell the truth. For once."

She shut her eyes.

He felt an awful burst of hate for her. "He has Matty! Because of you."

"Don't you say that," she said. "Don't you say it."

"Where is he?"

She was shaking her head. "I don't know."

"You're a liar."

Gray light. A thin wail of wind. She opened her eyes but didn't look at him. "I'm sorry."

"You're sorry."

"I told you when we met. I said to stay away from me."

He began to laugh wildly. "Yeah, Ava. And then you came to my house."

"I wanted to help you."

He sat looking at her. Every breath she took an act of treason. "Oh, really?"

"Yes. I tried to help."

"How'd he find us, then?"

She muttered, a strangled whisper: "You don't know anything. You don't know."

"Forget it. I know how he found us."

"You're wrong."

He didn't answer.

"I wouldn't hurt you," she said.

"I don't care. Whatever you say—it doesn't mean anything to me."

She turned her head and looked at him. Her hazel eyes. They said, *You are betraying me.* "Well. Good for you."

He turned away, toward the window. Trying to calm himself. Suck of air. Fill the lungs, drain them. Something broken that could not be fixed. He opened the car door and got out.

Snow blew sideways and pelted his face. He turned away from it, holding up the hood of his coat.

"Where are you going?"

She had gotten out of the car too. Frosty bits of snow gusted, swirled in her hair. She stood there watching him. Wounding him with her eyes. Her coat blowing. *My chest*, he thought. *My chest*. He shrugged.

"Don't do this," she said, her voice hostile. Cold.

"You did this. Not me."

He turned and started walking. The car door opened and slammed.

"Jack!"

"Just stop it."

He looked back to see her standing there in the road, her body stiff, warlike. The briefcase at her feet.

"You forgot this."

She pushed the briefcase across the snow to him.

They stood looking at each other. Everything so still. All of this like some ancient dream replaying. Constructed of air, soon to disappear.

So be it.

He picked up the briefcase. Then he stormed off, down the road.

XX

I am not like William Ernest Henley.
 My head is bloody,
  and it is bowed.

XIX

My father was right about one thing: What you put in your heart will make you hurt.

Right now, this heart is bleeding out.

And it hurts, it hurts.

But I am a stone. Smooth.

I roll with it.

Ava sits in the car with the engine idling and watches Jack walk away down the road in the snow. Holding the briefcase. The sweeping countryside beyond him shifts and warps in the snowfall. Stray trees standing out of the fields. Unmoving in the wind. She watches until she can't see him.

She sits for a long time, looking down the road the way he has gone. No one comes. The air in the car is cold. The windows fog. She starts to put the car into drive, and then she doesn't. She opens the glove box and inserts a battery into the cell phone. There are two bars. She sits and waits, the phone in her hand.

When she calls, he answers on the first ring. "Hello, bird."

She says nothing.

"Are you there?"

"I'm here."

Seconds pass. He says, "I think you want to ask me a question."

"Where is Matty?"

"He's with me."

"Are you going to kill him?"

"That's up to you."

"What do you want?"

"You know the answer."

She leans on the steering wheel, her forehead against her fist. Murmur of the engine. A hazy light. The snowflakes land on the windows.

"Don't say it," he says.

"Say what?"

"The thing people always say."

"What do they say?"

"They say, 'I'm begging you.'"

There is silence. She can hear him breathing into the receiver. She waits.

"See," he says. "You're better than that."

"You're going to kill him, aren't you?"

"I'm sorry."

"If you kill him, you won't get the money."

"I wouldn't worry about that."

"Tell me what you want."

"I don't have to tell you what you already know."

She waits. Games. Always games.

"I met your friend Jack. He has a pretty face. Doesn't he? Do you think his face will stay pretty?"

She twists on the wipers and watches the snow slide off the glass. She looks at the road. As if there is something there to be seen. But there isn't.

"Even so," he says, "you should try to save them."

"You want the money. But you want something else even more."

"Clever bird. Tell me. What do I want?"

His voice is soft. So full of need.

"We used to be friends," he says. "We aren't anymore. Why is that?"

"We were never friends."

"It's because of you. You made a choice. I can't take it away from you."

"No. You can't."

"Life is a labyrinth. Do you see? Every moment is a turning. The pattern is already there. A person's path through the world. The angles and curves. Dead ends. You've been in the tangle of it since you were born. You can lose yourself. Can't you? End, start, middle. You can get turned around."

"And maybe," she says, "you escape."

There is a pause.

"No, you don't. You don't. You don't."

She doesn't answer.

"You are mine, Ava. You are mine."

She doesn't answer.

She bites her lip, tastes blood.

"Where are you? Tell me where you are. Tell me."

She watches the road. She takes a breath. She asks the question: "Where are you?"

"Where I am doesn't matter. What matters is where I will be."

"Where will you be?"

"Think about it. You know."

After he disconnects, she just sits there. Watching the road. Snow twisting down. No sign of life. She turns off the engine. There is little gas left. She closes her eyes and exhales a breath of pale air and waits for Jack. He will come back. If she leaves, he won't know how to find her. She won't leave.

Because she knows where Bardem will be.

XVIII

This is one small story in an infinite number.
   But it is mine.

Doyle got to the motel about ten minutes after the call. In the parking lot were two county patrol cars with lights circling. On the sidewalk lay broken glass. An officer was questioning a woman sitting in the open back door of an ambulance.

Midge found him. "Madison County sheriff called. It's bad, Doyle. We got dead people all over the place."

"You checked for ID?"

"I got nothin'."

After he donned gloves he walked to the body lying by the truck and bent and brushed away the fine layer of snow. The man had been shot in the chest and neck, but his face was mostly intact. "You got casings?"

"Shotgun hulls and a couple nine millimeters."

He looked up toward the motel balcony. Measuring the

distance. The angle. A pink neon sign loomed above with the letter Os burned out. It read H T SH WERS.

"Up on the balcony you'll find a second victim," Midge said. "It ain't pretty."

"Shotgun?"

"Yup."

"What does that woman say?"

"Saw a man doin' jumpin' jacks, and then he shot at somebody. That's it."

"You find anybody alive?"

"Not yet."

He grimaced. "Where the hell's the DEA?"

"An hour away," she said. "There's more, Doyle. Go up them motel stairs."

They climbed the steps. Somebody had roped off what was left of the doorway. A trail of bootsteps led through the blood.

"It's Armageddon," Midge said. "Out-and-out carnage is what it is."

He stooped under the tape. There was no good way around what was left of the body, so he just stepped over it as best he could. The first thing he saw was a juice box on the nightstand. Rumpled bedcovers. He stood there for a minute. Then he saw something lying on the floor and went over and picked it up. A toy car. He turned it over in his hand.

"Maybe we had those Dahl boys here," Midge said. "Do you think?"

Doyle opened the dresser drawers. Box of cereal. Deck of

UNO cards. He went to the bed and dropped down and looked underneath it. Wooden bed slats. Dust. A dark shape in the corner. Eyes.

An animal was there.

He pushed the bed away from the wall, and the dog shot out from beneath. Midge jumped.

"Don't let it out."

The dog was little. Hunkering by the television. Scared. Doyle walked over slowly and crouched. No collar. He put out his hand.

The dog didn't move. Then it licked his fingers.

"Huh," Midge said.

He picked up the dog, his arm under its ribs, holding it awkwardly. When they got downstairs, an EMT was taking the witness's blood pressure. The witness looked pretty shook up.

Doyle took off his hat with one hand, still holding the dog in the other. "Ma'am, I wonder if I can ask you some questions?"

She nodded and blew her nose into a tissue.

"The man you saw doing jumping jacks—I wonder if there's anythin' you remember about him. How old would you say he was?"

"I think middle-aged. He was pretty far off."

"Dark hair?"

"Maybe."

Doyle shifted the dog on his hip. "Did he have a scar?"

"I think. Kinda across his face."

He put on his hat. "All right. I appreciate you talkin' to me."

He and Midge walked to his truck. He put the dog on the

passenger seat, and he thought about those boys. Maybe being hurt. Or maybe worse. He looked at Midge.

"He's out there. Bardem. I wish he wasn't, but he is."

"So are those kids. They need us."

"Get an APB on Bardem," Doyle said, "and a story on the news for the kids."

XVII

Sometimes you realize the things you thought you knew about the world might be a lie. You stop and see where you are, and everything's confused, and you understand that it's all chaos. The whole thing.

Snow covered the road and made humps over the dead crops on either side, and Jack let the humps guide him. Trudging the path before him. His steps hushed. The snow fluttering down. He didn't know where he was going.

He walked for a while and then he left the path and waded uphill through deeper snow across the field and climbed a narrow draw. Trees here. Gunmetal sky. He saw a rabbit that didn't try to run, and he stopped to watch it until the rabbit bounded off. He stood there looking at the tracks, and then he looked back the way he had come. He started to turn and go back, but then he didn't. He put down the briefcase and sat on a stump to think.

Matty could be anywhere.

He needed coffee—that was what he needed. Matty could be anywhere, could be somewhere cold, somewhere getting colder. If he was going to find Matty . . . He swallowed and breathed roughly. There was only one person in the world who could tell him.

He put his head down in his hands and accepted this fact like a wound. Ava was probably gone now. There was no chance of reconciliation. The things he'd said. She'd never forgive him. She was gone. He spoke aloud:

"She lied to me."

But she didn't. He knew that, deep down.

Sitting on the stump, he felt a wave of dizziness and waited for it to pass. Eventually the snow, the white branches, the briefcase, and the stump refocused. How long could a person go without sleep? Blood ran down his shoulder. There was no Ava to patch him up. No Ava to talk to.

He lifted his head, moaned faintly. His throat hurt.

You know. All the things she did for you. All she risked.

His eyes burned, and he closed them.

You found the one person on Earth you could count on, and you walked off.

With his eyes closed, he could see Ava standing in the road before him. Her steady gaze, her hair in the wind. The things she'd made him feel. He didn't like it.

He stood and picked up the briefcase, the handle a stone in his grip. He followed his tracks between the trees and to the road. She was going to be gone. But he had to try. *All she did was help, and you left her. You left her. And Matty could be anywhere.*

He trudged along, feeling a weird shakiness. There were stands of trees to his left, and miles of vague snow lay on the right. He stopped and looked back at his tracks, but the thinking stump was gone. When he turned around, he could see the car idling at the end of the road.

He started to run. When he got there, he pulled open the door and got in.

Silence.

"Hi," he said.

"Hi."

"I'm sorry I left you."

"I'm sorry he found us."

"I won't leave you again."

He looked at her, and she looked back. He needed to cry, but he didn't.

"I know where Matty is," she said.

His heart couldn't take all this. He wanted to ask if she thought he was alive, but he couldn't. Instead, he took a shaky breath.

She started the car. "We should go get him now."

"Okay."

XVI

I believed in second chances.
  And third chances.
  And fourth, and fifth.

They headed north on Route 20 toward Caribou-Targhee National Forest. The white roadway. Beyond the windows just the snow.

"We stick to the speed limit," Jack said. "Keep an eye out."

She nodded.

"The cops'll have everyone looking."

She nodded, her attention leveled on the road. Her hands gripped the wheel.

"Are you okay?" he asked.

She looked at him. Her pale skin. Her eyes amber in the twilight.

"He has a mountain house," she said, "near Island Park. This place he goes to be alone. *Live life in the woods.* You know? Like he thinks he's Thoreau or something."

"We're going there?"

She didn't answer. Her thoughts seemed elsewhere.

The falling snow. The soft hiss of the car heater. Jack shuddered. *You just have to stay calm.* "So we make a trade. The money for Matty."

"He'll find out what matters to you," she said. "He'll try to take it."

Jack hardly heard her. "We're all right. We just go and make a trade."

"He doesn't have weaknesses."

"What?"

"He's not like people. He doesn't have weaknesses. Except one."

"What do you mean?"

She turned her head and blinked at him. She looked stunned, like a person jerked back from some distant place by a tightened cord.

"Yeah," she said. "I mean, sort of."

"We're okay. We've got a way out of this."

"You're bleeding. Your shoulder."

"It's not bad."

She clutched tighter to the wheel.

He could hear her fear. He could taste it.

"We just have to stay calm," he said.

They drove. Looking out through the window at the road. The woods rising up ahead. A wind had begun to disturb the top of the spires, and in the swell, it looked like the waking of some sleeping creature, rising up among the crags of forest and granite.

Then the snow shifted—there was only the lift and fall of the wind.

"It's good," Jack said. "Right?"

"It's good."

"We'll get him back."

She looked at him abruptly. "Can you hold my hand?"

He pulled her hand into his.

It felt right. Her hand in his. He managed to drag in a breath.

The woods were just trees. There was nothing more.

"We're okay," she said.

"We're okay."

"And we always will be."

"Yes. We always will be."

XV

When you're scared of someone, you hate them, but you can't stop thinking about them. You try to know them. Feel their thoughts. You want to see through their eyes so you can know what they're going to do.

For a long time, I thought about what Bardem was going to do.

I'd thought about it all my life.

Sitting in that car, I didn't even have to try.

I knew him. And I knew me.

Bardem watched the rearview mirror. The yellow lights of a snow-plow shoveling along, down the highway. Distant in the valley. He turned onto a road invisible beneath stacking snow and skidded as he pushed on the gas. When he pulled up in front of the steel storage building, there were no wheel ruts on the road other than his own.

He got out and stood looking east. The weathered black pines strewn over the landscape. The snowtop dusted in pine needles, the shift of dark trees.

He pulled on gloves and made his way to the garage door. The wind rattled the steel. The snow was several feet high. He squatted and turned the key in the padlock and rolled up the door, his breath pluming.

Inside, the building was dark. He pulled the cover away from the snowmobile and checked the throttle. The oil and filter were fresh. He straddled the seat and grasped the handlebar and turned the key. When the sled fired up, he released the choke. A cold start needed time to idle, and he gave it ten minutes.

He drove out of the garage and stopped to lock the door behind him. Then he mounted the sled and brought it to a stop at the Land Rover. He pulled the rifle and the zippered bag from the cab and stowed the bag on the sled. The rifle he carried across his back. He walked around and opened the trunk. The dry box had shifted slightly during the drive. No sound came from inside. He heaved the box out of the trunk and let it thud to the ground. Clump of weight. Dead quiet.

He opened the cargo compartment and lifted out a double-braided nylon rope. It had plenty of strength and a bit of stretch. He looped the rope through the rear bumper of the sled and pulled the slack end to the box's carry handle and tied a square knot. He stood and examined the length of rope. Snow gusting. The wind wailing away between the pines. He walked to the idling sled and got on and drove into the woods, dragging the box behind him.

XIV

I sometimes watched Jack.

I did it without him knowing. I don't think there was a person on Earth who understood loneliness better than him.

They pulled into Last Chance General Store and parked in front of a gas pump. Jack sat looking out. The parking lot was empty save for one truck: an old Ford with a bumper sticker. LOST YOUR CAT? TRY LOOKING UNDER MY TIRES. Snow stacked on the windshield. Powder shreds wafting down. The gas station standing in the quiet white veil, and the ground untrodden. In the window was a sign: BEER.

Ava shut off the engine. "We need gas."

He nodded.

"You're covered in blood," she said.

He looked down. It was true.

"You go in and patch up your shoulder while I fill up. Try not to let anyone see you. And we should find you something to eat."

He looked at her.

"It's just—you're acting a bit off," she said.

"I want to find Matty."

"Me too. But it's not going to do us any good if you keel over before we get there."

This made sense. "Okay."

He reached down and opened the briefcase and withdrew a hundred-dollar bill and stuck it into his pocket. Then he went inside. The smell of fried food hung in the air. The man at the register watched television. Jack turned and went down an aisle. He found Krazy Glue and a bottle of hydrogen peroxide. A folded T-shirt at the top of a stack. He stuffed these things in his coat when the clerk wasn't looking.

He went in the restroom and set up everything on the sink. The coat he threw in the garbage. He pulled off the bloody thermal. His shoulder pulsing. The wound was still bleeding and had turned purple and black. He twisted the faucet and wet a paper towel and unscrewed the lid on the hydrogen peroxide. He poured it onto the paper towel and wiped away the blood. The wound burning like fire. After drying the gash, he opened the glue with his teeth and squeezed it over the wound and pinched the edges shut between his fingers while he counted to ten. It held.

He put on the T-shirt and washed his face and hands. He did all of this quickly. He took no great care. In the mirror he saw himself. The shirt showed an illustration of Sasquatch walking in the woods. Below the scene were the words *Never Stop Searching*.

When he reentered the store, Ava was standing at the counter. He went down the aisle toward her and picked up a little package of powdered dougnuts and a bottle of Coke. He looked for ibuprofen but didn't find any. A game show played on the small television hanging from the wall. The clerk was ringing up Ava. Jack looked out the window and saw a state trooper creep into view and come to a stop at the gas pump.

"Where you kids headin'?"

"What?"

"Well, I see you're just in that car."

Jack put down his things on the counter. He glanced at Ava. She was looking out the window, and then she looked at Jack.

"We got a cold front on the way, is all," the clerk said. "You kids don't seem too ready for what's comin'."

"We're just passing through," Jack said.

"Wrong time-a year for a trip, if you don't mind me sayin'. With most of the roads closed and all. You know? It's just you and the animals."

Jack looked out at the gas pumps. The trooper sitting there. His shoulder hurt.

Could he see the briefcase in the passenger seat?

The clerk went on.

"Well, the bears are hybernatin'. But there's moose—they're real dangerous—and then there's wolves, cougars. Where you goin' exactly?"

"How much are these?" Jack asked.

"A dollar forty-nine, and the soda's two. You got a place out this way?"

"Why do you keep asking?"

The clerk cleared his throat. "Well, you got no coat, is all. You gotta have good protection out here." He glanced at an oilskin coat hanging on a hook behind the counter. The clerk's own, Jack presumed.

Jack shifted uneasily.

"We'd like a big order of fries too," Ava said.

The clerk surveyed them. He wore a thick twill work shirt and a store vest. His name was embroidered on it: *Ed Tom*. He turned and slid open the door of the heated display case and scooped fries into a red-and-white checked paper sleeve and placed them on the counter.

"You don't run 'round these parts with no coat," he muttered.

"It's in the car," Jack said.

"Could you put everything in a bag?" Ava asked.

Ed Tom bagged the doughnuts and soda. A can of Pringles. Two bottled waters. Outside the window, the trooper headed onto the highway.

Jack glanced at Ava, who met his gaze.

"Well, we better get going—"

"Oh, yeah. Back on the road—"

Jack unfolded the hundred-dollar bill and placed it on the counter. The clerk looked at it and looked at Jack. "We don't take hundreds. See that sign? No large bills."

For a second, Jack just stood there. *Shit. Shit.* If this was what got them caught—

"Lotta money for a coupla kids your age."

Ava smiled. "Could you make an exception?"

A news bulletin came on the TV. *"Two teens are wanted in connection with a shooting that took place early this morning at this motel—"*

Jack turned and looked. A woman stood in the snow, holding a microphone. Police lights flared behind her. Then two photos appeared. School ID pictures. Ava and him.

The clerk's eyes widened.

"Time to go," Ava said.

She threw the fries at the clerk and he ducked in surprise, shielding his face with his hands. She scooped the bag of loot off the counter and made for the door. "Come on."

Jack just stood there, watching her.

She's incredible, he said to himself.

He reached across the register, grabbed the clerk's oilskin coat, and slung it over his shoulder.

The clerk straightened and blinked. "Hey!"

"Sorry," he said. "I'm sorry."

He backed to the door while the clerk picked up the phone, and then Jack turned and headed into the snow.

They came upon the steel building where the Land Rover was parked and pulled slowly alongside it. Several inches of new snow lay on the windshield. Ava sat looking at it, and then she shut off the engine.

Jack opened the door and got out. Snowflakes were floating down. A mountain wind. Ava got out and walked around the car and opened the rear door and put the food and drinks in a pack. Jack zipped up the clerk's coat and pulled on his gloves. Then he lifted the briefcase and shut the door. The hammer he tucked into his belt. Ava hoisted the pack over her shoulders. "Let's go," she said.

He looked around. "Is this it?"

"No. The road's closed. We'll have to go on foot."

Jack studied the building. "What's in there?"

"A snowmobile. He's taken it."

"Should we have a look?"

"It's locked."

"It might not be."

"You can go see. But it is."

Jack nodded. "Okay."

They looked at the snowmobile tracks. A thin layer of smooth snow lay over the deeper notches. Rectangular in shape. Ava stood frowning at them. Faint wisp of her breath: "He's dragging something."

"What do you think?"

She shook her head. "Let's go."

They tracked Bardem's path into the forest of pines. Between the draws fog rose off the ground in white vapor. Stands of thin needled trees on the slopes, and beyond, the stark alpine peaks stretching upward. Wind from the east. The snow drifting sideways and the conifers swaying. Stopping. Swaying again. The dying light, the cold. The two of them trudging side by side.

Hard going. The briefcase heavy. Throb of his shoulder. If he hurried, he only grew light-headed. They ate two of the powdered doughnuts and drank the water. It had started to freeze in the plastic. The snow came down in a curtain about them. There was no way to see anything far ahead. They climbed a ridge and stood at the summit and watched slow darkness fall over everything. The silent trees glowing. No tracks except for the long ribbon of the sled. The steel building lost behind them. He was coughing again, and she was shivering. He looked at her.

"We have to keep going," she said.

320

"I know."

"Do you want to rest?"

"No."

"We can rest."

He shook his head. "No."

"We just have to get there."

"I know."

They went on, night dropping fast. The wind arctic. He kept falling behind, and she waited for him. What they came to was a wood of subalpine firs. Their underbranches stiff and dark. The ragged light of the moon cast their thin shadows onto the snow. Rock and scrub lay beneath. Finally he stopped. Labored heaves of his breath. The air raw in his chest. He'd no notion of how far the cabin might be. He was floundering on his feet. *You have to keep going*, he told himself. *Hang on. For just a while longer.*

He dropped the briefcase.

He bent over with his hands on his knees and coughed.

The snow. The wind and the long, dry crack of cold limbs.

When he looked, the deer was little more than five yards away. Standing in the dark of the trees. It was a buck with its head up, looking at him. It was huge, gaunt as a trellis and laced with scars from endured battles. Winter coat battered and a long white head that showed its age. The beams of its antlers were heavy.

The next moment, he was gone.

The snow drifted into Jack's eyes. He straightened up and looked at Ava. She stood in the snow, looking back at him, her hair blowing out from under her hood. She was calling to him: "Stay with me."

They started again. Slogging along. Following the snowmobile's tracks. Before long, he was resting every few yards. He stopped and looked back and in the moonlight he watched the dark stand of trees, because he thought the buck might come again. But it didn't come.

They were higher. By now the snow was two feet deep. The air thinner. The wind had quit and most of the snow. Starlight, moon. Nothing moved in that cold high world. Jack struggled through the trees, pulling up dead branches where they stuck out of the snow, and his hands were numb. With each step, the snow swallowed his legs to the knees. Oh, he was tired. At every curve it looked as though the cabin might lay just ahead, but his eyes were seeing wrong—it was not.

"We're close," Ava called to him.

They came upon a vast high rim where a fire had passed through sometime long ago. The stand of black pines was dark and wasted but still strong enough to bear the snow. The cedar was all but black. Here Jack slowed, and he knew he couldn't go any farther. He looked across the field with the pale light of the winter moon painting the snow and tinging the thin twigs of pine, and in the violet dark, he could see the tracks of the snowmobile curve up and over the slope, and they kept going on and on. *But you are not going on*, he said. *You are coming to an end.*

He stopped.

He sat in the snow.

"He's the best kid," Jack said.

Ava trudged over and fell down beside him, cowled in her coat.

They sat there in silence. Frail snow whispering down. He tried to think of something to say, but he couldn't. He knew this feeling. Of time. The reality of the world. All of it wrong. How could it be named? The thought in the darkest part of him. The thing he believed to be true. "It's not good."

"What?"

"There's no plan. We don't have a plan."

She unsnapped the buttons at the throat of her coat and lowered her hood. She looked at him, saying nothing.

He tried to think of words to describe it. Put a candle to the dark. "The feeling never really leaves. This . . . wrongness. Like when you're dreaming, and you think you're awake, but you know something is off. Somewhere life has gone off the rails. It's not right. It's a fake. You can't convince yourself it's okay, even though you try. You just . . . know. This life isn't the way it should be."

The quiet, the cold. His heart beating.

"And you have to do something," he said. "Because you know it's out there—your right life. The real one. But you can't find it."

He watched her while she watched him. Her drawn face and those eyes. There would never be someone like her again.

"I'll find it," she said.

He believed her.

She got up and pulled him by the hand and lifted the briefcase. They went on. Bleak snow falling to the earth like ashes sprinkled by a grieving mother.

XIII

The light is dying now, but I will not go gentle there. I will rage.
  Life should spark and burn like meteors and end the same.
  Scorch hot as flames.
  I will blaze.
  And you, fate: Curse me, bless me. Do all the things you do.
  Night is near and dark is coming.
  But I will spark and burn and blaze.
  I will rage I will rage.

The first police vehicle pulled up to the storage building, followed by the second and then the third. It was almost dark. A hyperboreal twilight with red emergency lights flaring across the snow. Doyle got out of the truck and put on snowpants and tightened his shoulder holster. Midge got out of the passenger side and pulled down her fur hat around her ears.

"When do you aim to talk to them?" she asked.

"When I know what it is I'm sayin'."

Four men and a woman got out of the other vehicles. The law

enforcement officer for Caribou-Targhee National Forest stepped down into the snow in worn Carhartt overalls, old eyes looking out of the black balaclava that he wore. Belt with canteen and pistol and leather sheath for a knife. He was as rugged looking as the countryside. The rest were dressed in Kevlar vests and black parkas branded with DEA in white lettering. The woman wore a medical first-aid pack on her shoulders, and all of them carried Glock 17 pistols. Headlamps and tactical packs.

Doyle stood looking at the sled tracks. The faint bootprints that followed. Two sets. It was snowing slightly, and the wind set the woods to shuddering. The others unloaded snowmobiles from behind the truck trailers and stood waiting.

"The cabin," Doyle said, "is three miles up that mountain. The clerk at the gas station IDed Bardem and confirmed the cabin location. Any questions?"

The head DEA agent raised his hand.

"Sheriff Doyle," he said. "What do we know about Mr. Bardem?"

"If he aims at you, he ain't likely to miss."

The agent smiled. Like it was all a joke or something. Doyle looked at him steadily.

"We got kids out here," he said. "I don't want them hurt. You all understand?"

"Do they have the money?" one of the men asked.

Doyle stood watching the agents. He leaned and spat. "I'll say this once. If any of you hurt one hair on those kids' heads, I better be dead first."

Drift of snow. Wind rustled high in the pines.

They fired up the snowmobiles and drove out into the trees, headlights glaring and bouncing off the snow and into the night. Showing the path of Bardem's sled track. Midge mounted the remaining snowmobile behind Doyle's. "Nice speech. That was real inspirational."

"Smart-ass."

They headed upward.

"Let's go get this rat bastard," he shouted over the noise of the engine.

"Now you're talkin' English."

Beyond the trees and across the snow, Jack and Ava could see the shape of the cabin. Gray boards hewn of wood and the pitch of a timber roof. A brief light in the window. Strange and silent. Shrouded in the fog. The light was a fire. Jack could smell the smoke. He steadied himself and tried to observe his surroundings. His shoulder tingling in hot needle pricks. Ava stood with the briefcase, watching him.

"Stay close to me," she said.

The sled tracks led off behind the cabin, but Ava cut a perimeter inside the shelter of trees and approached slowly from the side. Across the porch. No marks in the snow at the door. They went to the window and looked in.

"There's no one here."

She put a finger to her lips. "Listen."

But there was nothing. The wind stirring in the pines. A distant creak of wood.

"We shouldn't go in."

"We have to," he said. "We're freezing."

"I don't think we should yet."

"We've got to find Matty."

"Let's just stop and watch for a minute."

"It's going to be okay. Come on."

He took the hammer from his belt in one hand and tried the doorknob with the other. It swung open with a groan. Like a bear waking out of hibernation. They stood and listened. In the hearth a fire hissed softly, the flames lighting up the walls. The darkened glass of the window. Jack knew he should think about that fire, and what it meant. Ava hadn't moved. They stepped into the small room. Creak of floorboards. Smell of meat cooking. To the left were a table and a chair. The bed was made neatly. A wardrobe chest. Across the room was a handmade kitchen counter, and on the cutting board—three potatoes. Carrots, celery. An open mason jar. On the cookstove, a pot boiled.

"Stay close to me," she said again.

He opened a door leading into a bathroom. Tiled shower, folded white towel. A metal sink. All of it spartan. Precise. Faint earthy smell. Like shaving oil. He went back to the main space, but there were no other adjoining rooms.

"Matty?" he said.

Nothing.

He took off his hat. In the kitchen, he raised the lid off the pot. The stew meat simmered in broth. It smelled delicious. He put the lid back and felt unsteady. On the mantel was a careful row of books. Plato, Immanuel Kant. A single brass picture frame propped up on metal legs contained a photo of a little girl. Nose covered in freckles, a crown of wildflowers strewn in her walnut hair. Ava. She was in the kitchen, opening and closing drawers. He watched her remove a steak knife from one. Bend and tuck it in her boot. Jack saw this, but he didn't see it. He went woozy and looked out the window. The barren trees on the ridgeline. Cold and black in the dark.

He sat at the table and put his head in his hands, his eyes brimming. Ava stood watching him. *Oh, Matty*, he thought. *Oh, my Matty.*

"They aren't here," he said.

She watched him, alert, saying nothing.

"They've left."

She shook her head and spoke softly. "He's here. He's playing with us," she said.

Utter silence. The pot bubbled.

"You're going to be okay," she said. "You both are. You have to be."

The wind shook the windows in their frames, and in Jack's chest rose a quickening. He looked at her. Why did she say such a thing?

Her bare face in the firelight. Her hair aglow, her eyes.

"You have my whole heart," she said.

Something beeped. Jack jerked up from the chair and listened. Shrill, again, came the beep. Electronic. Pulsing like an alarm. Ava didn't move at all. She was looking at the floor behind him with an expression of sudden comprehension on her face, and he turned. Between the boards under the bed, a light throbbed.

Ava pushed the bed. In the floor was a door or hatch, and it was locked with a shackle of hardened steel. From the table, Jack got the hammer. Kneeling over the hatch, he chopped and hacked at the wood around the hasp, and finally he jammed the claw under the staple and pried it up by the screws. The whole hasp came out from the wood with the shackle. His wound was throbbing. He lifted the hatch door and swung it up. A bluish light was down there. Stairs. The beep sounded louder.

Crouched by him, Ava whispered, "Jack."

He looked at her.

"You'll be okay," she said.

He pulled the hatch over and let it fall with a jolt to the floor.

He started down the rough slab steps. A biting cold. He could see earthen floor. He ducked and stepped down again and clutched the hammer. On the ceiling, ice glimmered. The cold was brutal. The light was a phone flaring in the dark, its beep echoing off the stone walls. Against the back wall stood a large box, aluminum. The phone flashed and vibrated on the lid.

He descended the final steps and approached the phone and swiped off the alarm. Warily, he picked it up. Just a phone. Nothing more. He pointed the screen away, using its glow to see. Punctured through the box's lid were rows of perfectly round drill marks.

Air holes.

Jack couldn't breathe.

"Matty," he whispered.

He pushed up on the lid, but it was locked.

"Jesus," he said. "Oh, Jesus."

He raised the hammer and struck one of the metal latches. The steel pinging. Gasp of his breath. The latch broke and skittered into the dark. He was going to throw up.

"God, please."

The paltry light. He'd dropped the phone. No time to look. He brought the hammer down on the second latch and wedged the claw under it until the latch snapped. He shoved open the lid.

Matty looked up, his wet and grimy face.

Jack shoved the hammer in his belt and bent to pick him up.

"Jack," Ava whispered.

He turned and looked at her crouching up there in the square of light, watching him from the room above. The briefcase near. Behind her were cowboy boots. Ironed jeans. A man. Ava didn't know he was there, and he raised the rifle and cracked the butt of it down on the side of her head. She fell to the wood floor and lay without moving.

Bardem bent and gazed at Jack. Then he lifted the hatch door and swung it over and slammed it shut.

XII

The colors went out of everything
    and the world swam away.

Black.

Pitch-black.

He fumbled for the box and gathered up Matty into his arms.
Faint warmth, the thin beat of his heart. Matty sagged without
moving at all. Jack unzipped his coat and held Matty against him.
An impenetrable dark. Cold as a tomb. He squatted, holding Matty
in his lap, and ran his hand across the uneven floor, searching for
the phone. Nowhere. The dull gleam of ice. "It's okay," he said.
"It's okay."

He looked toward the hatch into a blackness without dimen-
sion. *There's no way. You'll fall. You'll drop him.* He tried to breathe
but his chest was a vise. *Ava, oh, Ava!*

Her voice in the car: *He doesn't have weaknesses. Except one.*

His fingers touched the phone, and he pushed a button.

Spectral light. The foot of the steps. Matty drooped against him with no expression on his face at all. Above them, something heavy scraped across the floor. Then silence.

Jack stood with his pulse thudding and pulled Matty close and tried to listen. Bootsteps. They stopped. Then moved away. Bardem spoke not a word, the more disquieting for it. No bars on the phone. Useless. Useless. Matty's head lay buried in Jack's chest.

Matty stirred.

"You're okay," Jack said.

Jack could hear nothing, and they were freezing. He rubbed Matty's arms and legs. He took off his coat and covered Matty with it. No windows. There was nowhere to go but up. He could not hear Ava—he could not hear her. "We've got to go up," he said. "Okay?"

He carried Matty, stumbling across the floor. The phone went dark. He pushed the button again and tipped the light out into the darkness and started up the steps. Matty stayed huddled with eyes closed. When Jack reached the hatch, he put the phone down and pushed up on the wood. It groaned but didn't give. He shoved harder, sending a ripple of spasms down his side. But the door would not move.

From the other side of the hatch came not a sound.

He could not hear Ava.

He looked down at Matty. Slumped in the coats. Jack bent and kissed his filthy brow. "It's all right," he said. "We're all right."

XI

Here, at last, is the truth.

When she wakes the heat is roaring. The tops of the pine trees are there in the orange light and the dark of the woods and the moon. She is lying on a tarp. The snowmobile near. The briefcase. The man standing over her carries a rifle slung on his shoulder, and his arms are folded across his chest. He watches her.

"I'm tired of this life," Bardem says.

Dreams dissolve in this waking world. The heat is a fire. Built on the petrified snow in a stacked ring of deadfall limbs. The carbon edges. The flames lick the air, glinting strangely. Sparks of unknown futures carried slowly away in the night. She sits up, and her head throbs.

"Let's go somewhere," Bardem says.

He hasn't taken his eyes from her. She touches her head and watches the sparks rise and vanish. The world losing shape and focusing again. The woods and the dark branches. She can't see the cabin. She falls back on the tarp. Slow turn of the stars above. He has dragged her to this place. The right side of her forehead is wet. *Get up*, she thinks. *Get up.*

Bardem does not move. "We could start over."

The fire flares. Everything so still. Not even a breeze. *Maybe they are watching*, she thinks. *They are watching to see if you understand, here at the end. What it all means.*

She makes her way to her feet and stands before him. "Are they dead?"

"Probably they are. Now, or soon."

A wave of blackness comes over her, and she waits for it to pass.

"Try not to worry about it," he says.

Her gut twists. *Don't you do it. Don't you cry.*

In the air, something flutters. The butterfly lands on her hand. The quiver of wings, paper-thin. The butterfly flits away.

The sentry trees. The vast frozen sky.

She catches sight of her wrist. The heart there. Pierced black.

"I thought maybe I was like you," she says. "Without feelings."

He looks away, toward the darkness. "Last chance. You need to choose."

"I used to watch you shave when I was a little girl. Do you remember? The day you killed her. You told me not to cry. You said the things I choose to put in my heart will hurt. You said to be careful what I choose. I was careful."

"You have a choice now."

She stares at him. She goes on as if he hasn't spoken.

"I was so careful. Back then I only thought about what I didn't want in my heart. You. Anything that might hurt. *Anyone.* I didn't think about what I did want. Now I know."

"You don't know anything."

"I do. You don't think so. But I do."

He watches her, saying nothing. Blue eyes serene in the fire-light. Just beneath the surface lies something excruciating. Held there at bay.

"We're different," she says. "You and me."

"Don't say that."

"You hurt people."

"Not you. I never hurt you."

Her laugh sounds so strange in the silence. The watching trees. *It's all right,* she says to herself. *You need to be calm. Be steady. Last day on Earth.* "I used to dream all the time. Terrible dreams. Do you know what I learned? There is always a monster at the end of the dream."

"You chose the path, bird. Not me. All followed to this."

In the darkness she hears something coming. Snowmobiles.

"I didn't before," she says. "But I'm choosing now."

He smiles. His mouth is tight. He shakes his head very slowly. "Even though I could have told you how all of this would end, I want you to remember that I gave you this final chance. One last flicker of hope, before the light goes out."

"You are a killer."

"If you have a point to make, don't be subtle."

Stillness. The sound of the engines is gone.

The fire pops. *Hiss.*

"I'm ashamed of you," she says.

"At last, the truth."

"The truth—" Her voice catches. "The truth that breaks my heart."

Something moves behind her. She knows, because suddenly he cocks his head and gazes at something to her right. He stiffens and walks past her at a distance of several feet and unslings the rifle and lifts it up. She turns. Coming in the night between the trees are three men. Headlamps bobbing in the gloom. The cabin is there, in the distance. They are heading toward it.

Now.

She crouches and pulls the knife from her boot and straightens and raises it over Bardem and stabs down. He has already fired the rifle, and he swings around to face her with the handle of the knife sticking out of the left side of his neck. He looks into her eyes. Saying nothing. Making not a sound, he drags the knife from his neck. The blade glistens. She turns and sets off at a run into the woods. Away from Bardem, away from the cabin. Away from Matty and from Jack.

Her mind, as she runs, is almost quiet. Almost calm.

X

I run.

I know he'll follow.

I tear across the snow into a stand of dark trees and crash through branches and out onto open ground and cross into more woods on the other side. The deep furrows. I look toward the cabin, but I can see nothing. If I run he'll come for me. He won't go to the cabin for Matty, and he won't go for Jack. If they're alive, there's a chance for them. At a higher ridge I fall to the ground and swing my chin up over the snow to see.

And I am right. He follows.

IX

Jack shoved and heaved against the hatch, but it didn't budge. The pitiful light. Something heavy there, blocking it. He listened, holding Matty with difficulty. Ache of his shoulder. Beneath him, the stairs were moving. He could hear nothing. *Where is Ava, where is she?* He sat Matty on the slab step and tried to put the hammer in his hand. "Take it," he whispered. "Take it."

Matty shook his head. He was about to fall over.

Jack heard the sound of the rifle report as if through several feet of water. He put his arm around Matty and held him. "Don't be afraid," he said. "I have to go look for something to help us open the door. I'll come back. Do you understand? If the hatch opens, you swing the hammer and hit him. Do it hard. Do you understand? You can't hesitate."

Matty didn't answer.

Jack shone the phone on Matty. His ashen face. "Okay. It's okay. We'll go together."

He put the hammer in his belt and descended the stairs, holding Matty. The cellar was walled with stone. The phone was beginning to dim, and he pushed the button again. He could see nothing but the aluminum box. Rasp of air. The cold. He bent and coughed, rage filling his chest. *There is nothing. There is nothing. She's okay*, he thought. *She's okay.*

She's okay.

He started toward the steps, holding out the light. Leaning against the wall in a corner was a spade. He shifted Matty on his hip and grabbed the spade by the handle and headed up the steps. Matty unmoving, quiet as a stone.

"It's all right," Jack said. "See what I found."

He set the phone on the step. Soon it would die. He put Matty down and lifted the spade and wedged the corner of the blade under the door and pushed. Creak and groan. The hatch rose a few inches. He could feel something massive shift. He thrust his weight on the spade, and the opening widened. Moonlight. A crevice of hope.

VIII

I run.

Dark of the moon. The trees. Snow on the branches and needles. I don't look back. I can feel him there, aiming the rifle. His eye looking into the scope. *What you put in that circle is yours to take.*

I lurch and fall through the woods, the dark everywhere, until I crouch in a ditch and wait, gasping to find my breath. Pain in my lungs. Between ribs. The air temperature dropping fast. Behind me somewhere, a branch snaps. I reel backward and burst from the ditch, and am running. Black sky. Stars. My head, the dull throb and the thirst. Trees jump before my eyes and blur until they pass out of sight. Ahead, the ground advances in the dark like the jagged fringe of a mouth.

I stumble over a rock, and there's a glimmer of moonlight and then I'm down, rolling over and over in the icy snow, clawing with hands to grasp, trying to ward off limbs that scratch.

What do I remember?

My cheek on the snow. Lick dry lips. Warm here. The throb in my head is gone. Where is the cabin, where is the road, where are the gloves I was wearing? Slow the blood. Flex your hands.

Wait for the earth to come back.

For a moment Jack is lying beside me, the moonlight on his face. His breath on my skin. Sweet Jack, my shy Jack. His touch like a bright, yellow day. I am holding his hand. *What beauty there is in this world.*

I lift a palm to my head. Blood runs into my eye from my forehead. The world has stopped moving, but the tranquil sound remains: the hush of voices singing out there in the woods, very soft.

"Are you here?" I ask, but I don't hear myself ask it. And I don't hear an answer.

I stir and smile. Warmth, getting warmer. The hint of the song. I think that maybe they are near. They look for a thing that not even death can break, and maybe they see it. What tales will they tell?

I hope they like our story.

I know I do.

Something yanks me back into the woods.

An owl hoots.

A limb snaps. I jerk my cheek up.

The voices are gone. Quiet, not even a whisper. I wipe my eye with the sleeve of my coat and press it to my head. *I'll tell you what. Why don't you just get up?*

Stiff legs.

You need to move.

The trees regard me, solemn. I stagger to my feet and look up at a peaked snowcap. I can see him up there. Two hands. A rifle. His face.

What you put in that circle is yours.

I turn and careen into the pines, into cover.

Run.

Run.

I crash through a stand of deadfall limbs, the branches snared among the snow, and am free, running beneath the trees. *Away from the cabin, find the road, figure out what is wrong with your head.* These are the things to do. Smell of pine. Coldness. An instant or an hour. Heat, so hot. At my right, a dark creature crouches in the trees and rushes away. Cougar, or wolf. I veer away running. I can't hear him, nothing.

Quiet, these deep woods all the night. Tangle and web. You can get turned around. I burst over the crest of a ridge and find myself on the edge of an open field. Moon-splashed ground. The hard snow. I can't feel my legs. My hat is gone. By the time I'm halfway across the field, he is behind me at the tree line. Something zings near my ear and I look in time to see the moonlight reflect off the glass of his scope.

I watch him lower the rifle.

The long *craack* of the shot rolls toward me and caroms across the frozen blue field and into the trees. Mountains in the distance, rising up. *How far have you come?*

I turn and inhale.

And then I am weightless, flying over the snow. Nothing under my feet but air. Time. The reality of the world. It all breaks to pieces.

I don't remember the rest.

VII

To you girls I want to say
    Some men will shut you up.
    They will hide a girl from the world.
    But you.
    Smart you.
    Brave, beautiful you.
    You do not belong in a box.
    Break the door.
    Go, you.
    Walk in the sun.

VI

Jack heaved against the spade, and the burden on top of the hatch tipped and balanced for a second in midair and then crashed over on the floor. He lifted Matty through the hatch and laid him by the fallen wardrobe chest. He stood and swung the hatch over and let it slam down. The window, vague moonlight. The fire in the hearth, now out. Ava nowhere.

He's taken her.

He's taken her.

He picked up Matty in one arm and clutched the hammer with his free hand. Tore open the front door. He saw a police-issued coat, row of gilt buttons, a handgun, fur trapper hat. A badge shaped like a star.

"Where is she?" Jack shouted. "Where is she? Where is she?"

The woman on the porch looked at Jack in wary confusion. Standing in the snow behind her were two men and a woman in tactical gear, weapons in their hands. At the tree line, another figure held a long gun.

The female officer lowered her pistol.

"It's okay," she said. "Just . . . put down the hammer. You're okay."

He stood, gripping the handle. Matty was slumped into him, his arm slack around Jack's neck, his eyes closed. The woman raised her hand, and behind her, the weapons dropped.

"He's got her," Jack said.

The woman pushed back her trapper hat and looked into Jack's eyes—really looked. She had a kind face. She glanced at Matty. She spoke sofly. "Why don't you put down the hammer?"

"Okay."

She nodded, as if he'd answered a question correctly. "Is this your brother?"

"Yes. He's Matty."

"He looks hurt."

"I don't know what to do."

"I think you should let us look at him."

"Don't take my brother."

"We don't want to take him. We just want to make sure he's okay."

"Okay."

"Is there anyone else inside?"

"No."

She nodded again. Another woman came forward with a pack that had a white cross on it and pulled Matty from Jack's arms. She carried him into the cabin, followed by a couple of men. Bright lights flashed on. Jack blinked and turned a half pace. Matty lay on the bed, his little body wrapped in a space blanket, the medic bent over him, talking.

"Minor cuts and breathing's shallow. Body temperature is 93 degrees. I need an IV, fluids. Matty? If you can hear me, squeeze my hand. You're safe now. If you can hear me, squeeze my hand."

Jack moved his swollen tongue inside his mouth. He brought forth words: "Aluminum box."

The woman officer looked at Jack quickly. "Show me."

He didn't move. She watched him. "Okay," she said. "You just stay here. You're all right."

"He took Ava."

"We know. Doyle's out looking for them."

Other officers were appearing in the room. A man dressed in black said, "We got a medical transport coming. ETA ten minutes."

Jack swayed a little.

"Let's have you sit down," the woman officer said.

"I want to look for her."

"You can't."

"I have to."

"You can't. You're hurt, aren't you?"

"No."

"Maybe a little?"

"Yeah."

She sat him in the chair and crouched beside him. She took his hand and squeezed. "Look," she said. "You're kind've a mess. If you go out there searchin' for her, you will die. Okay? You need to stay here, with your brother. Doyle's out there. If anyone can find her, he can. Doyle's the best. He'll find her."

"He's looking for her?"

"Yeah."

"And he'll find her?"

"Yeah. He'll find her."

Jack stood there watching the medics work on Matty. Everything moving slow. He shook his head.

"I'm sorry. I have to look for her."

He pushed past her, into the snow.

V

The last time I had the dream, the stairs went higher than ever before. And they were high up. The weird, twisting stairs and the turns. The hallway longer. More narrow, stretching.

I'm running. I can hear myself breathing. I run so hard that I almost give up, but I don't. I get there, to the very top. Outside. The stairs just end, overlooking the night. Stars and black sky. And I freeze, looking out at all that dark. He follows. And he's right behind me. Breathing right into my soul.

Then I jump.

And I don't fall.

I fly.

When Bardem came down out of the woods, he had already ripped his shirt and wrapped the torn strip around his neck and shoulder and tied the ends under his opposite arm, like a sling. The shirt was wet through with blood. His head was foggy. He tried to think. The knife had pierced the muscle near his neck, perhaps four inches deep. If a major vessel had been knicked. He thought not.

He stopped and leaned his back against a tree, breathing. He swung the rifle from his arm and stood it in the snow and leaned on the forestalk. *Just stand here a minute.*

The pain took his breath. He spat, strands of bloody drool hanging from his lip. Bright red. He turned and looked back one last time at all the trees standing out of the gray snow, and he knew she was somewhere in those trees in the night, and he just stood there looking. The winter moon. Nothing moving. The silence.

He should have found her. But he had not.

He raised his head and let the rifle drop into the snow. It was still too dark to see, but he knew the black shape of the highway, and he walked toward it. Dawn almost upon him. The loom of granite burned to the horizon. Something imponderably still out there in the night. *Where are you? Where did you go?* Her tracks. Just gone.

His neck hurt.

His chest. His heart.

He should have found her, but he had not.

When he reached the highway, he waited until a late-model Lincoln Navigator with a lone driver came down the road. He walked out onto the road and stooped in the headlights. The SUV stopped in the middle of the lane, engine idling. The man watched him through the windshield. Bardem limped forward and raised his hands in supplication.

The door opened, and the man stepped out. "Hey, you okay?"

Bardem lowered his arms. Blood running down his back. "I need you to step away from the vehicle, and I need your shirt."

The man stood there, looking at him.

"Take off your shirt," Bardem said.

He unbuttoned his shirt. "Here. Take it. Take whatever you want."

Bardem reached and took hold of the shirt, flinching slightly. The man could see Bardem's pistol tucked in the waist of his pants.

"Please . . . just don't hurt me. I have a family."

"That's good." Bardem nodded. "Go home to your family."

The man watched Bardem get in the Navigator and close the door. He watched the car roll past him down the highway. He stood there in the road, watching the taillights until they disappeared in the snow.

IV

Doyle tracked the girl for four miles, and it was very cold. Tree-strewn hills with caps of white. The path just kept going. The footprints in the snow. The girl and, behind her, the man. Her father: Bardem. She had run hard and far. He found a red glove and followed the tracks across a wide field until the steps of the girl shallowed and then disappeared. No sign. Bardem had scoured the woods for her, but there was nothing. He had been bleeding. He had given up. The frigid snow had hardened in the night, and she was light. Doyle went back and examined the girl's tracks where they ended. He kept looking.

It was her hat he saw first. Lying on the lone hill. A short ways on, he came to her coat. Around him the trees were silent. The lightening sky. When he saw her, he coughed.

She lay with her walnut hair strewn across the snow.

He stopped.

He fell to his knees and bent his head.

III

They let Jack go to her and sit beside her in the snow. Just her and him. She had taken off her coat, and her hair was tangled and frozen and her skin was blue but she was still Ava. His Ava. He took a few breaths and just sat there and held her hand. The sun coming up in the cemetery trees and the glinting light all about her. This unbearable pain in his chest.

"I'm not ready," he said. "I'm not ready."

He stayed a long time. When he stopped crying he stood to go, but then he turned and came back. He lay down by her. He brushed the snow from her hair and kissed her head. The dried blood there. This vacuum of hushed loud space. When divinity enters a place and you feel it. He closed his eyes and talked to her. Things never said. *I love you. You have my whole heart too.* He kept his eyes closed and listened. *She knows. She knows.* "It's okay," he whispered. "It's okay it's okay." He held her hand and just stayed there. "I won't forget. I swear it."

All the things you did. You showed me.

I won't forget.

II

He was right.

What you put in your heart will make you hurt. But it will be the most spectacular kind of hurt. It will light you up and burn you. It will knock you down. It will break you apart.

And it will make you different.

Doyle unlatched the briefcase from Bardem's snowmobile and set it on the snow.

"You're bein' too hard on yourself," Midge said.

She waited for him to say something, but he didn't. He stood with his hands crossed in front of him. He looked at her.

She said, "We're gonna find Bardem."

They stood there. The sunlight in the trees, bouncing off the snow. The cold stack of firewood and the coals. After a little while, Doyle said: "I always thought I could fix things. Whatever trouble came along in this world. Well, I was wrong about it."

"You couldn't fix this."

"I could've followed her tracks better."

"Maybe you oughta ease up on yourself."

He kept looking at the briefcase. A shudder in his chest. His whole head was numb. He looked off into the trees. "She got away from him. How'd she do that?"

"I didn't know there was a way."

They stood with the briefcase between them. On the snow, the trail of blood and the tracks led into the woods. After a while, Doyle said, "I get why he left the snowmobile. How loud it is. Easy to hear. But why leave the money?"

Midge pulled down her hat. "Maybe he didn't want to leave it. Maybe it was too heavy to carry. He was bleedin' pretty bad."

"Or maybe somethin' else."

"Somethin' else like what?"

"Like sometimes you realize that the thing you wanted all this time isn't what you really wanted."

She stood watching him. Then she spoke, softly.

"I guess we all learn that. Sometime or other. Every one of us."

1

People say you shouldn't look back.
   But I do look back,
   and I am glad.

They stayed at the hospital for three days. When Jack wheeled Matty out the front doors, he looked down the road and then back at the hospital. A truck was coming. It was snowing lightly, and Jack just stood by the road and waited, holding the wheelchair. Doyle got out and came around and opened the passenger door.

"Well," he said. "Get in."

Jack lifted Matty into the truck. His golden hair stood up at angles. Matty looked at the sun peeking between clouds in the sky. He said, "It's a nice day."

Is it? Jack hoped so.

They went up a plowed drive, and Doyle parked in front of the house. The falling snow drifting about the car. Doyle got out. Jack collected Matty in the blanket and set him on his feet. "Hold on to my hand," he said.

They stood in front of the house, looking at it. There was a shoveled walk and a brick porch. Big windows. Beyond the house, a red barn. Doyle opened the door and took their coats and hung them on wall hooks. Warmth. A living room and a fire. Jack could smell a pot roast.

"Your stuff's in the upstairs bedroom," Doyle said. "I put it in the dresser. You can wash your hands, and then we'll eat. I got one rule: You take care of the dog."

The dog barked and ran up to Matty.

It was the puppy from the motel. Matty tugged at Jack's sleeve and got down on his knees. The puppy licked his hand. He looked up at Jack. "Does he have a name?"

"Not yet," Doyle said. "You'll have to give him one."

"I'll take care of him."

"Okay."

"Can he sleep with me?"

"Yeah. He can."

Jack risked the question, the only one that mattered. "How long can we stay?"

"You can stay as long as you want."

The woman officer named Midge squatted beside Matty and put her arms around him. "Hello," she said. "I am so glad to see you." She would come to visit sometimes, and she brought Matty books and read to him, or she baked bread. In the spring she helped plant a garden. Midge told them things about Doyle and his life. She said that sometimes a person who has survived losing everything builds the hardest shell over the tenderest soul.

There were fields behind the house and streams with brook trout that stood with silver fins raised in the white currents, and sometimes in the fall, deer came down from the hills. The air smelled of wheat. You could sit for a long time and, if you were quiet, you could see one. The gentle eyes, and the head that lifted. The soft ears. Once a doe and a fawn. Jack took Matty there, and sometimes they talked about her and remembered. Other times, Matty ran after the dog, and Jack lay in the field on the grass with his eyes closed and his heart searching. And searching. And he talked to her and he listened, and he didn't forget.

I broke my promise to Matty.

    But I kept it, in a way.

    I always come back.

Outside the living-room window, the sky blues bitter and cloud-less. Jack undresses and washes with the cloth and pot of water and then bandages his hands again. He gets clean jeans and a gray thermal from the highboy and stands in front of the stove. He is buttoning the jeans when he hears something in the front yard—what sounds like an engine. He pulls the thermal over his head and says to Matty, "Get behind the couch."

Matty doesn't move. He stands looking out the window. He speaks in a voice of sheer wonderment.

"It's a girl."

When Jack looks, he sees a girl getting out of a blue car.

Not just a girl. Ava.

"Shit," he whispers. He crouches down, keeping his eyes on the window. She comes toward the house, kicking her way through the snowdrifts to the shoveled path. He motions for Matty to get down, but Matty just stands there, looking out.

Matty smiles. Then he waves.

Her steps crunch on packed snow, then halt. Jack sinks low and waits. Hushed silence. Strangely quiet. Then she knocks.

He slinks behind the couch. Matty grins at the window.

"Get down," Jack hisses.

The next thing he knows, Matty has the door open. Jack straightens from behind the couch, flushing, and walks to the door. She's no more than two feet from him. Her cheeks are slapped red from the cold. On her head she wears a knit hat, and from it her hair scatters out in a flyaway mess. Her coat falls to just above her knees and is made of battered wool, a juniper green with tarnished brass buttons. It looks like some relic from World War II. These details he sees in a haze. She smells like something warm: nutmeg or ginger.

"Hi," she says.

"Hi."

ACKNOWLEDGMENTS

One of the happiest pleasures of writing *What Beauty There Is* is reaching the point where I can at last say thank you.

So thank you to all those readers who have seen something of yourselves in Ava, and in Jack and Matty, who have opened your minds and hearts to their experience. The story matters because of you, and for this I am blessed.

Special thanks to Lindsay Auld of Writers House, who found *What Beauty There Is* in her slush pile and saw potential, who championed my work with tireless enthusiasm and skill. I'm grateful to call Lindsay my agent.

Many thanks, also, to my editor and publisher, Jennifer Besser, at Roaring Brook Press. I am reminded of my elated response when I learned Jen had requested the book: "Jen Besser! Is this asking too much of the universe?" Jen has been as fantastic an editor as I imagined she'd be, and more.

My sincere appreciation goes to the many souls at Macmillan and Roaring Brook Press who have worked without fanfare behind the scenes. Mary Van Akin, I won the lottery with your publicity expertise. Elizabeth Clark and Sara Wood, the cover is gorgeous, and, Luisa Beguiristaín, you've guided this novice through thick and thin with talent and kindness. My highest praise goes to the team of bighearted heroes at Macmillan Children's, with gratitude to Morgan Kane, Katie Quinn, Kenya Baker, Gabriella Salpeter, and Kristen Luby.

And thank you to the many editors and translators—with special thanks to Anthea Townsend at Random House UK—who have worked to bring *What Beauty There Is* to a worldwide audience. I appreciate your efforts. Greatly.

So many toil away quietly, unseen, to bring books into the world. I recall at a particularly rough point in the writing, I received a note that said, "Belief, like love, is a shaft of light in the darkness. I believe in you." I'd be neglectful if I didn't single out the shafts of light who have labored with unending support, and lots of cups of tea, including Marion Jensen, Margot Hovley, John Dursema, Josi Kilpack, Jennifer Moore, Nancy Campbell Allen, Mette Harrison, Christy Monson, Kenneth Lee, Shanna Hovley, Steven Jensen, my ever-faithful writers group, and my parents, Garald and Eileen Anderson.

And finally to my children, Brady and Kate. I wrote this story for you: first, last, and always. You taught me about love, and you have my whole heart.